HELL

Recent Titles by Hilary Norman

The Sam Becket Mysteries

MIND GAMES
LAST RUN *
SHIMMER *
CAGED *
HELL *

BLIND FEAR
CHATEAU ELLA
COMPULSION
DEADLY GAMES
FASCINATION
GUILT
IN LOVE AND FRIENDSHIP
LAURA
NO ESCAPE
THE PACT
RALPH'S CHILDREN *
SHATTERED STARS
SPELLBOUND
SUSANNA
TOO CLOSE
TWISTED MINDS

IF I SHOULD DIE (written as Alexandra Henry)

** available from Severn House*

HELL

A Sam Becket Thriller

Hilary Norman

This first world edition published 2011
in Great Britain and in the USA by
SEVERN HOUSE PUBLISHERS LTD of
9–15 High Street, Sutton, Surrey, England, SM1 1DF.
Trade paperback edition first published
in Great Britain and the USA 2012 by
SEVERN HOUSE PUBLISHERS LTD.

British Library Cataloguing in Publication Data

Norman, Hilary.
Hell. – (Sam Becket mysteries)
1. Becket, Sam (Fictitious character) – Fiction.
2. Police – Florida – Miami – Fiction. 3. Serial murder
Investigation – Fiction. 4. Detective and mystery stories.
I. Title II. Series
823.9'2-dc22

ISBN-13: 978-0-7278-8074-1 (cased)
ISBN-13: 978-1-84751-378-6 (trade paper)

All Severn House titles are printed on acid-free paper.

Severn House Publishers support The Forest Stewardship Council [FSC],
the leading international forest certification organisation. All our titles that
are printed on Greenpeace-approved FSC-certified paper carry the FSC logo.

Typeset by Palimpsest Book Production Ltd.,
Falkirk, Stirlingshire, Scotland.
Printed and bound in Great Britain by
MPG Books Ltd., Bodmin, Cornwall.

For Poppy, and all the other beautiful family dogs
we've been lucky enough to share our lives with.
Great characters, every single one.

ACKNOWLEDGEMENTS

My thanks to the following:

Howard Barmad; Batya Brykman; Special Agent Paul Marcus and Julie Marcus, to whom I owe so much for putting up with my endless questions yet *again* (and how would I ever manage without the 'real' Sam and Grace?). Grateful thanks to Amanda Stewart (who I'm going to miss so much); many thanks to James Nightingale; and to Euan Thorneycroft. Thanks, too, to Helmut Pesch, Carolin Besting, Rainer Schumacher and Wolfgang Neuhaus; and, as always, to Sebastian Ritscher. Very special thanks to Helen Rose – always there to answer my questions! Thanks to Jeanne Skipper. And as always, I'm so very grateful to Dr Jonathan Tarlow – and to Sharon Tarlow, who also helped with this one.

And finally, and most especially, as always, to Jonathan.

'Hell is watching the woman you love most in all the world falling into the pit of a nightmare – and not being able to do a damned thing to help her.'

Sam Becket

'Hell can wait.'

Jerome Cooper

ONE

April 12

If Jason Leonard, Grace Lucca Becket's first patient of the day, had not arrived early, and if she had not been running a little late after getting Joshua, her two-and-a-half-year-old son, to his preschool, then Jason would not have been kept waiting for her out on the deck, and it might have been Grace who'd spotted it first.

It.

After which she would almost certainly have called Sam – her husband, a detective in the Violent Crimes Unit of the Miami Beach Police Department – who would probably have come straight home. And Sam might have taken a look and then called the bomb squad, who might have decided to detonate a controlled explosion (better safe than sorry), in which case they might not have found out for a while, if ever, what exactly had been inside the package.

As it turned out, however, Jason had been alone when he'd noticed it.

And being fourteen years old, and bored and a little edgy – since, though he found Doc Lucca pretty cool for a shrink, their sessions had been getting tougher of late – and since one of his *things* was that he couldn't look at nice stuff without wanting to touch it, wanting to make it his *own*, that was just what he had done.

Because it looked neat.

And kind of weird too.

Which made it irresistible.

It had been the dinghy he'd noticed first – a mini-dinghy, like a kid's inflatable toy – tied up to a cleat on the dock piling beyond the Doc's deck, bobbing up and down in the water, bright yellow plastic shining in the sunlight.

Something inside it.

A plastic box, like a Tupperware container.

Something else inside that.

Jason had looked around before he'd squatted and reached down into the dinghy, in case someone was watching him, in case this was a trick – someone trying to catch him out, maybe – though no one except his mom and the Doc knew he was here, so it couldn't have anything to do with him.

Which meant, he guessed, that it probably had something to do with the Doc's little kid, though Joshua was only two, so Jason doubted he was allowed near the water . . .

And all he wanted was a closer look at what was inside the box.

Which was, as it turned out, *another* box, one of those fancy gift types – red with a white ribbon fixed to the lid, so you didn't have to untie anything, just ease off the top . . .

A second plastic container.

Something else inside that.

Something weird.

Jason stopped, stayed very still, listening for sounds of Dr Lucca. He already knew that what he ought to do was leave this alone, put the lid back on the gift box, stick that back in the bigger plastic container, put the whole creepy thing back in the little boat.

Because, to tell the truth, it *was* creeping him out now.

But the fact was, Jason was incapable of doing the *right* thing at moments like these. He could never seem to stop himself from looking at things he was not allowed to see, like the filing cabinet beside his dad's desk when he visited him at his office, and the drawer in which his mom stacked her panties and brassieres, but where she also kept the gross pink vibrator that he knew she'd die rather than have him see – and *that* was an image to make him sick to his stomach . . .

Same deal with any of the things he'd stolen.

He couldn't help himself.

Didn't really *want* to help himself, he'd admitted once to the Doc, probably because the stuff he wasn't meant to see or possess was usually way more interesting than the stuff he was allowed access to.

So now he did what he'd known he would all along.

He opened the box.

Grace had just shut Woody, the family's dachshund-miniature schnauzer cross, into the den, because Jason Leonard was not easy around dogs, when she heard the teenager's cry.

Of fear, she thought, instantly, or maybe pain, her own alarm rising as she quickened her pace, hurried through the kitchen out to the deck, and saw the teenager backed up against the wall of the house.

'Jason, what's wrong?'

He didn't answer, but he was on his feet, did not appear injured.

He was staring at something – a number of things – lying near the guard rail between the deck and the water, and Grace's own gaze flicked over them, took in plastic containers, a scarlet box, white ribbon.

And then she saw that it was none of those things that transfixed him.

It was something else, something a darker, shinier red.

Blood.

Grace looked back at Jason, scanned him from his red hair right down to his scuffed gray Keds. 'Jason, where are you hurt?'

'I'm not.' The boy's voice was scared, guilty. 'I'm sorry, Doc.'

Grace's eyes flicked back to the mess.

Saw that it wasn't *just* blood on the ground.

'Dear God,' she said, just as the bad smell of it reached her.

Fleeting relief washed over her that Joshua would be safe at preschool until noon. And then that relief was gone, because this was *trouble* again; this was, at the very least, more unpleasantness, right in their own backyard.

'It was in that box,' Jason said.

Grace looked at the scarlet box, its white-ribboned lid beside it, and at the two empty Tupperware-type containers close by.

'I knew I shouldn't have looked,' the teenager went on. 'But that is *way* disgusting, Doc. You know what it is, don't you?'

Jason knew, because he'd seen one just like it in a horror DVD he and Alex Bailey had ripped off a week or two back.

'I know what it is,' Grace said quietly.

Anatomy 101.

No doubting it.

It was a human heart.

No bomb squad, but a different kind of explosion of activity happening out on the Beckets' deck now.

Detective Sam Becket and his partner, Alejandro Martinez, were on the scene, checking things out for themselves because, though the Becket house was in the official jurisdiction of the Bay Harbor Islands Police Department, and – where violent crime was suspected, in the authority of Miami-Dade – this was *home* for Sam, his wife, Grace, a respected child and adolescent psychologist, and their young son, and no one was raising objections.

Crime Scene had been there a while, but Dr Elliot Sanders, recently appointed Chief Medical Examiner for the county – still overweight, still smoking and drinking more whiskey than was good for him, but also still the best ME Sam or Martinez knew – had dropped everything to come take a look too; his own special courtesy for a detective he'd come to know well and to respect over a number of years. Along with Sanders, there was a small team of technicians from his office, and after everyone had finished photographing *in situ*, making sketches of the scene and gathering what evidence they could, the little yellow dinghy, the quarter-inch polypropylene line that had secured it to the cleat with a rolling hitch knot, and its mysterious, grisly contents would be removed to the Medical Examiner's Office.

And the process would begin to trace the person to whom the heart belonged.

Best-case scenario, it might turn out to be someone already deceased; an organ donor, perhaps – a heinous enough crime, given the heart's lifesaving transplant potential.

Or it could be something else altogether.

A homicide victim, mutilated post-mortem.

'Or maybe before.' Martinez, a stocky, middle-aged Cuban-American, voiced the thought, his rounded, expressive face and sharp dark eyes conjuring up images that disgusted him.

'Don't even go there,' Sam told him.

He was looking at Grace, a few feet away in their lanai, seeing the new strain on her lovely face and hoping against hope that the tying up of the miniature dinghy to their property had been a random choice, that this thing might just as easily have happened to any of the island's other residents.

Except Sam did not believe that.

Had good reason not to.

And he could see, from Grace's expression, that neither did she.

TWO

The New Epistle of Cal the Hater

Giving up the killing was the hardest thing I ever did.

Damned hard.

Even for a damned man.

And they don't come much more damned than me.

The rest wasn't so bad. When you've already lost everything that mattered to you, you get so down on life that you don't worry about where your next meal is coming from, let alone your next fuck. Don't really care, sometimes, if you live or die.

Except for the hell and damnation thing.

But I missed the killing worse than anything.

I tried hard. For a long, long time. Punished myself whenever I felt the need sneaking up on me, the way I used to, the way my mother taught me.

Good old, *dead* old, Jewel.

I thought she'd be my last.

I really meant to stop.

Really.

I guess I'm just weaker than I figured.

THREE

The month had started out so sweetly.

Springtime in Miami.

Lovers everywhere, strolling hand-in-hand, young and old. Two of them, on the first Sunday afternoon of April, older than most, taking a walk along the beach around 95th Street in Surfside, shoes off, enjoying the feel of the sand, not too far from where they'd just finished lunching with family.

Celebrating.

Because Dr David Becket, aged sixty-five, a recently retired paediatrician, and Miss Mildred Bleeker – whose age was known only to her and, presumably, to her parents and the New York City Department of Records – had become engaged to be married.

The whole gang sitting around a big table outside La Goulue in Bal Harbour. Sam, Grace, Joshua and Cathy – their twenty-three-year-old adopted daughter, so uncannily like Grace with long legs, butter-gold hair and eyes a similar striking blue, that strangers assumed they were biological mother and daughter; Grace's sister Claudia and her family, recently returned after several years in Seattle; and Saul Becket, Sam's much younger adoptive brother – only one year between him and Cathy; Sam and Saul a generation apart, but as close and beloved as any brothers could be.

'Adoption in our blood,' David liked to say, because he and his late wife, Judy, had started the family tradition one year after he'd first happened upon Sam, aged seven, a shocked, confused African-American boy stranded in an ER following an accident which had killed his parents and sister.

Forty-three years old now, six-three with powerful shoulders, Grace's cooking his best excuse for not being quite as rangy as he had been, though he still had the same keen-boned face and loose-limbed, well-muscled body; a tough cop when he needed to be, but soft at his core. His father as proud of him now as he had been every day of their life together.

Meeting Grace the best thing that had ever happened to Sam.

Mildred disagreed with that. 'Second best,' she had once pointed out to David. 'Samuel met you first.'

'OK,' David had acquiesced to a degree. 'My son's a lucky man.' And then he'd paused. 'Almost as lucky as me, finding you.'

'Goes both ways, old man,' Mildred had said.

Sam knew that his father and Mildred had been slow to declare their feelings because of their concerns for his and Saul's sensibilities, Judy Becket, their mom, having passed away almost four years ago.

First chance they'd had, they'd reassured David. In the first place, they'd both heard their mom say that she wanted him to find companionship again; and in the second place, both Judy's sons – and the rest of the family – had grown to love Mildred as much as David had.

Respect had come first for them all. For a woman whose life's journey had been rougher than any of them could properly imagine.

A woman from a conventional family background who had given up so much for the man she loved, and then, having lost him, had turned her back on comfort and convention and chosen life on the streets.

Which was where Sam had first come to know her, shortly before violence, in the shape of a psychotic killer – self-styled Cal the Hater – had robbed her of that life too, but had also, fortuitously, brought her to Sam's family and into all their lives.

Cal the Hater, presumed dead until last spring, when he'd written to Sam.

Not dead, after all.

Still alive and, thereby, a threat to the whole Becket family.

Because Cal the Hater, a multiple killer, was also Grace's step-brother, Jerome Cooper, son of Frank Lucca's second wife, a young man who had been brought up to hate both Grace and Claudia.

Though the person he had come to hate most profoundly of all was Sam, because Jerome Cooper had also been raised a racist, and Samuel Lincoln Becket was an African-American, adopted, barmitz-vahed Jew, *and* he was married to one of the women Cooper loathed, *and* he had, as the killer saw it, caused him to lose everything he had held dear.

Cal-Cooper still out there someplace.

But for the time being, at least, there was happiness in the Becket clan through the joining of two more lives.

FOUR

April 13

No hearts or any other vital organs had been reported missing from laboratories or hospitals. No bodies stolen from morgues or funeral homes or hospitals or any place else.

No body had turned up minus a heart.

Yet.

But Sam would have bet all he owned that this was a homicide.

Attempts would be made to match the heart's DNA to the CODIS database, but until either that brought success, or a mutilated body was found, or a missing persons report elicited a match, there was little to investigate. No prints on the scarlet gift box or ribbon or on the polypropylene line – not as strong as nylon, Martinez had learned, and hard on the hands, but still used by some as inexpensive anchor line.

'Also used by waterskiers as tow-rope,' he told Sam in his lightly-accented voice, 'and by campers, and even for clothesline.' He shrugged. 'Common as bugs in the fucking Everglades, in other words.'

'Almost, I guess,' Sam said.

Like the other items, all readily available from any number of retail stores or online; though Miami-Dade had faint hopes of tracking down the source and, who knew, the purchaser of the toy dinghy.

Not in Miami Beach's jurisdiction, but the two detectives working the case were good guys, and Sam and Martinez had enough work in any event to be going on with, as was usual in the Violent Crimes Unit. Two aggravated batteries in the last two weeks, three domestic violence cases in the same period, and the rapist of a sixty-five-year-old widow in the North Shore was being urgently sought before he struck again.

And for Sam, on the home front, his father's wedding to help organize.

Although it had been Sam who had first come to know Mildred Bleeker in her homeless days, it was Grace who'd been the first to be granted real insight into the older woman's personal history.

Mildred had begun working for her about eighteen months earlier, assisting her in the office and rapidly making herself indispensable – which came as no surprise to David, whose own office she'd already organized – and the two women had viewed one another with quiet warmth and mutual respect.

Respect the key to Mildred's secrets, and that only over time.

They'd known, until early last year, just the barest facts. That Mildred had once been engaged to a man named Donny who had died long ago. That since then she had slept for the most part on a bench near the promenade in South Beach, a few blocks from Miami Beach PD headquarters. That Mildred was intelligent and courageous – and that something about Sam's manner and his kindness to her had begun to ease open her suspicious heart.

David Becket following suit.

And then, one afternoon last February, Mildred had asked for a few hours off to visit her late fiancé's grave because it was the anniversary of his passing. Grace had offered her a ride, and by the end of the afternoon, she knew that Mildred had been a secretary in New York, living with her parents in Queens, when she'd taken a Florida vacation and had met Donny Andrews, a postal worker estranged from his wealthy family after refusing to join their banking business. It was an instant love match, Donny travelling back with her to New York to meet her family, but Mildred's mother had disapproved, and her father had always taken his wife's side even when he didn't entirely agree with her. Donny, desperate not to lose her, had proposed, Mildred had accepted, and they had returned to Miami.

'We never married though,' she'd told Grace. 'I told Donny that I was proud to be his fiancée, but that I couldn't picture an actual marriage until we found a way of winning my father's blessing.'

There was no blessing, but Donny had bought Mildred a ring, and they'd settled into a blissful existence in a small rental in Little Havana. Until Donny had been diagnosed with clinical depression and had left the post office.

'I went behind his back and sold the ring to pay some bills, and when he found out, Donny swore he'd buy me another.' Mildred's expression was faraway. 'But three months later, he got in the way of a shooting by a drug dealer. What they call an "innocent bystander" in the newspapers.'

'Oh, Mildred,' Grace said, softly.

'I never did get that second ring,' Mildred had said.

Her wedding to David Becket was set for April 22nd – after the short engagement they'd both agreed was sensible at their age – and would take place in the lanai at Sam and Grace's house. Family and close friends invited, with Grace and Cathy – who was studying for an associate degree at Johnson & Wales University's College of Culinary Arts in North Miami – in charge of catering the party.

Labors of love always welcome, so far as they were concerned.

Grace was trying hard to get the heart out of her thoughts, but the jarringly unpleasant incident – so frightening for poor Jason Leonard – and the awareness of the ongoing police investigation into it, was preying on her mind.

Bringing back other memories, infinitely worse.

The terrors of last March and others; older flashes, but still painful.

It had been a struggle to get over what had happened to her and

Sam, realizing how close they had come to losing their lives, remembering what had been done to them. But they had survived, almost intact, though even Sam, strong as he was, psychologically and physically, still had nightmares about it, as she did.

Bad things came and went again, if you were lucky, and they had been infinitely luckier than the other victims of that horror, and before that their little son – still just a baby then – had survived abduction by Jerome Cooper, and before *that*, there had been . . .

How many times could one be lucky?

When did your luck run out?

There was an edginess in Grace sometimes these days that had never been there in the past, a tendency toward irrational fears. Only last week she had been playing with Joshua in the pretty little park opposite their house when she'd had a feeling they were being watched.

Her skin had prickled, and she'd moved quickly to pick up her little son, and Joshua had felt her fear, had stared into her face, surprised, and she'd told him it was all right, that everything was fine, but all the same she'd walked quickly out of the park and across the road to home and safety.

There had been no one there, of course, she'd realized within minutes.

Imagination.

Jerome's fault, and those other monsters, and Grace guessed it didn't help that her husband's daily life still revolved around wickedness, that he, like Martinez and their colleagues, was at risk every time he went to work. Yet that was nothing new, and in the past she'd coped with it well enough, having no real choice, as she saw it, because Sam's work was important to him, and he was a fine detective, and anyway, it had become an integral part of him, and she would never ask him to give it up.

But her protective shell had taken a few too many hits, was wearing a little thinner, and Grace wasn't happy about her new tendency to overreact. Sam had enough to worry about without having to stress about her, and Joshua certainly needed and deserved a calm, capable mom to take care of him.

Not a woman who jumped at shadows.

Or memories.

FIVE

April 18

It was a child who noticed it first: the bright yellow toy dinghy bobbing in the Round Pool at the Fontainebleau. The girl, Monique Lazar, aged nine, whose parents and two siblings had been enjoying the lavish wonders (including a 32-inch flat screen television, digital safe and butler service) of one of the family cabanas surrounding the pool, looked around for the dinghy's owner, saw no one who seemed to be playing with it, and took tentative possession of it.

No one was watching her. Her father was engrossed on the phone, her older brother Lucien was asleep, his iPod in his ears, her mom was at the beauty parlor and her little sister was playing in the kids' area with her nanny.

The package inside the dinghy was the most attractive thing about it.

Compelling.

Scarlet, with white satin ribbon.

Monique knew about private property, about finders keepers being wrong, and she was pretty sure that whoever this did belong to would be back for it soon enough, so she didn't plan to touch the package, but she saw nothing wrong in retrieving her Palm Beach Swimsuit Barbie from her bag, getting in the water, popping Barbie in the dinghy and towing her around, chatting to the doll about what might be in the gift box.

It was five minutes or so before Edouard Lazar came to check on her, and Monique waited for him to ask her about the dinghy (Maman would have noticed right away) but Papa just asked if she was OK and told her to be careful in the water, and then he was back in the cabana and turning on his MacBook . . .

So Monique went on playing with Barbie.

Until Lucien showed up.

'*Qu'est-ce que c'est*?' he asked. 'Whose is it?'

'I don't know,' Monique said. 'No one's.'

'It must be someone's.' Lucien looked around, shrugged, squatted on the edge and eyed the package. 'I guess we should check if that's valuable, and hand it in.'

Monique asked if she could just play with it a while longer, but Lucien said no, and what her big brother said usually went.

'Can I open it?' she asked.

He shook his head. 'Give it to me.'

Monique passed the package up to him, stroked Barbie's hair, sat her back down in the empty dinghy and looked up at her brother.

He had taken the top off the box, was looking down into it, puzzled.

'What's the matter?' Monique asked.

'There's a plastic box in here,' Lucien said.

'Open it,' she said.

'I'm not sure.'

'Maybe it's just someone's lunch,' Monique suggested.

Lucien stood up, eased the lid off the container.

'*Merde!*'

Violently, he threw the box away from himself, and its contents fell into the water right in front of Monique.

Who began to scream.

Edouard Lazar leapt to his feet, and all the other people in and around the Round Pool came to see what she was screaming at.

And in another second, she was not the only one.

Only the one plastic container this time, Sam and Martinez noted, but otherwise the packaging and contents seemed, at least superficially, identical, though the MO this time around had been far bolder, the intent clearly to shock more publicly. Not like the first, tied up to a private property.

The Beckets' property.

The same evidence of savagery in both cases. Another human heart.

A second unknown victim, waiting to be found.

And this time, a Miami Beach case.

The Lazar children were traumatized, but being well cared for by their parents, who had permitted their gentle and brief questioning, though with neither of them witness to any crime, their evidence was plainly limited to discovery.

On the plus side, there was plenty of CCTV around the security-conscious resort, and management and personnel were horrified, cooperative and highly efficient, keen to assist the police and anxious to have the Round Pool reopened and returned to normality as swiftly as possible.

A good chance, therefore, the detectives figured as they went through the security camera recordings, that they would at least see the moment when the dinghy had been placed into the pool. They anticipated a disguise, and almost certainly someone in no way directly connected to the perpetrator, someone paid to undertake the task.

'Shit,' Martinez said.

Neither of them had anticipated what they saw.

A young child, probably aged no more than five or six, all covered up by a too-long, hooded toweling robe, making immediate or even future identification impossible, making it hard even to be certain if the small person clutching the yellow dinghy was male or female.

'Could be – ' Martinez hesitated – 'what do we say these days – a little person?'

'It's a child,' Sam said. 'Look at the walk, the movements.'

'I don't know,' his partner said. 'Remember that creepy movie, where Donald Sutherland thought it was a kid in a raincoat.'

Sam shook his head. 'This is a child.'

And only a small and unsatisfactory part of the story, because when the dinghy had splashed down in the Round Pool, it had been *empty*, and the hooded child had turned around and walked, through a throng of resort guests, along one of the paved pathways away from the pool area – and had disappeared from view.

'Someone waiting, maybe, to take off the robe,' Sam said. 'Make the kid even more unrecognizable.'

Ten minutes further into the recordings, they watched a game taking place in the pool between a dozen or so youngsters horsing around, boisterous enough to send a few would-be quieter swimmers for cover.

When the game was over, the scarlet box was in the dinghy.

They watched it over and over.

'Nothing,' Sam said.

Not so much as a hint of who had placed it there.

Nor any trace of the hooded child after he or she had left the area.

Their best hope of an ID would come when the footage had been enhanced and examined more thoroughly, but by then that child would almost certainly be long gone and less easy to trace. It was not hard for casual visitors to come and go, either to eat at one of the restaurants or at the deli or café, or just to check the place out. And if the child was a legitimate guest who had, perhaps, been asked to carry the dinghy as, say, part of a game, and if they did manage to ID the kid, his or her parents would probably raise objections to any kind of interrogation, and anyway, the child might not know the identity of, or even be able to describe, the person who'd given them the goddamned thing.

Still, Crime Scene and the ME and his team were on the case, and resort staff were being asked to view the recordings in the vain hope that someone might recognize the robed child.

So far, no evidence had been found of violence in any bedroom or suite or anyplace else in the resort that had been made accessible to the police.

And a second human heart was on its way to Elliot Sanders's office.

SIX

April 19

Today was the anniversary of Sampson Becket's death.

Sam's first beloved son, born to him and his first wife, Althea, more than twenty-one years ago, their marriage a painful casualty of the accident that had robbed them of their beautiful boy.

That loss eighteen years ago this day. The memories of the anguish never really fading, only the ability to keep them at bay growing stronger with time.

Most years, Sam went up to Sarasota on the anniversary, laid Sampson's favorite colored seashells on his grave, sang him a lullaby or two in his baritone voice. Sometimes he went alone, sometimes with Grace; a couple of times his dad had come along, and twice Saul, and some day Sam planned to take Joshua, but this year he had his father's wedding to prepare for, and David had asked if he minded the date being so close to the anniversary, and Sam had told him he could not be happier.

No visit to Sarasota this year. Too much to be done.

Life going on.

And a killer to catch.

With so much to do and with an excited two-year-old to contend with, Grace had scheduled no appointments for the whole week leading up to the wedding. Cathy would be at JWU until the day before, but Saul had been more than pulling his weight and, despite all Grace's protestations, the bride herself had been unstoppable.

'I'll stop one day before and not a minute sooner,' Mildred had told David and Grace a month ago. 'And if anyone tries to keep me from helping with my own wedding, I'll call the whole thing off, and then see how *you* – ' this last to David – 'like that.'

'It might be easier than being married to a cantankerous woman,' he said.

'You think you've seen cantankerous?' Mildred countered. 'You try getting me to put my feet up again when I've important things to do, and you'll know what cantankerous really means.'

But though the transformation of the lanai was taking shape and the wedding outfits were hanging under covers in various walk-in closets, and the preparations for the luncheon could not be tackled much before Wednesday and the morning itself, Grace was still glad she'd kept her calendar free.

Come this cool, wet Monday morning, however – and Grace hoped to heaven it would not be like this on Thursday – when Sara Mankowitz telephoned and Grace heard the awful strain in her voice, she knew that if she refused to see Pete, Sara's son, she'd have no peace of mind for the rest of the day.

'I'm desperate,' Sara had said.

Not a hysterical woman, for the most part, besides which – though Grace would not have admitted it to anyone else – some patients were just a little more special than others.

Ten-year-old Pete Mankowitz was a sweet-natured boy who suffered from panic disorder and had lately been developing signs of agoraphobia and, in general, worrying hell out of his mom, whose husband had walked out three years ago.

Working in cooperation with the family doctor, Grace had used relaxation techniques and cognitive therapy, but it was beginning to seem that they might soon have to resort to drug therapy. Sara was understandably resistant, given that some of the safest medications sometimes aggravated depression and, even when they did not, tolerance could occur in the long term. But with Pete often absent from school, and increasingly unable to interact socially . . .

For today, a house call.

'You could kill two birds,' Mildred suggested. 'Have lunch with your sister.'

The bride-to-be working today, no one daring to challenge her, and she had a good point, since Claudia's new house on Key Biscayne was little more than a mile from Pete's.

'There isn't really time for that,' Grace said.

'So make time,' Mildred told her. 'I'll pick up Joshua.'

'You're getting married in three days,' Grace said.

'I don't need reminding,' Mildred said.

'But you must have so much to do,' Grace said.

Mildred's smile was beatific. 'I guess some of us are just better at time management than others.'

Same deal as with the first heart.

No reported thefts of bodies from anyplace. No reported mutilations of cadavers from hospitals or similar facilities.

Neither heart had come from long-term laboratory storage, and in any case the ME had swiftly ruled out any possibility that the organs had been intended for transplant because the removal technique had, to say the least, been unskilled.

'Not performed by any surgeon this side of hell,' Sanders had told Sam.

No bodies brought in with organs missing.

No DNA matches.

But something real bad was happening in and around Miami Beach.

Worse to come, Sam was way too certain.

Pete Mankowitz, with his tow-colored hair and frantic hazel eyes, had been about as bad as Grace had ever seen him when she'd arrived at the one-storey house near Crandon Park.

Full-blown panic attack, textbook style. Except this was no book; this was a living, breathing, suffering boy, and though Grace had managed, finally, to calm him down with techniques she had taught him over time, she had wondered at the severity of the attack.

'What triggered this, do you know?' she asked his mother, once the youngster was finally resting in his bedroom.

'I don't have a clue.' Sara, a pretty brunette in her early thirties, sat on the edge of one of her gray leather armchairs, exhausted. 'We'd been talking about going out for a burger with a friend this evening, but he seemed OK with that, and Pete knows if he starts feeling bad, we can get takeout or just come straight home.'

'Is this your new friend?' Grace asked.

'Charles Duggan, yes.'

She'd met him a couple of months back, had mentioned him to

Grace because she liked the man, but had been trying keep the relationship low-key in case it upset her son, though Pete had expressed no concerns.

'Have you noticed any worsening of Pete's problems when Mr Duggan's around, or when he knows he might be coming around?'

'Not especially,' Sara said. 'Or not until today.' Her expression grew more desolate. 'I'll have to stop seeing Charlie, won't I?'

'Not if he's a good man.' Grace smiled. 'They're hard enough to come by, Lord knows.' She paused. 'But with a boy as sensitive as Pete, you may have to tread extra carefully.'

'I thought I had been.' Sara was fighting back tears again, had been weeping when Grace had arrived. 'I'm sorry.'

'Don't be, Sara.' Grace was gentle. 'This is so hard on you. The last thing I want is to deprive you of any kind of comfort.'

Sara shook her head again. 'It's no comfort if it makes Pete unhappier.'

'We don't know if it has anything to do with your friendship. The chances are today's attack had nothing to do with your plans for the evening.'

'I've called Charlie,' Sara said. 'We're taking a rain check.'

'Probably just as well,' Grace said. 'At least for tonight.'

Daniel Brownley, Claudia's architect husband, had named their new house Névé because he loved snow-covered mountains almost as much as he loved the ocean, and in the midst of designing its soaring lines of solar glass and white steel, he'd thought of the word for the snow at the summit of a glacier, and no one had been able to dissuade him.

Névé's beauty was a little stark for his wife's personal tastes, but Daniel had returned to Florida purely for her sake, and Claudia thought she might have lived in a hovel if it made Dan happy.

Névé was certainly no hovel, but it was extraordinary. The house overlooked the ocean in the Village of Key Biscayne, and the materials Daniel had used were designed to adapt to weather shifts – a tough call in South Florida. When it was sunny and hot, the huge expanses of smart glass darkened and cooled to comfortable levels; when storm clouds and thunderheads gathered over Biscayne Bay, their dramatic displays were reflected by equally 'smart' wallcoverings.

Grace liked the house more with each visit. Like Claudia, she had initially found its high-ceilinged open spaces and white tiled floors daunting – not to mention its state-of-the-art security system, with a siren loud enough to wake all the dead of Miami. Time, however, was softening her opinion, and whenever she stepped outside on to the terraces Daniel had created on both levels of the house, she realized that her brother-in-law had somehow managed to create an environment wholly in keeping with the island.

Today, Claudia, delighted by her unexpected visit, had rustled up a lunch of crab cakes and salad, which they were eating in one of the surprising, comfortable nooks, some large enough for the whole family, some designed for one or two, all on the ocean side of the house; this one a cozy corner with a sleek bio-fireplace that would make it perfect for relaxing come winter.

'Now I feel guilty,' Grace said.

'Whatever for?' Claudia asked.

'I turned down patients this week so I could organize the wedding, and now Mildred's taking care of Joshua, and here I am living the life of Riley.'

'A shrink should know better than to ruin simple pleasures with guilt.'

'Point taken,' Grace said.

She looked through the glass wall at the rain-soaked terrace and smooth Brazilian hardwood deck, looked past the swimming pool toward the gate in the security-alarmed white fence that led on to public, sandy, palm-planted grassland, the beach and bay beyond, and felt they might almost have been back on Islamorada in the Keys, where Claudia had been so happy before Daniel's work-motivated move to Seattle and the rocky personal times that had lain ahead.

Grace looked at her now, thought how peaceful she seemed, her dark eyes alive, her sense of contentment almost palpable.

Almost contagious.

The tranquility remained with Grace for most of the drive home.

Until she stopped at La Tienda Fiesta, a party store in Little Havana where she'd placed a large order for the wedding. She'd hoped to double-check Wednesday's delivery with Luis, the manager, but the place was hectic, and he seemed embroiled with a purposeful woman wielding a clipboard. Spotting Grace, however, Luis gave her a thumbs-up, which she supposed was reassurance enough, but while she was here, she thought she'd check for some party extras for the lanai.

An attractive leather-bound guest book caught her eye, a possible keepsake for Mildred and David.

She stooped to pick it up.

Something brushed the back of her neck.

Startled, she straightened up and turned.

No one there.

Just a couple a few feet away, intent on their own shopping, and an elderly blue rinse lady to her left who looked a little confused.

But it had felt like fingertips. Like a *caress*.

So much so that as she'd turned around, she'd half expected to see Sam standing behind her, laughing.

Thrown, Grace looked left and right again up the aisle.

And saw a figure just disappearing around the corner at the rear exit end.

Male, average height, slim, with silvery-blond hair.

Familiar.

Suspicion hit her hard, like a small, sick punch to her chest.

'No,' she said out loud, and took off, sprinting to the rear exit, wanting desperately, even as she ran, to be *wrong*.

Out in the parking lot, no men who looked like *him*.

An assortment of cars, all ordinary, anonymous. She scanned the lot through the mist of rain, saw a young couple, laden with bags, clambering into their truck, saw an old red VW Beetle and a motorcycle with a big-bellied guy – no helmet and little hair – heading for the exit.

Just her imagination then.

Like last week in the park opposite their house.

She waited for relief, but instead she felt jolted, nauseated.

Dragged sharply back again to last year – not just her imagination that time, because Sam had thought he'd seen him too . . .

Come on, Grace.

This had been nothing. Just someone accidentally brushing against her. Another customer or a salesperson walking behind her, maybe even a piece of fabric that had felt like fingers on her neck.

Standing here now in the rain, she lifted her right hand and rubbed the spot with her own fingers, the place just below the nape of her neck, exposed today, her hair twisted and pinned up.

The place that Sam often touched that way, kissed.

Come *on*.

No one there. Neither today, nor last week.

No one.

Certainly not *him*.

SEVEN

April 20

The sun was out again.

And a body had been found.

Washed up on the sand at 53rd Street Beach.

Partially decomposed, partially devoured by marine creatures, though they had not been responsible for the large wound in the center of the individual's chest.

That had been caused – according to the ME's preliminary findings – by the amateur surgeon, the *butcher*, who had carved his or her way into the male victim's body, then cracked and spread open the ribcage, before cutting out the heart.

The victim had been African-American, probably in his mid-twenties, and he had been strangled to death with a ligature, taken from behind.

'Nothing more for you yet,' Elliot Sanders told Sam and Martinez.

Not the first time they'd all come together to a beach homicide scene, with all its inherent difficulties; constantly shifting sand and who knew how many members of the public having passed by since the body had washed in.

'How long before we know if either of the hearts are a match?'

Sam asked the question, knowing all too well that such things took a whole lot longer than any of them hoped, including Sanders.

'It's a priority,' the ME said, grimly.

Though whether a match was, or was not, found, they already knew for sure that another sick killer had come to Miami Beach.

'Was there anything else?' Grace asked Sam late that night.

'Such as?'

They were sitting at their big old oak kitchen table, and Sam had already told her about the John Doe while she'd heated up clam sauce and cooked spaghetti, had kept the details sparse, but she had seen the first heart for herself, and he felt it was only right for her to know.

'I don't know,' she said. 'Anything familiar?'

Sam took a long look at her.

It was not like Grace to prevaricate.

Yet he knew damned well what she was asking, not least because he had asked himself the same thing earlier in the day. Because it came to mind, because of the strangulation with a ligature and the victim being taken from behind and being black.

Mainly, of course, because both hearts had been placed in dinghies.

The first tied up to their home mooring.

'The body wasn't found in a dinghy or rowboat, and the victim's skin was not raked,' he told her, since that was what she wanted to know, because that had been a big part of Jerome Cooper's MO.

'Could you tell that for sure?' Grace asked, knowing about the condition of the body.

'Yes,' Sam said. 'And as to the strangling, you wouldn't like to know how many people are killed that way every year in the US.'

Not too many African-American males in Miami-Dade, Grace would bet, but did not say.

She did, however, share with him yesterday's experience in the party store.

Strictly speaking, her *non*-experience, though it had not felt that way.

'Just me, I guess, being jumpy,' she said. 'Again.'

'Which is not like you,' Sam said. 'And I wish you'd told me yesterday.'

'I knew it was nothing.'

'Still,' he said. 'I thought we had a deal.'

They did. Anything that significantly worried either of them, they shared.

'I'm sorry.' Grace paused. 'The dinghy thing's still bugging me.'

'Me too,' Sam told her.

'MO's change, don't they?' she said.

'Sometimes.'

'What if it is him?'

'Then we'll catch him.'

'You didn't before,' she said.

'If it is him,' Sam said, 'this time we will.'

EIGHT

April 21

The fact was, Jerome Cooper, aka Cal the Hater, had been back on Miami Beach PD's Most Wanted list since he had sent Sam Becket a handwritten letter last year and ceased being presumed dead. And everyone in their line of work knew that it was hard as hell for some attention-seeking psychos to stay in hiding for too long, and right now, what Sam wanted to be happening most was for every boat in every marina and at every mooring in the whole of Miami-Dade to be searched; every boat big enough, that was, to hold one man and a dead body.

'Not gonna happen,' Martinez said.

Which Sam already knew.

What he did *not* want one day before his father's big day (and today was his brother Saul's birthday, too, though they'd agreed to celebrate tomorrow) was a homicide investigation laid in his lap, but Beth Riley – promoted to Sergeant when Mike Alvarez had made Lieutenant – knew same as everyone else in the unit that there were some parallels here that had to make it Sam Becket's case.

So here they were in their open-plan office on the third floor at 1100 Washington Avenue, going through their starters' paces, with no real crime scene to focus on and no immediate hopes of a name to put to their John Doe. And the temptation was to go ahead and pin this crime on Cooper, but in so doing they risked letting some other killer continue about his business while they pulled out all the stops on the wrong man.

In other words, Sam knew they had to go by the book.

Detectives Mary Cutter and Joe Sheldon – a recent recruit to Violent Crimes, a young New Yorker married to a Miami Beach doctor – were out on day two of a neighborhood canvass in hopes of finding a witness. Ideally some insomniac with a telescope or binoculars, who'd been scanning the ocean at first light and had seen the victim being dumped from a boat.

'About as much hope of that as finding icicles under the Venetian

Causeway,' Cutter had said as they'd started out the previous afternoon.

'I heard it snowed this January,' Sheldon said.

'You believe all the crap you hear?' Cutter had said.

An appeal for witnesses had gone out this morning on Channel 7, and the story of the grisly find had appeared on the Channel 10 website. People were already calling in, as they often did in the early stages, some well-meaning, sharp-eyed folk with information worth imparting; but outweighing those callers were the attention seekers and cranks and sometimes, worst of all, those citizens with nasty minds and little better to do than try to lead the police astray.

Nothing of value yet.

Lieutenant Alvarez had okayed Sam's absence for tomorrow afternoon – the wedding not scheduled till four o'clock – but still, Sam, the *host*, for crying out loud, not to mention the man the bride had asked to give her away – was now going to be working right down to the wire; and Martinez, who'd put in for a day the instant he'd been invited, was going to miss the ceremony for sure, though he still hoped to make it for a little partying before the newly-weds departed on their honeymoon.

'What's eating you, man?' Martinez asked Sam around noon Wednesday. 'If it's tomorrow, you know we'll get you there on time.'

'It's not that,' Sam said.

He'd swung by the party store first thing and spoken to Luis Delgado, the manager, and Delgado had said he wanted to help, but their security camera had been busted for over a week, and the boss hadn't gotten around to having it fixed.

'What if it was Cooper Grace saw on Monday?' Sam said now.

'You don't think she was just being jumpy?'

Sam shrugged. 'You know how I am with coincidences.'

'Me too,' Martinez said.

'But if she was right . . .'

Sam stopped, because sweet Jesus, that thought scared him, because there were just too many connections here. As he'd pointed out to Grace last night, Cal the Hater's trademark raking of flesh had been absent in this case, and the whole macabre heart thing was totally new. But the rest could not be so easily ruled out as coincidence, not with the first toy boat so deliberately tied up at their home.

Which put Cooper, at the very least, high on their list of suspects.

List of *one*, in fact, for the time being.

Man, but that scared him.

NINE

April 22

The morning of the wedding was sunny and gorgeous, perfect weather forecast for the rest of the day.

Preparations in the Becket house well underway.

And for Sam and Martinez, a missing persons report of interest.

'Andrew Victor.' Joe Sheldon brought it to them at nine fifty. 'Twenty-seven, African-American, five-eleven, around a hundred and fifty pounds, reported missing by his housemate – ' he glanced down at his notes – 'Ms Gail Tewkesbury, who says Mr Victor sometimes goes AWOL for a week or so, but he went out almost two weeks ago and she has a real bad feeling about our John Doe.'

'Tell her we're on our way,' Sam said.

'She's going to stay home till you get there.' Sheldon handed Martinez the address. 'Condo at 50 Biscayne.'

'Fancy,' Martinez said.

Gail Tewkesbury was diminutive in stature and visibly upset, but with her sharp facial features, intent gray eyes and dressed for work in a well-cut suit, she looked like a force to be reckoned with.

'I was told you couldn't show me a photograph,' she said right after she'd let them in, and briefly her narrow mouth trembled, as if she might cry. 'So I've found Andy's comb for you because I know that might help you with the ID.' She had her emotions under control. 'And his toothbrush is in the bathroom. I'm afraid I'd already touched the comb before I thought of it, but I knew you wouldn't want me to touch the toothbrush.'

'You were right,' Sam said. 'That's very helpful.'

'I haven't touched anything in his bedroom either.' The pitch of her voice rose. 'And I have the name of his dentist, because I know that might help too.'

'It will,' Sam said. 'Thank you.'

'Do you have any reason to think that something might have happened in his bedroom, ma'am?' Martinez asked.

'No,' she said. 'Of course not. But if this . . .' She shut her eyes, took a shaky breath.

'Hey,' Sam said, gently. 'Take it easy.'

She opened her eyes, went on. 'If this were to turn out to be Andy, I just assumed you'd need to see his things.'

'We would,' Sam said. 'But let's hope it doesn't come to that. Let's hope he shows up tonight, and you can yell at him.'

'And call us,' Martinez added.

'God, yes,' she said. 'Right away.'

They got her to sit down in her blue and white living room, and she assented gratefully to Martinez going to her kitchen and getting her a small bottle of Evian, from which she sipped while she told them about Andrew Victor.

'I met him almost three years ago, while we were both working for the same downtown bank. I worked up in investments, and Andy was a teller on the first floor, but we got talking one day and just hit it off, and then last year, when I moved in here and was looking for a housemate, it all worked out beautifully because Andy's just the sweetest guy.'

'Do you still work together?' Sam asked.

'Not any more,' Gail Tewkesbury said. 'They let him go.'

Neither detective took that further, would do so only if the missing man was confirmed as the victim.

'Which bank do you work at, ma'am?' Martinez asked.

'The Starr Banking Corporation of Miami on West Flagler Street.'

Martinez made a note.

'In your call,' Sam said, 'you said this wasn't the first time Mr Victor's gone missing.'

'Not missing, exactly,' the young woman said. 'He just stays out sometimes for a week or more, and I've asked him to call and tell me so I don't worry, but Andy laughs at me and says I'm more like his mom than his real mother, and he's right, of course, except that we're friends, and friends do worry about each other.'

'Yes, they do,' Martinez said.

This time, she went on, Andrew Victor had gone out on the evening of Saturday the ninth – she had no idea where he'd been going, had just arrived back from work as he was leaving, though she remembered telling him he looked good.

'"Spiffy," I think I said. And I told him to be careful, too. I was always doing that. I guess he was right about my sounding like a mom.'

'Did you have any particular reason to tell him to be careful?' Sam asked.

'Partly because he was taking his pushbike,' she said.

That jolted both detectives.

Jerome Cooper had owned a tandem that he had named Daisy. He had used it, they knew from what he'd called his *Epistles* – a long stream of writings in a collection of exercise books found in his South Beach hidey-hole two years back – to attract lovers and tricks and victims.

If the John Doe was Andy Victor, therefore, they were looking for a bicycle that might have been dumped near the crime scene. Unless the killer had appropriated it.

'What kind of a pushbike?' Sam asked.

'It's red,' Gail Tewkesbury answered. 'I don't know what make.' She paused. 'But I took a photo of him once, posing on it, outside the bank.'

'Could you find the photo, ma'am?' Martinez asked.

'Sure,' she said. 'Shall I do that now?'

'If you don't mind,' Sam said.

She was back with them in less than five minutes, held out the photograph, and Sam took it first, studied it briefly, looked at the young, laughing face, then passed it to Martinez.

'Can you tell the make?' she asked.

'I can't,' Sam said.

'Me neither,' Martinez said. 'But we got people who can.'

'Did you have any other reasons for telling Andy to be careful?' Sam asked.

'He used to ride the pushbike with his iPod in his ears,' she said.

'Did he take the iPod that evening?' Martinez asked.

'I think so,' she said. 'I haven't seen it since.' She paused. 'Andy takes people at face value,' she went on. 'He's gay, but he hasn't had a partner for a while, and I know he goes to clubs and parties and he loves talking to strangers, and I think that can be dangerous.'

'I think you're right,' Sam said.

Gail Tewkesbury's hesitation was palpable.

'Something else you want to tell us?' Sam asked after a moment.

She shifted uneasily in her chair. 'I feel so disloyal.'

'If your friend comes home,' Sam said, 'and we hope he will, then whatever you tell us today will go no further.'

'OK,' she said. 'Andy sometimes went looking for sexual encounters.'

'Do you know where he went?' Martinez asked.

'Different places. He didn't tell me much because he knew it upset me.'

'But he still told you some stuff, didn't he?' Martinez said. 'Enough for you to get upset.'

'I guess.' She rubbed her face abruptly with her palms, left pink tracks on both cheeks. 'I already said he went to clubs.'

'Which ones?' Martinez asked.

'I don't know their names,' she said. 'Except they were in South Beach.' She gave a ragged kind of sigh. 'He went to the beach, too, at night, looking for new "friends".' She made air quotes with her right index finger. 'So dangerous, I couldn't stand to hear about it.'

'A lot of people do the same thing,' Martinez said gently.

'Doesn't make it safer,' Gail said, and her eyes filled. 'Poor Andy.'

'Any place more specific that you can remember him mentioning?' Sam asked. 'A particular section of beach, maybe?'

'He talked about the dunes,' she said.

'Always in South Beach?' Sam said.

Jerome Cooper's old hunting ground.

'I don't know,' she said.

'So do you think this could be him?' she asked, and her voice shook.

'We don't know,' Sam answered.

The knuckles on Gail Tewkesbury's clasped hands whitened. 'Is the reason you can't show me a photo because of something that's happened to his face?' Tears sprang suddenly into her eyes. 'Andy's not vain, but he takes a pride in his appearance, you know?'

'The body was in the ocean,' Sam told her, gently. 'That's why.'

She nodded. 'How long will it take to find out if this is him?'

'That's hard to say, ma'am,' he said.

'It can take time,' Martinez told her.

'But everything you've given us will help,' Sam said.

It was after eleven thirty by the time they came away. Gail Tewkesbury had all but begged them to tape off Andrew Victor's room because she could not bear the thought of potentially vital evidence being lost should it be bad news, but with no positive ID there had been little for the detectives to do but take a swift look at the room.

Nothing of immediate interest or use leapt out at them. There was no computer, and Gail told them that Andy's laptop had crashed and died due to a virus, so after he'd left the bank, he'd sometimes borrowed hers, which they were welcome to inspect at any time. His datebook bore a handful of names, and just a few appointments, on various pages from January through to mid-April, with a few more future plans, sundry birthday reminders and memory joggers set down for the rest of the year.

The names – all set down with no other information, no clues as to who they might be – were mostly male first names; few surnames, one of which Gail said she believed to be the name of a potential employer with whom Andy had interviewed in February.

The room was orderly, but not excessively so, nor did it appear to have been recently cleaned by anyone who might have been trying to conceal evidence. It was the well-cared for room of a man in his twenties whose taste in clothes and accessories seemed to favor Gap, Nike and Timbuk2, with just one photograph of a woman of around thirty – his sister, Ms Tewkesbury said – with her husband and three children; and a wall of movie posters featuring Denzel Washington, James Dean, Richard Gere, Wesley Snipes and Keanu Reeves.

Conventional tastes, it seemed to Sam, as he regarded the posters. None of Andy's possible heroes even remotely resembling the weasel-like Jerome Cooper. Or the David Bowie characters that Cooper aka Cal the Hater had modeled himself on during his last spree.

Getting *way* too far ahead, he told himself as they got back in Martinez's Chevy Impala.

'So what are you thinking?' Martinez asked.

'Nothing you're not thinking too,' Sam said. 'If it's Victor, the gay factor's another check against Cooper.' He paused. 'And South Beach, of course.'

'The pushbike, maybe, too,' Martinez said. 'Or a copycat.'

'Could be,' Sam said.

The copycat theory had already been raised at the department before the John Doe had washed up, everyone well aware that Joshua's kidnapping a couple of years back had hit the local headlines, publicizing the link between Cooper and the Miami Beach cop and his family.

Which meant that the first dinghy could have been tied up to the Beckets' piling three days after Andrew Victor had gone missing, by the by – by some other crazy crawling out of the rock, sand, marl and muck on which Miami was built. Or, now that the case had become more complex, some other murdering scumbag, not crazy at all, just evil.

'You're not buying it though,' his partner said.

They were good friends as well as partners, had long shared histories between them, some good, some bad, some sad as hell.

'I don't know what I'm buying,' Sam said. 'But copycat or not, coincidences or not, I still want Cooper behind bars.'

Because the fact remained that if it was him out there doing these things, there was no telling what kind of danger his wife and son could be in.

Again.

'We need to check Lost and Found for a red bike and iPod,' he said.

'Some hopes,' Martinez said. 'Where next?'

'Doc Sanders's office,' Sam said.

The Miami-Dade County Medical Examiner's Office on Bob Hope Road. A place they'd both had too many reasons to visit through the years.

Bearing gifts for him today. One toothbrush, one comb and the name and address of Andrew Victor's dentist. Gifts of life and death.

Just a matter of time.

'And after that,' Martinez said, 'you're going home.'

A wedding to organize.

On a scale of one to ten, Sam hoped that today ought to score about a seven for security. A family wedding at a cop's home on one of the two Bay Harbor Islands, which sported one of the lowest crime rates in Miami-Dade.

Except this was Cooper they might be talking about: a man who had stolen the same cop's baby son out of his crib while his mom had slept in the next room.

No one was really safe, ever. Sam had too many reasons to know that.

So once he got home, he was going to be keeping his eyes open for the slightest hint of trouble.

The *slightest*.

And once the day was over, he'd made up his mind to request a Bay Harbor Islands PD watch on their house and on his wife and son. And in the past, Grace might have objected to that, but now he was not at all sure that she would.

That made him sad.

And mad as hell.

* * *

David Becket's wedding afternoon.

The day still gorgeous, the sky a clear blue, not too hot.

Perfect.

His first wedding was an old, hazy memory now, existing for his two sons only in the silver-framed photographs of the occasion, but if David shut his eyes, he could travel right back to that day, could see Judy standing beside him beneath the chuppah in their temple in her beautiful white dress and veil.

Mildred knew better than anyone that she could never compete with that memory or with all the years of sharing, of everyday *living* together, just as David would never come to replace the short, but ineradicably sweet memories of her life with Donny. Neither of them wanted to compete or to replace; that was one of the things that made their decision to marry so fine.

So right. For both of them.

Not entered into lightly, that was for sure.

Though it was a fact that they had seemed to slip right into place beside each other after Mildred had first agreed to come and live in the shelter of David's home; and care, tenderness and, ultimately, love had come easily and gently after that.

Nothing wrong with easy or gentle.

Nothing wrong about *right*.

There were white roses around the front door and through the hallway, marking out the route for the guests into the lanai, which had become, for one day only, wholly unrecognizable.

No chuppah today, but Saul, his father's best man – a carpenter by profession, his furniture increasingly in local demand – had built an indoor pergola and threaded roses through its trellis roof.

Beneath which he now stood beside his father.

Waiting, as Sam brought Mildred down the short, narrow aisle.

To David, her husband-to-be.

Grace waited, too, to one side, in a dress of pale gray silk, her hair in a chignon, smiling first at the bride, then at Sam – seeing him stoop somewhat, Mildred tiny beside him, but *so* handsome in his dark suit and the new, modern Italian silk cravat she had bought for him; then smiling down with pride at Joshua, standing very straight in his new Diesel polo shirt and pants, clutching her hand, wide-eyed at the goings-on – and then looking over at Cathy, standing on the other side of the pergola, gorgeous in a cornflower-blue halter dress with her new ultra-feminine urchin haircut.

Mildred's own suit was champagne silk, her face wreathed in smiles as her adored son-in-law-to-be guided her to her groom. Handsome too in his hawk-nosed, craggy way, in his new gray suit – not looking rumpled for once – a white rose in his buttonhole, his silver hair elegantly combed, his eyes behind his spectacles intent only on her and filled with warmth.

Her David.

They had exchanged their vows, been declared husband and wife by Judge Helen Dawkins, an old friend of the groom's, had kissed, held hands, signed their names, been congratulated and embraced, had laughed with pleasure, and had both come close to shedding tears of pure joy.

And now, together with their family and close friends, they were partying, eating, drinking and dancing.

Saul was dancing with Mel Ambonetti, a twenty-one-year-old student in the Anthropology Department at the University of Miami, a tall, blue-eyed brunette, with an elegant aquiline nose and long, shining hair that swung as she moved. Three months together, and the first woman who had gotten to Saul for a long time.

The whole Becket clan here today, along with good friends and neighbors, and a fistful of cops, too: Martinez, of course – who'd hurried in just after six – and Beth Riley and Mike Alvarez, too, both having become friends of the groom's over time.

No family there for Mildred. Her parents, still living in Queens, had claimed frailty as their reason for not attending – and David had asked Mildred if she might like to go back to New York City for their honeymoon, but Mildred had said she was determined that nothing and no one would spoil their special time.

'Though it seems a shame,' David had persisted after they'd chosen Boston as their destination, 'to be so close and not go see your parents at all.' He'd shrugged. 'They can't be getting any younger.'

'I guess you're right,' Mildred had said. 'And heaven knows I've never had much time for unforgiving people, so maybe we could go at the end of the vacation.' She'd paused. 'But I wouldn't want to stay with them, even if they ask us to, which they probably will not.'

'We'll be in a hotel,' David had assured her.

The Ritz Carlton in Boston, first, and he'd reserved a park view room at the Plaza in Manhattan for the last five days before their return, and that about summed up what David wanted for Mildred

– that, and good health for them both, and as long a shared old age as the good Lord would grant them.

Beautiful food and surroundings today, a two-tier wedding cake and a birthday cake for Saul, both baked and decorated by Grace and Cathy, the same way that everything had been arranged and prepared by them, with love.

A wonderful party, and a wonderful day.

No troubles.

Not a single one.

The happy couple going on their way finally, though Sam and Grace had suggested they wait till next day to leave, since their flight would not reach Boston until gone midnight, but David and Mildred had been determined to do it their way.

'Plenty of time to rest when we get there,' Mildred had reassured them.

'Plenty of time to rest when we're dead,' David had added.

TEN

April 23

Early next morning, Sam met with a lieutenant in patrol at the Bay Harbor Islands Police Department – a man he'd had cause to meet a few times – to explain his concerns for his family's safety with regard to the suspected return to Miami-Dade of Jerome Cooper.

Having been a sergeant at the time of the kidnapping, the lieutenant did not need asking twice.

'I'd really appreciate this being kept informal,' Sam said.

'You don't want your wife to know?' the lieutenant asked.

'She'll know,' Sam said. 'But this is really a just-in-case.'

'Better safe than sorry,' the other man said.

'I owe you,' Sam told him.

Grace felt tired Friday morning, but good. Happy and relaxed, the way she always felt after a family party had gone beautifully. The kids had helped with most of the clearing up, and she had taken Joshua to preschool before settling down to the tasks that remained.

Sam had called to tell her about the patrol cars that were going to be coming around every now and then till they could be sure Cooper was not on the scene.

'Are you sure it's necessary?' she had asked.

'I'm hoping it's *un*necessary,' he'd said. 'But if you don't mind, I'd sooner err on the side of caution.'

'I think I mind a good deal,' Grace had said. 'But I'm not sure I feel like arguing the point either.'

She was still feeling good – getting the job done, thinking about the newly-weds' first Boston morning, hoping their flowers had arrived – as she took out yet another bag of trash just after eleven, ahead of going to collect Joshua, when a gray four-door sedan came around the bend in their road and slowed to a crawl opposite their house.

Tinted windows closed.

Someone watching.

This time, she was *certain*.

Woody, at her heels, growled softly.

'It's OK,' she told him, and bent to pick him up.

The car had not moved.

Grace's heartbeat grew rapid, her mouth dry. She looked up and down the road, wishing for a black-and-white to appear *now*.

No such luck.

In her arms, Woody growled again.

The sedan was still there.

Quickly, Grace turned and hurried back into the house, shut and locked the front door, walked swiftly into the kitchen to do the same, then to the lanai.

And then she called Sam.

'Nothing to worry about, Detective,' one of the patrol officers assured Sam as soon as he pulled up. 'We'd have called you if there was.'

They had been aware of the car in question, the officer said, had been observing the gray Ford Fusion right outside the Becket house, had been parked just around the bend in the road, had noted Grace's reaction too.

The Ford had begun to move away right after she'd gone inside, and the cops had made their own move in response, signaling the driver to pull over.

Totally innocent.

'Just a guy out with his wife looking at properties,' the officer told Sam. 'Whole bunch of printed details with them in the car. They were embarrassed, said they'd just wanted to get the feel of the island, were interested in the kind of people living here, the way people do, you know.'

'Sure,' Sam said.

'They said they were real sorry if they'd upset the lady, but the guy said he figured that if he rolled down the window and spoke to her, that might have freaked her out more.' The officer's grin was relaxed. 'His words.'

'And they checked out?' Sam asked.

'Goes without saying, Detective,' the officer said.

'I'm grateful to you,' Sam told him.

The guy's partner looked a little awkward.

'Mrs Becket sure looked edgy,' he said.

'She has good cause,' Sam said.

'I guess she does,' the other man said.

Some good news for Gail Tewkesbury.

Comparison of Andrew Victor's dental records proved that he was not their John Doe, though her concern for him remained undiminished, especially as it was too soon to say if Victor's DNA was a match for the heart found three days after his disappearance.

'Nice woman,' Martinez remarked after Sam had gotten off the phone, having assured her that her fears for her friend were still being taken seriously.

'Very,' Sam agreed.

'One link less to Cooper,' Martinez said.

That particular gay connection having been wiped out.

Which ought, perhaps, have been allowing Sam to feel easier about his family's safety, but was doing no such thing, because the news had reduced his justification for any kind of patrol at their house.

No one had suggested that the dinghy and contents tied up to their mooring had been a random act, but the location of the second heart had been wholly unconnected to them, added to which Sam feared that Grace's visible jitters might stop some people taking his concerns as seriously as they ought.

Especially with the copycat theory gaining strength.

'Anything I can do, man?' Martinez asked.

'I wish,' Sam said.

'Patrol's still out there,' his friend said.

'For now,' Sam said.

Just before six, more news in from Ida Lowenstein in the ME's office.

A DNA match.

The second heart – the one found in the pool at the Fontainebleau – belonged to their John Doe.

The turnaround for DNA checking in Miami-Dade usually a *whole* lot longer.

'Guess Ida came through for you again,' Martinez said.

He was always claiming that the lady had a soft spot for Sam – though they both knew this was Doc Sanders himself leaning on the lab to speed things up.

No body yet for the heart left outside the Becket house – that possible DNA matching still in the system's backlog.

No more missing persons reports to help ID the Doe.

'This I hate,' Sam said.

'Know what you mean,' Martinez said.

They all felt bad about unnamed victims. No one able to mourn them and no solid start at chasing down the perpetrators, let alone getting justice for the deceased.

And this case, with its disturbing but inconclusive links to Cal-Cooper . . .

Sam had never wished for great wealth, knew he had a good life, that he was blessed with more comforts than he had a right to, that he had all the things that really counted. Family, love, good health, a home he loved; the ability to help make his dad's wedding day memorable; occasional extravagances like the tickets he'd bought months ago for tomorrow night's performance of *Don Pasquale* – opera a big thing with Sam, though he hadn't sung for a long while now.

Lucky man, and he knew it.

But just for once, he would have liked to be rich enough to whisk every member of his family away to safety. Just until they put away this killer – copycat or Cooper.

Then, and only then, would Sam feel able to rest.

ELEVEN

April 24

Late Saturday evening, in the hubbub of a semi-wild party at a warehouse on NE 2nd Avenue in Wynwood, the man just embarked on his latest mission took his first look around the throng of flailing dancers and drinkers – and knew.

Soon as he set eyes on him.

It was, he had begun to think, his greatest talent.

Knowing who to pick out for his boss.

Not for himself – he'd never been gifted in that department, but for the *man* he seemed to get it right almost every time, which was one of the main reasons he was still on the payroll.

Not the only reason though.

He took a slug of the lousy vodka someone had handed him, and made his way through the crowd.

Eye contact already established.

Eyes were very important to the *man*, and this guy's were just about perfect. Darkly dancing. Friendly and bold.

He was up for it, no question.

'Hey,' he said.

'Hey,' the other man said back, in a low, warm voice.

The Boss liked good voices too.

'Feel like getting out of here?'

No reason to linger.

Every reason not to.

'Sure,' the other guy said. 'Why not?'

He smelled OK, so far as it was possible to be certain in this stinkhole of cheap perfume, body odors and all kinds of smoke.

Fragrance was another plus.

'I'm Rico,' the target said.

Somewhere deeper inside the warehouse there was a bang and women shrieked, and then there was raucous laughter and more loud banging, cracking, like fireworks, maybe.

'You got a name?' Rico wanted to know.

'You can call me Toy.'

'I like that,' Rico said.

From a distance, they heard sirens, coming closer.

'Let's get out of here,' Toy said.

Mission, Stage One: check.

TWELVE

April 25

Anticlimax hit Grace hard on Sunday.

Post-wedding, post-opera, those fine distractions past, as if all the preparations and the big day itself and, finally, last night's outing with Sam, had formed a kind of protective bubble, keeping out the inky darkness of the threat she still felt looming over them.

All her unease was back today.

Sam was at work on the John Doe killing with Martinez – both of them, she knew, feeling the frustration that came with working blind – and she knew, too, that Sam had been behind Cathy's and Saul's insistence that she and Joshua come for lunch at the apartment they shared in Sunny Isles Beach, which irked her just a little because it brought home the fact that he was worried by her edginess.

Not that she wasn't glad to be with them, and she was touched by their concern, but long after they'd eaten and lazed around for a couple of hours, they were still encouraging her to stay, plainly trying to keep her there till Sam got home.

'We're not playing that game,' she told them both. 'Bay Harbor PD are still patrolling, and even if they weren't, I'm sure I'd be perfectly safe.'

'At least let Saul go back with you,' Cathy said. 'Check the place out.'

'It would make me a whole lot happier,' Saul said.

'Oh, for heaven's sake,' Grace said. 'It's so unnecessary.'

'We don't think so,' Cathy said. 'Nor would Sam.'

Grace and Sam were her parents in every sense that mattered, but Cathy had never called them 'Mom' or 'Dad'. Her biological father had been an evil man. Her mother and beloved stepfather – the first man to have adopted her – had both been horrifically murdered. 'Mom' and 'Dad' bore too many bad connotations. Sam and Grace had been Cathy's fresh start.

'All right,' Grace said now, giving in.

She told them she was doing it for their peace of mind, but the truth was that she *did* feel idiotically relieved watching her young brother-in-law checking around the place until he was satisfied.

'You sure you want me to go?' Saul asked when he was done.

'Of course I want you to go,' Grace said.

She looked and sounded light-hearted, confident and calm.

Little point, after all, in letting Saul know the worst of her fears – the ones she hoped and prayed were mostly in her mind.

That if she and Joshua were not really safe while Cooper was still at large, then *none* of them were safe.

Stage Two had gone even more perfectly.

Toy had realized that as soon as he'd seen the Boss's face.

The *man* was pleased with the night's selection, no doubt about that.

And all Toy had to do was make the intro.

He got it right, etiquette-wise, which was another of his skills.

'Tom O'Hagen,' he had said, 'this is Rico.'

The Boss first, every time. Always the superior first.

'Hello, Rico,' the man said.

Which had been when Toy had seen just *how* pleased he was.

'Can I get you anything else, Mr O'Hagen,' Toy had asked.

O'Hagen's eyes had not left Rico's face.

'Not another thing, Toy,' he said.

Which was Stage Two done with.

Easy as blinking.

Not quite so easy inside.

In the part of Toy that had once housed his conscience. The part that had gone AWOL not long after he'd met Tom O'Hagen and sold his soul.

Not to the Devil, exactly.

But almost certainly to one of his cohorts.

Toy couldn't know that for sure – he didn't know anything for *sure*, not about what happened to guys like Rico after he'd delivered them to the Boss.

Except that he never saw them again.

For which he was devoutly thankful.

He *knew* it, though. Knew that bad things happened to them.

Stage Three.

Not his business.

He hoped, with all that remained of his soul, to keep it that way.

There were things Toy was prepared to do, and things he was not.

He'd done plenty for O'Hagen, and hoped to go on doing more.

Not just for the money, either, though Christ knew he needed it.

Tom O'Hagen certainly knew.

And for now, anyway, the Boss's gratitude was solid.

All that really counted, for Toy.

On Sunday evening, Grace was still alone.

Sam had called a while back to say he might not be able to get home before dark, and she'd told him a little crankily that she was fine, that there was no reason for him to worry.

'When have I ever stressed about being alone after dark?' she'd said. 'Besides, I have our son and dog for company, so I'm not alone, am I?'

Which had, she knew, hardly filled Sam with confidence, given that less than two years ago, Woody had accepted doped meat from Jerome Cooper, clearing the way for the killer to kidnap Joshua.

A hard thing for either of them to forget.

Still, she'd been working calmly enough in her office, and had made a small snack of Cheddar and crackers, and aside from going upstairs to check on Joshua – borderline obsessively – every fifteen minutes, she was doing just fine.

Until she heard the sounds.

Like shuffling – not inside, but someplace *close*, one minute seeming to come from around the back, then at the side of the house – creepy sounds – but she just couldn't identify exactly *where* they were coming from.

'Woody?' She looked down at the dog by her feet.

Not so much as a cocked ear, let alone a growl.

'OK,' she said.

She went upstairs to check on Joshua again, then back down to her desk.

'OK,' she said again. 'Relax.'

She heard it again.

'Come on, guy,' she told Woody.

Phone in one hand, little dog at her heels, she took another slow walk around the house, checked every window, double-locked the front and back doors, switched on the outside lights to take a look around.

Nothing. No one.

She *hated* feeling this way, had never been like this in the past. Enough cause, Lord knew, but that made her resent it no less.

New sound.

The Saab entering the driveway.

Pure relief, then a kind of frustration, almost anger.

'This is not me,' she told herself, quietly.

And went to greet her husband.

THIRTEEN

April 26

At seven twenty on Monday morning, two miles east of Baker's Haulover Cut, soon after Ron Emett had taken a dive off his pontoon boat to try and find out what was amiss with the Danforth anchor, he surfaced gasping and ashen-faced.

'Call the cops!' he yelled up to his wife, Rachel.

'What happened?' She leaned over the side, stretched out her hand to try to help him as he began scrambling wildly back on board. 'What's wrong with the anchor?'

'What's wrong with it,' he told her, 'is there's a *body* attached to it.'

Goddamned flesh and bone snared right around one of the flukes.

Ron Emett had never felt so sick.

'You just call the cops and stay on this boat,' he told Rachel. 'You don't ever want to see what I just saw, honey. Not ever.'

Not *ever.*

They came in droves.

Not just the cops and Sam and Martinez and Crime Scene and Doc Sanders, and more members of the media circus than any of them had seen in a long time, but any number of small private boats, plus a horde of rubberneckers with binoculars on the beaches, no one put off by the storm warnings forecast for the day. And who the hell had gotten word out so fast, Sam didn't know, but none of it really mattered, because there was and would be nothing much for them to see, because the remains of that poor human being would be kept under wraps until the ME was ready to commence his exam back on dry land.

And so far as the detectives were concerned, they, too, were going to be pretty much treading water until Elliot Sanders had something to tell them.

Could be days or weeks.

And maybe it was some kind of perverse wishful thinking, or maybe it was one of Sam Becket's well-known hunches, which made no sense, given that this could be anyone: a lone sailor gone overboard or a drunk or a swimmer who'd gotten in a jam with no one to help him. *Anyone.*

But Sam knew it was another victim.

He just knew it.

FOURTEEN

April 28

He was right.

And this time it was bad news for Gail Tewkesbury, among others, because they had a match.

The body that had come to rest beneath Ron and Rachel Emett's pontoon was that of Andrew Victor, Ms Tewkesbury's housemate and friend.

Like the first body – still a John Doe – this poor guy was minus his heart, not to mention various fingers, toes and other parts of his anatomy, courtesy of nature and the ocean's scavengers.

He still had his teeth, though, a perfect match for Victor's dental records.

Which meant that Sam and Martinez and the rest of the squad were now in business with a full-blown homicide investigation.

'No clear evidence of skin raking,' Lieutenant Alvarez pointed out at a squad meeting. 'The heart not Cooper's MO, so far as we know.'

'But Andrew Victor was African-American, gay, was known to go looking for sex in South Beach, was probably strangled with a ligature from behind, all of which makes him a candidate for Cooper,' Sam responded. 'And no, his heart wasn't the one stuck in a dinghy and tied to my house, but that message was as personal as Cooper's note to me last March.'

'Any idea why he'd graduate to cutting out hearts?' Joe Sheldon asked.

'Because he's the sickest fuck we've ever had to deal with,' Martinez said.

'Maybe it'll turn out to be just black hearts,' Sam said, then shrugged. 'Cal was always an exhibitionist.'

'And he may not be raking his victims' chests these days,' Martinez said, 'but I'm betting the fruitcake still beats himself up.'

'Only one way to prove that,' Sergeant Riley said. 'Find him.'

The squad's number one task.

No one wanting that to happen more than Sam Becket.

He had woken up that morning with something else on his mind.

Their home was not secure enough, his wife was still jittery, even if she wasn't admitting it, and the fact was, none of them could be truly safe so long as Cooper was at large.

Time to do something.

He called Grace just before he and Martinez left for the Tewkesbury apartment.

'I want us all to move to Dan and Claudia's house until we know things are safer. Cathy and Saul too.'

Security and family all under one roof.

Made sense to him.

'Sam, we can't do that.' Grace was startled. 'We can't impose on them.'

'I talked to Dan an hour ago. He and Claudia are all for it.'

'You've all been talking about this?' She felt a surge of irritation.

'Gracie, don't get mad,' Sam said. 'One conversation, one hour ago.'

She shook her head. 'But why now? I mean, I know they found this poor person, but what's changed?'

'Nothing's changed,' he said. 'But too much still points to Jerome being back, and that's a risk I don't want to take.'

Her anger had gone, replaced by a sinking sensation.

'You think it was him at the party shop last week,' she said.

'I don't know, but I guess I'm just not prepared to take the chance that it might have been,' he said. 'And you can't deny that your sister's house is a much nicer proposition than some hotel room or safe house.'

'That's not the point,' Grace said.

'I'd say it's exactly the point.'

Daniel Brownley's security system had been set up so that any occupant could check any part of Névé, internal and external, from several locations around the house. The smart materials created primarily for comfort could also be used to fool would-be intruders into believing that the house was occupied when it was empty. And the alarm system was directed through to the Village of Key Biscayne Police Department and a private security firm.

It was everything Sam and Grace both ordinarily hated.

But these were not ordinary times.

'I'm not going to leave you or our son unprotected again,' Sam said. 'And the same goes for Cathy and Saul.'

'We could make our own house more secure,' Grace said.

'Is that what you want?' Sam asked.

Grace was silent for a moment, picturing alarms and bars at their windows, hating it as he knew she would.

'Is there anything you haven't told me?' she asked. 'Any threats?'

'Nothing I haven't told you,' he said. 'Just common sense.'

She took another moment.

'What do we do about preschool?'

'We keep Joshua with us till this is over,' Sam said.

Another pause.

'What do you want me to do?'

'Get packed, lock up, pick up Joshua and get over to your sister's.'

'I have two patients this afternoon,' Grace said.

'Are they emergencies?'

She considered the cases: an eight-year-old and a young teen. Both doing quite well, neither in crisis.

'I can postpone,' she said. 'What about Cathy and Saul?'

'Leave them to me,' Sam said.

'You know you're scaring me now,' Grace said.

'I don't mean to,' he said. 'That's the whole point.'

Gail Tewkesbury was heartsick, but she was still exactly the kind of intelligent, clear-minded person that Sam and Martinez needed to assist them. Staying calm and cooperative as the investigative machine got underway around her, she offered the detectives coffee and water and then began, all over again, to tell them everything she could about Andrew Victor and the friendship they'd first formed at the Starr Banking Corporation.

He had, she divulged to them now, been fired after three warnings for bad timekeeping and, finally, for swearing at his boss.

'And I guess he could have his moments, but he was still the nicest man I ever met,' Gail said in the sitting room. 'Any time I needed help with anything, or got sick or just blue, Andy was there for me – and to be honest, I think maybe his weaknesses made me even fonder of him.' Her shrug was sorrowful. 'I already told you he said I sometimes mothered him a little, but he liked it – maybe because his own mom wasn't the easiest.'

'How much did he tell you about his family?' Sam asked.

'Just that it hadn't gone too well when he came out. His dad got mad, his mom was more embarrassed than anything, Andy thought. He said they were both relieved when he moved away.'

'His sister, Anne, is flying in today,' Martinez told her.

'I know,' Gail said. 'She texted me first thing. I never met her, but I'm sure she must be broken up. It was important to Andy that she stayed in touch with him.' She paused. 'Do you think you could make sure she knows that? In case I don't get to meet her.'

'I expect you will,' Sam said.

'We'll tell her though,' Martinez said.

Andrew Victor's bedroom yielded no more of obvious interest than it had a week earlier, when its occupant had still been a missing person, not yet a victim of homicide.

No love notes, no hidden cache of photographs, erotic or otherwise. No illegal drugs, no prescription medications of the kind that might have been subject to abuse. No threatening or even reproachful letters from lovers, current or past. Just the neatly kept room of a young man thought by his landlady and friend to be 'the sweetest guy'.

'There's nothing in his waste basket,' Sam said to Gail. 'Did you empty it?'

She shook her head. 'Andy must have before he went out.'

The garbage collections long since gone.

They looked harder, but failed to find a cellphone or address book. They removed the datebook they had previously glanced at, with its few names to try following up, but little else to help them; meetings that might or might not have been dates or even potential sexual encounters, but no helpful notes either anticipatory or reviewing. And only the last four months to scrutinize, last year's diary not yet in evidence.

'Not a "Dear Diary" kind of a guy,' Martinez commented.

'More's the pity,' Sam said.

The chances were, of course, that even if they did turn up any of the men named on those pages, they would turn out to be irrelevant to the investigation, because the likelihood was that Andrew Victor had happened upon his killer on a street or on a beach or at a private party or at a nightclub – an encounter, wherever it had taken place, that would have given poor Andy no chance to log the person's name in his datebook.

They sat down again with Gail, went through each entry with her, but she had beaten them to the punch, had already compiled a list of names of her own.

'This is everyone I can remember Andy ever mentioning,' she said, handing it over. 'Though I've probably forgotten people – my brain's turned to mush.'

'Hardly surprising.' Sam looked at her list. 'This is good.'

She'd supplied more than names. Relationships with the deceased, as far as she knew, were printed beside each one, together with phone numbers and suggested possible addresses.

'This is more than good,' he said after a moment.

'Except I can't imagine that any of them could be of any use,' Gail said sorrowfully. 'I mean, how's the guy who Andy said kept new releases for him at a DVD rental place going to help find his . . .?'

She stopped, unable to bring herself to speak the word.

They gave her a few moments.

'How about I make you a cup of tea?' Martinez offered.

She shook her head. 'I'm OK.'

'Going back to the lifestyle risks you mentioned last time we met,' Sam said.

'Yes.' Her voice was soft, sadder than ever.

'You mentioned clubs and the beach,' Sam reminded her.

'I still don't know which clubs,' she said.

'Anything else you've thought of?'

'He went to parties, sometimes,' Gail said.

'Friends' parties?' Sam asked.

'Mostly not,' she said. 'The open kind, I guess – he said he got to hear about them on the Internet, in chat rooms, maybe.' Her eyes moved to her VAIO notebook on a desk in the corner. 'As I told you, he sometimes used my laptop, so please feel free to look at it, or take it if you need to.'

Martinez leaned forward, his dark eyes intent. 'Did Andy ever mention any chat rooms in particular?'

'Or any websites you can remember?' Sam asked.

'I don't think so,' Gail said. 'But I guess if he visited any of them here, they might still be in the cache.'

They'd told her on arrival that their search warrant would extend to her private space and property, and she'd said they didn't need a warrant, that she wanted nothing more than to assist them, but Sam had explained about the wisdom of ensuring search warrants were in place even in cases where consent had been given.

Few things more soul-destroying to a cop than watching hard evidence rendered inadmissible in court by a technicality.

'Any other gizmos of yours he shared?' Martinez asked.

She shook her head.

'Your cellphone?' Sam said.

'He had his own iPhone.' She smiled. 'We went into the Apple store on Lincoln Road last month because I'm thinking of getting the iPad, but Andy was too busy flirting with one of the Genius guys to take much notice of anything else.' Once again her eyes began to brim. 'I'm sorry.'

'Don't be,' Martinez said. 'You're doing great.'

'Did he and the Genius guy make contact after that?' Sam asked.

'No way,' Gail said.

'You're sure?' Sam said.

'He was straight,' Gail said. 'Andy said it was a waste.'

Deep sadness in her eyes again.

They called a halt, knowing there was no more to be gleaned from her this day, but Sam asked her – knowing it was unnecessary, that the young woman would do little else for a long while – to keep on thinking, going over past conversations, small everyday events.

'You just never know when something trivial can lead somewhere,' he said.

'You think I might have a clue buried someplace in my head,' she said.

'It happens,' Martinez said.

Her face seemed to alter for an instant, a frown puckering her brow. 'I don't suppose . . .'

'Go on,' Sam said.

She shook her head. 'I feel selfish even thinking it, but it hadn't occurred to me till just now that I might conceivably be in some kind of danger.'

'I'd say that was unlikely,' Sam said.

'Unless you think you might know the killer,' Martinez said.

They were already at the door, ready to leave, but willing to give her another hour or more, and it wouldn't have been the first time that an innocent afterthought had taken them someplace worthwhile.

'In a way, I wish I did,' Gail said. 'Believe me, if I had the smallest inkling, you'd already know it.'

Sam believed her.

Though the days had long gone since he'd taken any stranger at face value.

Life's lessons had been too hard.

A man had to be a damned fool not to heed them.

He took an hour mid-afternoon to collect Cathy from JWU and bring her back to Sunny Isles Beach, where Saul was waiting at their apartment.

'The fact is,' Sam told them, 'that until Jerome Cooper is either locked up or on a slab at the morgue, I want my family taking special measures.'

'So we're all going to Claudia's?' Saul said.

Sam nodded. 'It's pretty much ideal, and Dan and Claudia say they're happy about it.'

'I'm not,' Cathy said. 'I go to college in North Miami.'

'I'll drive you,' Saul said, 'morning and afternoon.'

'How lovely,' she said. 'In your beautiful pickup.'

'Snob,' her uncle said.

'What about your workshop?' Cathy was serious. 'You have zero security.'

'I'll buy a new lock,' he said.

'I'd rather you took time off,' Sam told his brother.

'I have a commission,' Saul said. 'And it's not movable.' He paused. 'But I've been thinking I could use a little help from Hal with one of the big pieces, so maybe now could be a good time for that.'

'Hal's not exactly bodyguard material,' Cathy said.

Hal Liebmann was a buddy of Saul's, went back a long way.

'He's tough enough,' Saul said.

'So long as you make sure you're never alone,' Sam said. 'Which applies to you too,' he told Cathy. 'Grace and I aren't too happy about you going to college.'

'I'll stay with the crowd,' Cathy said. 'I know better than to take chances.'

'I know you do,' Sam said. 'But for now, we all live on Key Biscayne, OK?'

'I guess,' Cathy said.

'Sounds like fun,' Saul said.

Sam stood up. 'I'll leave you guys to pack.'

'You want us to drive together?' Saul asked.

'I'd honestly rather have my own car,' Cathy said. 'No offense intended.'

'I'd rather you go together,' Sam said.

'Do you really think Cooper might make a move on us?' Cathy asked.

'I doubt it,' Sam said.

'You're just going to be happier having us all under one roof,' Saul said.

'I'll be happier,' Sam said, 'when this is over.'

When Anne Dover – Andrew Victor's thirty-two-year-old sister – arrived at Miami International soon after six, Sam and Martinez were waiting.

It was not the way they ordinarily chose to proceed, preferring wherever possible to allow grieving relatives at least a little breathing space before bringing down a load of painful questions on their heads. But Mrs Dover had spoken first to Lieutenant Alvarez, and then to Sam, and had made it clear that she wanted to be of assistance, if possible, the instant she landed.

And the fact was they might never get an ID on the first John Doe because, sad to say, that happened too damned often. Which meant they needed every detail from every person they could find in Andrew Victor's life.

She looked older than her years, wore a black suit and small hat, giving her a look, Sam thought, of the fifties, making him wonder if she'd borrowed it from her mother, the woman who had, according to Gail Tewkesbury, made her son feel that she was embarrassed by him.

'Please don't be nice to me,' Anne Dover told them, within moments of meeting. 'I don't deserve it, and I don't really want it, if it's all the same to you.'

'If it's all the same to you,' Sam said, 'I think we're going to find it hard not to be nice to you.'

Anne Dover's smile was wan. 'Just do your best,' she said.

'We will, ma'am,' Martinez told her.

They wanted to take her to her downtown hotel, but she wanted to talk to them right away, so they went to Starbucks in the terminal and, without preamble, she explained to them the cause of her shame.

'It hit our parents very hard, finding out Andy was gay,' Anne said, 'and I know he kept on hoping things would change, but they never did. Our father was angry about it – as if it was something Andy could have changed, like his clothes – but our mother seemed to find it socially unacceptable, which always seemed much worse to me.' She shook her head. 'I was worse than either of them.'

Sam and Martinez both waited as Anne Dover stirred her coffee, but she remained silent, locked in another world.

'What did you do?' Sam asked, finally.

'Nothing,' she said. 'Not one damned thing.'

'Your brother's friend, Gail, says that you stayed in touch with him,' Sam told her. 'She said that meant a lot to Andrew.'

'It's nice of her to say that,' Anne Dover said.

'I'd say she meant it,' Martinez said.

'More than I deserve then,' she said, and took a breath. 'So tell me, gentlemen, what I can do for my brother now. When it's all too late. I'm assuming you don't know who did this to him?'

Sam leaned in to the table. 'How much did he tell you about his life?'

'Not much,' she said. 'But I've brought all his letters, just in case there's anything in any of them that might help you.' She reached down, patted her black trolley case. 'I thought I might look through them on the flight, but I found I couldn't.'

'There's time,' Sam said.

'I don't think there's anything there,' she said. 'I can't remember him telling me about anything bad happening – except when he got fired from the bank. Did you know about that?'

'We did,' Martinez said.

'That upset Andy so much,' his sister said. 'But he didn't blame anyone except himself. He was never resentful.'

'Did you speak often?' Sam asked.

'I called him about once a month. Andy always liked to hear about my children – two boys and a girl. My husband's home, taking care of them.'

'Your brother kept a photo of you all in his room,' Sam told her.

She nodded. 'I guess you've been through all his things already.'

'I'm afraid we had no choice,' Martinez said.

'I know,' Anne Dover said. 'I just think Andy would have hated that.'

She had nothing of use to share with them, but she promised to make herself available at any time of day or night while she was in Miami. Her parents, she said, had no plans to fly down, and she would be making the arrangements to bring her brother home when formalities permitted.

She refused their offer of a ride into the city, apologized for not being able to help them in any way as yet apparent, and asked them to keep her in touch with the investigation.

'Sackcloth routine a little hard to take?' Sam said to Martinez as they headed back to the car.

'You think?' Martinez said, and rolled his eyes.

'I guess her pain's genuine enough,' Sam said.

'A genuine pain,' Martinez said.

The air was still balmy just after eight thirty when Sam's old Saab growled its way past Névé's steel security gate and lights blazed out in the driveway.

Grace's Toyota and Cathy's Mazda – not Saul's Dodge pickup, after all – stood alongside the other family cars, and the front door was already opening, and Mike, Grace's older nephew – an athletic, handsome seventeen – was emerging with a welcoming smile.

They were a warm, natural, easygoing family, yet their front door was solid steel masked by a snow-white façade, complete with biometric fingerprint entry system. And Lord knew security was just what Sam craved for his own family right now, but he had wondered at it more than once, at the gentle-mannered architect who'd gone to such semi-paranoid lengths.

'Hey,' Mike said. 'Need a hand?'

'Hey yourself,' Sam said, pulling his bag out of the trunk. 'No hand needed, thanks. How're you coping with all this?'

'It's great to have you here,' Mike said. 'Everyone's out back. Dad's barbecuing.' He led the way inside, and the door closed with a soft whoosh and click behind them. 'Mom said I should ask if you want to freshen up or come right on through and have a beer?'

'Beer, no contest,' Sam said.

He was off-duty till morning, with Cutter and Sheldon taking the late shift to start calling in at some of the South Beach nightclubs that a guy like Andrew Victor – a 'risk-taker', according to Gail Tewkesbury – might have visited on the evening of Saturday, April 9, on what might have been the last night of his life.

Sam dumped his bag along with those thoughts and followed Mike across the vast open-plan living space that formed much of the first floor of their home, through to the illuminated rear of the house, with its expanse of terrace, deck, pool and barbecue area – where Daniel and his younger son, Robbie – fifteen years old, living mostly for food and his electronic gizmos – were hard at work, wearing 'Danger, Men Cooking' aprons.

'Hi, guys,' Sam said, and Woody came trotting over with Ludo, the three-legged spaniel rescued by the family last year in Seattle.

'You made it.' Grace, looking relaxed in jeans, got up off her lounger and came to kiss him. 'Joshua's asleep upstairs, tired out from being spoiled the instant we got here.'

'Hey, bro,' Saul said from another lounger.

Mike brought him over his beer, and Sam thanked him and made his way across to their host, gave him and Robbie a hug.

'Thanks don't seem enough for this, Dan,' he said.

'More than enough,' Daniel told him.

Sam looked at the tall, angular, green-eyed, bespectacled man, a little stooped from decades of leaning over drawing boards, but still driven and vital and fundamentally kind, and thought again how glad he and Grace were that he and Claudia had gotten over their bad patch a couple of years ago.

'If you're wondering where your daughter is,' Daniel said, 'she's helping Claudia in the kitchen and looking lovelier than ever.'

'She's very happy at JWU, thank God,' Sam said.

'She deserves all the happiness she can get,' Daniel said.

* * *

Grace came with him upstairs – up a steel and glass staircase softly lit from within – to show Sam the guest suite, which was more comfortable than any hotel they'd ever stayed in.

'Cathy's going to be downstairs in another guest room with en-suite shower,' Grace said. 'Saul's sharing with Mike, and Joshua's in with Robbie.'

Sam checked out the room, put away his gun and holster in a bedside drawer. 'I thought he'd be with us.'

'Robbie really wants to have him,' Grace said, 'though we can always turn things around if anyone's unhappy.'

She came into the bathroom while he showered.

'We need to talk about my patients,' she said.

'I thought you'd have them come here,' Sam said, reaching for a towel.

'I can't do that,' she said. 'It's too far, and there'd be confidentiality issues with so many people coming and going – not to mention the inconvenience for Claudia and Dan.'

Sam went back into the bedroom and rummaged in his bag for shorts and a T-shirt. 'So what's your plan?'

'House calls?'

'Not safe enough.' He sat on the bed, pulled on sneakers. 'Any chance Magda would let you share her setup for a little while?'

Magda Shrike – Grace's mentor, friend and occasional psychologist – had recently relocated both home and office into a prime building in Bal Harbour.

'Twenty-four hour doorman,' he said. 'Decent security.'

'I'm not sure she'd have the space, let alone the inclination.'

'But you don't hate the idea?' Sam asked.

'I hate all of it,' Grace said.

'Will you call her?'

'We'd have to look at our insurance policies.'

'Sure,' Sam said. 'So will you call her?'

Grace smiled at him.

'First thing tomorrow,' she said.

The rest of the evening was almost pure pleasure. Daniel was glad to let Sam and Saul lend a hand with the cooking, while Grace and Claudia sipped wine and ate themselves to a standstill. Mike and Robbie and Cathy swam and ate and laughed a lot and everyone took turns to go upstairs to check on Joshua, and even the dogs hung out happily together.

'It's so beautiful out here,' Grace said to Sam.

'Sure is,' he agreed.

He was trying not to stare out past the white, alarmed, monitored fence to the dark bay beyond, trying not to imagine Cooper out there somewhere with a long-range night scope trained on them – maybe even a high-powered rifle sight – almost the entire Becket family laid out for him in one fell swoop . . .

'Stop it, Sam,' Grace told him quietly.

Which told him it was nothing she hadn't considered too.

Both their imaginations running riot.

'We have to live,' she said. 'Make the most of this.'

Sam nodded. 'Special time.'

'And not just because it could get taken away,' Grace said. 'OK?'

They'd spoken in the past about whether or not they might have benefited from therapy after what they'd gone through a year ago, and Sam had been offered counseling through the EAP, but had turned it down because, shaken as he was, he'd felt so damned happy to be alive. And they both knew, more than most, what damage could be done by unresolved post-traumatic issues, yet still they'd both stubbornly, perhaps foolishly, chosen to get by on the sheer relief of survival.

Lately, though, Sam had become increasingly concerned that it might have been the wrong decision for Grace. Not just because her jumpiness was so uncharacteristic – if justifiable – but also because it seemed to him that she was up and down, in and out of denial.

Which was not healthy, and not like her.

Another reason, perhaps, why working with Magda might be a good plan, because if anyone could persuade Grace to get some counseling before things got out of hand, it was Dr Magda Shrike.

Yet this evening, here and now, Grace was the one making sense.

The way she almost always did.

Sam lifted his beer bottle.

'Damned straight,' he said.

FIFTEEN

April 29

They all went about their business Thursday morning – all except Grace, who was waiting for Magda to return her call, and as things stood, she guessed it would be Monday before she could even hope to start seeing patients again.

It was all so *very* wrong, she thought, then rebuked herself, because here she was, safe in her sister's stunning home, which meant that her biggest concern right now was making sure Joshua kept away from the pool.

'There's no way he could wander outside on his own,' Claudia had already assured her.

Biometric systems on all exits, not just the front door.

No concerns at all, then, Grace told herself, as her sister brewed fresh coffee.

Unless she counted their psycho stepbrother.

'Hey,' Claudia said, seeing her face. 'Can't you at least try and think of this as a vacation?'

Grace looked at her sister and gave herself a swift kick.

'You bet I can,' she said.

Nothing had come of Cutter's and Sheldon's nightclub trawl, but Sam and Martinez were planning to continue it tonight.

With Cal the Hater's old hunting grounds in mind. Hot-Hot-Hot and Menagerie two of the killer's favorite clubs – not forgetting the promenade along which the self-styled 'Joy Boy' had been swaggering when Mildred had first laid eyes on him two years back.

David had called this morning from Boston, had tried Sam on his cellphone because the machine had picked up at the house, and Sam and Grace had agreed that the honeymooners did not need to know what was going on until their return.

'Everything OK, son?' David had asked.

'Everything's peachy, Dad,' Sam had said.

'You sure?'

Always hard to fool, Sam's father.

'Has the bride had enough of you yet?' Sam had tried steering the conversation away.

'The bride said I looked splendid last night, as a matter of fact.'

'Give her our love,' Sam had told him.

'Is Grace with you?' David had asked.

'Of course not, Dad,' Sam had said. 'I'm at work, and Grace and Joshua are spending the day at Claudia's.'

Which had finally appeased David Becket.

Leaving Sam free to organize the rest of the day, during which the team were going to be paying low-key visits to as many of Miami's marinas and moorings as humanly possible.

The *Baby*, Cooper's old cruiser – blown up by him before his disappearance – in their thoughts.

The kill-site during his last known rampage.

All the way through to matricide.

Though with the incalculable number of boats and vessels of all shapes and sizes docked and traveling through Miami's waterways, Biscayne Bay and the ocean beyond, the chances of finding the bastard and some new boat without any kind of hard intelligence or a tip-off were almost nil.

All the more reason for Sam to be grateful for Névé.

Safe haven.

SIXTEEN

May 3

Sam and Martinez had worked through the weekend, keeping their own trawl through the marinas downbeat, aware of the risks of Cooper upping anchor and disappearing again.

A master of that, Cal the Hater.

And no new leads to point the detectives in any other direction.

Open minds needed, eyes and ears – their own, the rest of the squad's, and their regular street informants' – trained on *anything* that might lead them to the 'Heart Killer', as the media had tagged the perp.

* * *

Magda had come better than good, had welcomed Grace on Sunday afternoon with open arms, a spare bedroom already transformed into a consulting room, even a waiting room ready for her patients' use.

'But it's your dining room,' Grace had protested.

'I don't give dinner parties,' Magda had said. 'This will be the first time the room has been used since I moved in.'

'It's such an imposition,' Grace had said.

'You're paying rent.'

'Not enough.'

'Take it or leave it,' Magda had said.

They had agreed little more than a token payment, just enough to keep things on a professional footing, because Magda refused to countenance profiting from their troubles.

'It makes me wonder,' the older woman said now on Monday morning, regarding the setup again, 'why we've never thought of joining forces before.'

'You were in California,' Grace pointed out. 'And then Joshua came along.'

'And one of these days he'll be at real school and have a bunch of friends he'll want to have visit or sleep over, and maybe you and Sam will enjoy the idea of having one more room at home.' Magda's smile was touched with regret. 'It's different for me – my empty spaces feel like a reproach.'

She had divorced her unfaithful orthopedic surgeon husband almost a decade ago and their only son, a plastic surgeon, lived in DC with a family she rarely got to see.

'Sharing's a tempting thought in some ways,' Grace said. 'Though my home office has always suited us.'

'I know,' Magda said, easily. 'Just something to mull over.'

Only three patients for Grace to see this first day (the mother of the fourth put off by the change of location, though the Shrike apartment was less than a mile from their house), but enough for her to realize, as the morning progressed, that there might be something efficient, even calming about this kind of compartmentalization.

Although the den and deck where she saw her patients at home had always seemed to relax them, and Grace firmly believed she could do a better job for troubled youngsters in an easygoing environment.

Easygoing, relaxed and stable.

Unlike her mind, currently.

The move had been easy to organize, files brought across, phone calls diverted, and she'd contacted the parents of two of her more critical patients – Sara Mankowitz, for one – to let them know where she'd be in case of emergency.

Her organization not *quite* infallible, though, she realized after lunch, finding she'd left a file at home that she would need first thing Tuesday. Which meant she'd have to go to the house to fetch it, and the deal she'd agreed with Sam was that she would drive herself to and from Bal Harbour so long as she stuck to daylight hours, and call if anything out of the ordinary occurred.

A swift visit to their house just after five p.m. definitely did not necessitate a call, Grace decided. And while she was home, she could take another swift scan around to make sure there was nothing else they might have left behind.

Everything seemed OK when she walked through the front door.

No warning prickles of intuition – just sadness because the house felt so empty, because they'd chosen to abandon it.

Not *chosen*, she reminded herself.

And went about her business.

She located the file, added two others, slipped them into her attaché case, then went upstairs to the bedroom and into the walk-in closet – where nothing sprang to her attention – then back to her dressing table.

An extra lipstick, maybe, she decided, and some perfume, and maybe some headache pills . . .

She wandered into the bathroom.

And *knew* instantly.

Someone had been in here.

She could *smell* it.

She took a step forward, her heart hammering, palms damp.

And saw it.

'*Holy Mary*' – all the way from early childhood and her late mother's influence – flew into her mind.

She stared down into the bathtub for an interminable moment.

And then she turned, one hand covering her mouth, the other stretched out to steady herself as she went out through the bedroom and back down the stairs.

Carefully – she couldn't afford to fall, not now.

Not here all alone, with no one knowing where she was . . .

She waited until she was outside on the sidewalk before letting herself turn to look back again at the house. The home she'd made a long while before she'd met Sam. Lovely small white house with its red-tiled roof and the old familiar bottle brush tree and twin palms in the yard.

Perhaps this, finally, of all that had happened here over the years, might be what drove her and Sam away for good.

And then, suddenly aware of how violently she was trembling, she went to the Toyota, got inside, locked the doors.

And called her husband.

'How in *hell* could he have gotten in without anyone seeing him?'

Sam's anger and frustration were at boiling point.

He had already erupted at Grace for going to the house alone – getting no argument from her because she knew that he was right.

'Though if I hadn't gone,' she had said, lamely, 'we wouldn't have known it was there.' She'd seen his expression. 'I know you'd have come with me if I'd asked, but you were working on the case.'

He'd been at the Starr Banking Corporation, talking to former colleagues of the late Andrew Victor, had left the office of the dead man's manager within seconds of receiving Grace's call.

About *it.*

A third heart.

Carved out of Lord only knew what poor person.

'Oh, man,' Martinez said now, regarding the *thing* in his friends' bathtub. 'I've said it before and I'll say it again, but if there is a sicker fuck in this world than this total shitbag, I sure as hell don't want to know about him.'

'Goes double for me,' said Sam.

'Make that a triple,' Elliot Sanders said.

The ME had come in person as soon as he'd gotten word of the find, primarily because of his involvement in the two other heart cases, but also because this one had been left inside the Becket house.

They already knew *how* the intruder – whether Cooper himself or some unknown accomplice, or another altogether unconnected individual who was just *maybe* taking some leaves out of Cal the Hater's book and bringing his or her own creativity for the rest – had gotten into the house.

Through the lanai, cutting and breaking their way in.

And Grace had not ventured into that part of the house, had not come to check over the place, had simply dropped by to retrieve her files and personal items and had, consequently, been wholly unaware until she'd entered the bathroom.

With the family gone, the specific watch on the house had ceased, and Mary Cutter's and Joe Sheldon's early inquiries up and down the street indicated that no one had seen the intruder, nor had anyone noticed the presence of any unknown vehicle or visitors that afternoon.

'Could have been morning,' Sanders said.

No box or plastic container this time.

Nothing between the heart and Sam and Grace's white porcelain tub.

Crime Scene were here now, crawling all over the scene, but by the time they had eliminated the Becket family's prints and DNA, Sam was betting they'd have nothing to speak of.

The first time he'd met Jerome Cooper, he'd taken him for a fool.

No longer.

SEVENTEEN

The New Epistle of Cal the Hater

Starting over took time.

I was always good at dress-up.

Got myself out of Florida fast as I could. Stole a couple of boats, took the bus, hitched rides and ended up in Georgia.

In Savannah.

Problem was, I only knew two ways to make money.

Fucking and killing.

Fucking, mostly.

Sex kept me alive, I guess.

Savannah, Georgia, being known for its Southern charms.

At my lowest point, I was giving blow jobs in alleyways and abandoned buildings for twenty bucks, and then I moved up a notch or two to motels – though after I'd gotten myself infested with goddamned crabs I went back to one of those holes with a sack of roaches and liberated them before I got the hell out.

I'm good at running.

In the old days, it was always Jewel I was running from.

After she was gone, it was hell I was more afraid of.

Life goes on, though, as they say, and the longer it went on, the more I started remembering what Cal was best at: which was being the Joy Boy. Which meant what I had to do was start believing in Cal again, and making other people – the ones with more than a fifty in their wallets, the ones with something about them – believe in Cal too. And soon enough, little by little, the good old, bad old Joy Boy was out there again, walking his cool walk, drawing people's eyes and their cash too.

Only thing Cal and I didn't have was what we wanted most.

Only thing we never gave up was hating.

Samuel Lincoln Becket most of all.

EIGHTEEN

It was ten to midnight before Sam got back to Key Biscayne that night, but, just as she had waited up after countless late shifts at home, Grace was still awake and waiting for him in the kitchen.

Granite, steel and glass, same snowy white floors as the rest of the first floor. Almost too gorgeous to use.

'I made *Cacciucco*,' Grace told him. 'I made enough for the whole family, but the person I really made it for was you.'

'Thank you, Gracie,' Sam said.

It was an Italian fish stew, and a special favorite because it had been his first taste of Grace's cooking and had become one of their big comfort dinners, and also her equivalent to a bunch of roses when she felt a need to apologize.

'I forgave you already,' Sam said now.

'Aren't you hungry?' she asked.

'I'm more tired than hungry.' The aroma got to him. 'But I guess I could manage that.'

'Good.' Grace began ladling stew into a bowl. 'Because I need to tell you something.' She set the bowl in front of him, added a hunk of ciabatta and poured him a glass of Chianti.

'The whole shebang,' Sam said wryly. 'You must feel guilty.'

'I do,' Grace said. 'For being so dumb.' She pulled out a chair and sat down beside him. 'And I need you to know – really to believe – that if I needed one more thing to make me accept the reality of our situation, walking into our bathroom and seeing *that* was it for me.'

'Glad to hear it,' Sam said.

'I also need you to know – ' she hadn't finished – 'that you don't have to spend another minute stressing about me pulling a stunt like that again, OK?'

'OK,' he said. 'Have a glass of wine with me.'

'From now on, I'll drive to Magda's and straight back here again, and if anything unusual comes up, I'll call you right away.'

'And by "unusual", you mean what exactly?'

'You know there's no way of knowing that until it happens.'

'And what if "it" happens and you can't reach me?'

'Sam, I don't know exactly,' Grace said. 'But bottom line, I promise not to do anything careless.' She smiled. 'At least not until you have him locked up. OK?'

His eyes were suddenly deadly serious. 'Do you know what it would do to me if anything bad happened to you?'

'Yes, I do. Same as if it were you.'

'Not to mention how much Joshua needs his mom.'

'And his dad.' Now Grace got up and poured herself a half glass of wine. 'Any breaks?'

'Not yet.'

'You'll get him,' she said.

'You bet we will,' Sam said.

NINETEEN

May 5

It was three a.m. Wednesday morning when all hell broke loose.

Ear-splitting sirens that ripped the whole extended family from their beds – Cathy down on the first floor, the others spilling into the upstairs hallway.

'It's OK,' Claudia told Sam and Grace and the others, her voice raised over the alarm – which promptly ceased, leaving her last syllable hanging shrilly in the silence. 'Dan's dealing with it.'

He emerged on cue from their bedroom. 'Just the usual. I've called it in.'

'We have to call the cops and the security firm with the code,' Mike said.

'The usual?' Sam asked, pulling a T-shirt over his head.

'He's a local character,' Daniel said. 'An old drunk, harmless.'

'You sure about that?'

'Come take a look.' Daniel beckoned Sam into the master bedroom, where one of the closet doors hung open, revealing a bank of monitors with an overview of every entry point into the property. 'Number four – see?'

He played back a recording of a bulky gray-hooded figure knocking clumsily into the fence at the rear, then stumbling away.

'You sure he's gone?' Sam said. 'I'd like to check him out.'

'Long gone,' Daniel said. 'We're used to him.'

'How long's he been around?' Sam wasn't taking anything at face value.

'Way before we moved in, according to the neighbors,' Daniel said.

'He's harmless.' Claudia was in the room, tying the belt of her robe. 'A bit of a train wreck – some people call him Clouseau, but no one knows his real name.'

'Poor guy,' said Saul, from the doorway.

'Pain in the ass,' Robbie said.

Everyone was in the bedroom now, Grace holding Joshua, who was sleepy and undisturbed.

Sam's eyes were still scanning the monitors. 'You sure it's the same guy? You can't see his face.'

'Sure as I can be,' Daniel said. 'Body language, height.'

'OK,' Sam said. 'I'd still like to take a look around.'

'If it makes you feel better,' Daniel said.

'There's no one around now,' Mike said. 'The cameras are sensitive to body heat and motion, even movement of air.'

'Even so,' Sam said, heading for the door.

Daniel smiled at his older son. 'He's a cop, Mike. What can I tell you?'

'Sam, please be careful,' Grace said.

'I'll go with him,' Robbie said.

'No way,' Daniel said. 'I'll go.'

'I thought the whole point of all this stuff – ' Claudia motioned at the screens as the two men headed toward the staircase – 'is we never have to put ourselves at risk.'

'And we don't.' Mike put an arm around his mother's shoulders. 'It's just Uncle Sam doing his thing.'

'Unkie Sam,' Joshua repeated, rubbing his eyes.

'That's right,' Grace said. 'Your Daddy.'

'Why don't we put this guy back in his bed?' Cathy suggested.

'As soon as they're back inside,' Grace said.

Quietly, more calmly than she felt.

Suddenly having as little faith as Sam in Daniel's box of security tricks.

In the light of morning, everything felt different.

Better, the way things generally did.

Even with a killer on the loose.

No killer here at Névé last night, though, and even Sam was convinced, because Daniel had blown up the shots of the drunk and confirmed that he was indeed their regular guy, and Sam had seen for himself that he bore no resemblance to Cooper.

He felt better all round this morning, more accepting again that his family was safer here than most other places he could think of.

At least, so long as they *were* here.

'All of you guys,' he said, first thing, 'be careful.'

'Stop worrying so much,' Cathy told him.

'Never,' Sam said. 'That goes for all of you,' he said, taking in Mike and Robbie.

'Cross our hearts,' Saul and the brothers said, almost in unison.

And Joshua giggled.

It was a busy day for Grace.

No cancellations, all her pre-arranged appointments kept without complaint, and a last-minute consultation arranged for four p.m., when she had expected to be leaving.

She called Claudia before accepting that final appointment, to make sure she would have no problem taking care of Joshua until her return.

'Are you kidding?' her sister said. 'I'm loving every minute.'

Grace called Sam, too, just before four.

'Just telling you because I promised,' she said.

'Thank you,' he said.

'How's it going?'

'All systems at full power,' Sam said. 'Sucking up every creep in Miami-Dade, seems to us.'

'But not the one you're looking for,' Grace said.

'Not yet,' he said.

Grace told him that she loved him, and he reciprocated.

'More than ever, Dr Lucca,' he told her.

Remembering, abruptly, sweetly, the first time he'd ever seen her, the long legs and Scandinavian cool, and that much warmer Italian *something* lingering below the surface. All still present and correct. Lucky, lucky man.

'What?' Grace asked, hearing loaded silence.

'Later,' he said.

Grace thought, as she took the Julia Tuttle Causeway to I-95 on her way back to Key Biscayne after that last consultation – with a six-year-old girl displaying signs of anorexia nervosa – about her role as psychologist versus mom.

Today had worked out efficiently, and she'd enjoyed grabbing lunch with Magda, had appreciated the smooth, uninterrupted hours of work. But she had missed Joshua badly, and as good as it was to be spending time with Claudia – and they were all being so kind, so relaxed about their staying – Grace was missing her own home, too. She wanted – *needed* – to get back as soon as possible to deal with what had happened there, before it took root in her mind, grew out of control.

The bathroom – perhaps the whole house – would have to be steam-cleaned, and they were going to have to rip that tub out and put a new one in if she was ever to be happy soaking again. And Sam had once said that he thought a Jacuzzi-type tub might be kind of nice, one big enough for them to share . . .

'It'll be OK,' she told herself out loud.

And it would be fine, the house, the new bathtub, their *normal* family life.

As soon as *he* was done with.

It was on 95, at the junction with South Dixie Highway, that she became aware that an old red VW Beetle convertible that she'd first noticed on Julia Tuttle was still behind her. It was a model she had a fondness for because Claudia had driven one years ago, and they'd had some good times together in that car, top down . . .

Something else about the car was prodding at her, and she groped for the memory, then, abruptly and more unpleasantly, remembered that there had been a red VW Beetle in the parking lot at the party store a few days before David's wedding – though if that VW had been a convertible, she couldn't remember.

She took SE 26th on to the Rickenbacker Causeway and checked her rear-view mirror, saw that the car was still there, and for the first time she was able to catch a better glimpse of the driver . . .

Impossible to see his face, hidden by baseball cap and sunglasses, and she knew it was a crazy thought, it was *nothing*, but still it was creeping her out.

Call Sam.

Grace reached for her phone on the dash, took another look in the mirror, saw that the VW's indicator was flashing, saw the car dropping back and taking one of the Hobie Beach exits.

Gone.

The relief was great enough to make her laugh out loud.

Nerves *really* getting out of hand.

She drove on into the Village of Key Biscayne, to her family.

TWENTY

The New Epistle of Cal the Hater

I knew I'd met the *one* – my meal ticket, my very own fleshpot, my passage to Easy Street, and all those vulgar clichés rolled into one – when I met Blossom.

Blossom van Heusen was old and fat, but she was also pale-skinned and fragrant as her name suggested, and she was kind and she liked to laugh, and she knew more about sex than anyone I ever met, and she knew me right off for what I was.

Not the killing part. She never knew about that side of me, and I'll always be glad about that, because I really liked Blossom – maybe I even loved her – and I never wanted her to think badly about me, and I never, ever wanted to harm a hair on her head.

Blossom was rich, too. She'd made her money from prostitution and two wealthy marriages, but when I came into her life, she was lonely and sick, and I made her laugh and, better than that, I gave her the best orgasms anyone ever had, because I was the Joy Boy again. And I never once laughed at her, only *with* her, and I took care of her when she was sick, and it seemed to me for a while that there was nothing I would not have done for her if she'd asked me.

'You're everything to me,' I told her once.

'I do hope not,' Blossom said, because she wanted more for me.

'You're everything my mother never was,' I told her, 'and I love you for it.'

That was when she told me she'd been going to put me in her Will, but then she'd figured that might bring me trouble, bring me to the notice of the *authorities*, and she knew I wouldn't want that, so why, she said, didn't she just give me my share before she passed on?

'Sounds good to me,' I told her, and she laughed.

She told me then that she wanted just one thing in return, my help with her own passing, because it seemed too far off for her liking. I cried like a baby when she asked me for that, and I said I couldn't do that to her, I just couldn't, and she cried too, because she knew then that I *really* cared for her, and she knew, too, that I was going to leave her before she passed on, but she gave me the money anyway.

'No strings,' she said.

I didn't know then how much it was.

'Don't look at it until you've gone,' Blossom told me.

I don't think I'd have minded if it had been ten dollars.

Because I really loved that lady.

I did what I could before I went. I was there when she wrote her last letter *To Whom It May Concern*, telling whoever found her that she wanted to die, that she'd suffered enough from her cancer, and that no one had helped her. Which made me weep again, but I still helped her as much as I could stand to. I washed her and made her hair nice and her make-up the way she liked it, and there was nothing else I could do for her, no food I could make for her, because she couldn't manage eating anymore.

And I was weeping again when I walked out of Blossom's front door for the last time, and I guess that was when I knew why.

Because I hadn't been Cal the Hater since I'd met her.

And when I looked at what she had given me, I think I sobbed for a while longer, just like a goddamned crybaby.

And then I dried my eyes, checked into the Bohemian Hotel on the riverfront, put the envelope into the safe, went shopping on River Street, bought myself a money belt and some decent clothes, then came back and drank more toasts to Blossom van Heusen than I can remember.

And the next day, I left Savannah.

TWENTY-ONE

May 6

Plenty of tough and tedious days and nights ahead, Sam knew, until they caught the killer. Everyone working hard to cover the work that came with any new major violent crime, let alone a double – probably triple – homicide, while, at the same time continuing the manhunt for the prime suspect.

Not for the first time – and they'd *almost* had him then.

'Almost' not good enough.

Ask Andrew Victor.

Ask his friend, Gail, and his sister Anne, both of whom had called yesterday hoping for news, neither heaping blame on the detectives' shoulders for their lack of success.

Nothing to tell them.

They had appealed to the public for information. There was a press release on the department's website, and Fox, CNN, 7 News, CBS 4 and Channel 6 – along with the local Spanish stations, Channels 51 and 23 – were all taking the item.

Calls flooding in.

A lot of them from crazies, as always, taking up time and manpower calling in phony information.

Other calls, too, from good citizens.

Taking them nowhere yet.

It didn't help that their photographs of Cooper were out of date, and there was no way of knowing what he might have done to his appearance. If (and it was still a big if) it had been Cooper that Grace had seen at La Tienda Fiesta on April 19, it gave them nothing to go on.

'Male, average height, slim, with silvery-blond hair.'

Someone who *might* have walked up behind her and had enough nerve to brush his fingers against her neck.

Might have been fingers. No certainty even of that.

If the new homicides were down to Cooper – and Sam, at least, had all too few doubts left on that score since yesterday's grisly discovery – then he doubted he'd still be using the same head-to-foot silver get-up in which he'd strutted the South Beach promenade in his earlier, bold killing days . Though if it was Cal the Hater luring unsuspecting men like Andy Victor into his horror web, then he might still be acting out the 'joy boy, joy giver' character he'd written about in his *Epistles*.

At three fourteen Thursday afternoon, the squad got wind of another missing persons report that sounded warning bells.

Ricardo Torres, age nineteen, from Hallandale Beach, had been reported missing by his mother, Mrs Lilian Torres, after her son had failed to come home for the fourth night in a row. Mrs Torres said that she knew Ricardo had been going out to a party two Saturdays back, on April 24, but she didn't know who'd invited him or where the party had been.

The report had been filed with the local police department, and if there was cause to suspect a sinister reason for the young man's disappearance, any crime would lie in Broward County's jurisdiction.

Little more than dumb luck, therefore, that word had filtered through to MBPD's Violent Crimes Unit, but now they had it, and by five thirty, Sam and Martinez were in the Torres apartment, not far from Hallandale Beach Boulevard.

Mrs Torres was a well-rounded woman with dark, distraught eyes, but she took time to invite them to sit on her narrow balcony, offered them fresh lemonade and home-baked sugar cookies.

'This is wonderful,' Sam told her. 'It's not often we get treated so well.'

'Perhaps you'd like coffee instead?' Lilian Torres's anxiety stretched to giving them the right kind of hospitality. 'I should have asked.'

'Ma'am, this is great,' Martinez assured her.

'I can tell you it made me nervous right away – ' Mrs Torres got down to her fears – 'that he wouldn't tell me about the party, because usually my Ricardo tells me where he's going, but if he's planning something he thinks I might not like, it's like shutters come down over his eyes, and there's nothing I can do.'

'Is Ricardo a student, Mrs Torres?' Martinez asked.

'Not any more,' she said. 'He works in a shoe store in Aventura, in the mall.' She shook her head. 'If his father was still with us, Ricardo would still be at college and he would not feel able to disappear like this.'

'Where is Ricardo's father?' Sam asked.

'Gone,' she said flatly. 'I don't know where.'

'Might Ricardo know?' Sam asked.

'No,' she answered.

'So there's no chance your son might be with his dad?' Martinez asked.

'Not unless he's been keeping that from me too.'

'Does Ricardo have close friends?' Sam asked.

'None of them know where he is.'

'What about a girlfriend?' Martinez asked.

Closest way he could think to ask if the young man was gay.

'No,' Mrs Torres said.

Martinez's take on the situation as they left the building was that Ricardo Torres might not be missing at all.

'Deadbeat dad, mom unable to control her kid.'

'I don't know,' Sam said. 'He's been gone twelve days.'

He'd seen other things up in the Torres apartment: photographs of a boy with sweet, dark eyes and skin several shades lighter than his own, but still dark, and maybe straight, maybe not, but either way still the kind that Jerome Cooper loved to hate.

To mutilate and destroy.

A young man whose natural wish for independence might have pushed him straight into Cal the Hater's path.

Or maybe not.

'I hope to God you're right,' he told his partner as they got back in the Chevy.

Martinez still remembered what Cooper's previous victims had looked like.

'Me too,' he said.

Grace's cellphone rang at six forty-seven Thursday evening.

Sam had called earlier to say he'd be working late. Daniel was having dinner with clients and Mike was going to a party, but the rest of the clan were home. Grace had bathed Joshua and put him to bed, and Cathy had volunteered to cook, and in a little while Claudia was going to open a bottle of Napa Sauvignon Blanc . . .

She answered the phone.

'Oh, Grace, thank God,' Sara Mankowitz said.

High-octane stress in her voice, which had to mean that Pete, Grace's young patient, was in trouble again.

'Sara, what's happened?'

'I'm so sorry to call, but I didn't know what else to do, and there's no way Pete's going to listen to Charlie—'

'This is Charlie, your new friend?' Grace wanted clarity.

'Yes, and he knows Pete trusts you, which is why he told me to call.'

'Sara, slow down.'

'I can't,' the other woman said. 'Charlie was working on Virginia Key today, and he suggested we might like to go to Jimbo's—'

'Jimbo's? Really?' Grace's surprise showed, because Jimbo's Place, a shrimp shack at the end of the road on Virginia Key, was a local institution, but in no way suitable for a nervous boy.

'I know,' Sara said. 'But Charlie said he thought it could be just what Pete needed.' She was talking rapidly, tearfully. 'Some of the types out there unnerved Pete, so we left, but the more Charlie tried to calm him down the worse he got, and then, when Charlie slowed the car down at a junction, Pete jumped *out*, and we've tried everything to get him back, and Charlie's backed right off now, but Pete still won't shift, and I'm scared to death he'll—'

'Sara, where are you?' Grace cut in, alarmed. 'And where exactly is Pete?'

'We're in a pull-off by Crandon Boulevard across from the tennis center, near the big parking lot.' Her voice shook, but Sara kept going. 'And he's taken cover in the shrubbery near some trees. I can see him, he's OK for now, but if he takes off he could get into the park or even cross the highway—'

'Sara, you need to call Fire and Rescue,' Grace cut in again.

'That would *terrify* him, you know it would.' Sara's voice was pitched even higher. 'Grace, I'm so sorry to ask this of you, but you told me you're staying nearby, and you're the only person who can get through to Pete when he's freaked out. He's just so worked up, he's crouched down in the bushes like some scared animal, and please, *please* say you'll come.'

Grace glanced at her watch – not quite seven, and still light, and dinner was a way off, and she hadn't drunk a drop of wine yet, and this *was* a true emergency – though she was glad she was alone, because if Claudia or the kids knew, they'd be jumping all over her saying she couldn't go.

But she had to go. There was not a fragment of doubt in her mind.

'I'll be on my way in five minutes,' she told Sara. 'Keep your line clear so you can talk me in when I get closer.'

She checked that her own phone was fully charged, dropped it into her purse, dragged on her sneakers, looked in on Joshua – thankfully, sound asleep – then ran downstairs.

Claudia was in one of the nooks, watching TV.

'I have an emergency,' Grace said. 'No time to explain—'

'What kind of emergency?'

'I'll lock my doors there and back, and I'll call Sam from the car, and please make sure Saul and Robbie stay here with you, or Sam will ground me for life.'

Claudia was on her feet. 'At least tell me where you're going.'

'Not far.' Grace headed for the front door. 'Sis, it's a patient, and I think it's a life or death situation.'

Saul and Cathy both emerged from the kitchen at the same time.

'What's up?' Saul asked.

But Grace had already gone.

Sam and Martinez were doing another tour of marinas.

They'd been to Flamingo Marina – at the end of 16th Street, not far from the Lincoln Road Mall – twice already. They knew there was no logical way they'd strike lucky here of all places, because this was where Cooper had kept his old cruiser, the *Baby*, neatly tied up all through his first killing spree, taking her out mostly to dispose of remains and evidence. The last place therefore, at least for a *sane* person, to return to, but Cal the Hater was a million miles from that, and anyway, if this was Cal-Cooper playing new games with Sam and his family, maybe if they kept on coming by, something might give.

'Who the fuck knows with this creep?' Martinez said.

Too many people around the first couple of times they'd come to call, and they hadn't shown Cooper's old photos around this place, wanting to keep a low profile, though that was a hard one to call; but it was quiet this evening, felt like a better time to mooch around, and it was the longest shot, yet both men had felt drawn back . . .

Nothing. Again.
And then:
'Hey,' Sam said, on their way back to the road.
Looking at a small handbill pinned up on a noticeboard near the entrance.

Special deal at Sadie's Boatyard
More than you'd expect
Come soon!

The thing about it – the thing that had attracted Sam's attention – was that it looked brand new, unlike the other notices, many of which had been laminated long since to protect them from the elements.
This one was not laminated, yet it looked crisp, recently posted.
Maybe by someone who'd expected them back . . .
'Sadie's Boatyard,' Martinez said. 'S.B.? Special message for Sam Becket, you think?'
'I'd say that's a long shot,' Sam said. 'You ever hear of Sadie's Boatyard?'
'Uh-uh,' Martinez said.
'"More than you'd expect",' Sam read out loud off the handbill.
His gut already recoiling, almost certainly irrationally, at the thought of what the 'more' might be.
'Probably nothing,' he said.
'But we're going anyway, right?'
'Nothing to lose,' Sam said.
Martinez took an evidence bag and glove from his pocket, noted the address on the bill, then unpinned the handbill and bagged it.
On their way.

Grace's cellphone had lost its signal.
No way of calling Sam till it came back.
Nor of ascertaining Sara and Pete's location.
She'd never had signal problems here before tonight.
'Murphy's Law,' she said out loud.
Any minute now, it would come back.
Knock on wood.

* * *

Martinez was driving, and Sam was reminding himself that this was most likely another waste of time, except this was not just one of his hunches, this was his partner feeling the same.

Traffic was heavy, but they were in no big rush, and Sam's PDA had yielded no listing for Sadie's Boatyard, which, according to the handbill, was on South River Drive not far from NW 9th Avenue – along with a whole bunch of boatyards, and not a spot they'd have picked for an evening drop-in.

But if they were right about this being *something*, then one key question was exactly when had the handbill been posted, and Sam couldn't picture Cooper himself risking it, but he might have slipped a few bucks to someone, in which case they'd need to find that individual. And if it was down to Cooper, he couldn't have known they'd go to the Flamingo Marina again this evening, so maybe there were bills pinned up at other locations too.

Too many ifs and maybes.

And almost certainly a dead end anyway.

The missing, sweet-eyed Ricardo Torres came into Sam's mind, and he said a swift, silent prayer for Lilian Torres, then cleared his mind.

Probably just an innocent handbill from a boatyard looking for business.

Probably nothing.

Grace's phone had a full signal now, but Sam's phone was going to voicemail, and leaving a message felt too much like the easy way out, like cheating on her promise.

She knew that if he'd been with her when Sara had called, he'd never have let her go without him, and it had still been light when Sara had called, but darkness was already descending, and there was an unusual clog of traffic on Crandon Boulevard, the ten minute trip taking much longer . . .

Turn the car around.

It would make sense, whatever Sara said, to call Fire and Rescue, identify herself as Pete's psychologist, tell them the score, maybe arrange for them to take her along to lessen his panic.

But Pete Mankowitz was a child in need.

He needed Grace, and he needed her *now.*

So she made no call, left no message on Sam's phone, and kept on crawling along.

* * *

Sadie T. Marshall's Boatyard – to give it its full name – was dark and deserted.

'*No one does it better than Sadie*,' read an aged beat-up sign.

Maybe once upon a time, but now the place looked more like a boat graveyard than a working establishment, and if security had ever been high on Sadie T. Marshall's list of priorities, they were non-existent now. Any fool, it seemed to Sam and Martinez, checking over the place with flashlights, could have made off with the cruddy, leaking old tubs here this evening.

Not that anyone would notice, let alone care.

'See anything?' Martinez asked softly.

'Not yet.'

The handbill was growing more suspect by the second, both men keeping a hand on the holsters under their jackets.

No 'special deal' here, at least not of any legitimate variety.

And then Sam saw it.

'There,' he said, his voice low, stilling the beam of his flashlight so his partner could see what he'd spotted.

Twenty feet or so to their right, tied to a hook.

Another toy dinghy.

'Oh, man,' Martinez murmured.

They both drew their weapons simultaneously, smoothly, took a long, slow sweep-around with the flashlights, both men high-tuned to the possibility of ambush.

No sounds except traffic and night birds . . . A dog barking somewhere . . .

Sam's cellphone rang in his pocket.

He winced, silenced it.

They waited another long moment.

'Let's go take a look,' he said, grimly.

She had no choice now but to leave a message, because the traffic had eased, and any second she'd have to call Sara, and Grace had been mulling over why this Charlie guy had chosen to take Pete to Jimbo's, though maybe he had meant well, maybe he was just clueless about troubled children, and he was probably feeling guilty as hell now . . .

She heard Sam's voice, took a breath.

'Sam, please don't get mad, but I had an emergency call from Sara Mankowitz – remember I've told you about her son, Pete – and they're in big trouble, and she needs me to settle him, so I'm going to get them back to their place and call a doc to help arrange his meds. And I've tried you a few times, and I'll call you soon as I'm through, and don't worry about me, I'm being very careful – and there's no violence in Pete, just fear, and I love you, and you please take care.'

She ended the call and made another.

'Sara, I'm almost with you. Tell me exactly where to find you.'

There was a plastic container in the dinghy.

No doubts remaining.

Except about the contents.

'Could be anything, man,' Martinez said. 'Could be a friggin bomb.'

'Could be,' Sam agreed.

He crouched low, close as he could get.

The dinghy was about four feet away, bobbing gently.

'You don't want to be touching it,' Martinez said.

'Just looking.'

'We need to back off, call this in.'

'I know,' Sam said.

Except that calling in the City of Miami bomb squad was going to take time, and this was Jerome Cooper's doing, and Sam did not *feel* that it was a bomb, not for one second. And if that scumbag somehow knew that he and Martinez were here right now, that could mean he might be about to make a move on Grace or the rest of the family, and even if they were safe and sound in Daniel's Home Knox, he could not afford to waste one more minute than he had to.

'You back off, Al,' he said, quietly, 'and cover me.'

'No way,' Martinez said. 'I'm calling it in.'

'Go ahead,' Sam said. 'But I'm taking a look first.'

'Fuck's sake, man, you got the family to think of.'

'That's why I'm not waiting around.'

'Shit,' Martinez said. 'So let me open it. I got no one.'

'You got plenty,' Sam said. 'But that message was for me, not you.'

The S.B. in Sadie's Boatyard not such a long shot after all.

'I still can't see you,' Grace told Sara.

'I'm wearing white, waving my arms.'

The highway itself was well lit, but as Grace peered into the darkness to her right, she became suddenly aware of a new kind of fear taking root, because it was one thing trying to help a frightened child in his home or in a consulting room, but this was something else altogether, and she should not have agreed to this, she was too edgy to . . .

There.

A flash of white, arms flailing.

'I see you,' Grace said.

Saw the exit to the pull-off, and took it.

No bomb.

No heart either.

Just a small single piece of paper torn from a spiral-bound notebook.

Handwritten, the script familiar to Sam.

From the New Epistle of Cal the Hater

When you know you're going to hell anyway, you know you have nothing to lose.

All at your door, Samuel Lincoln Becket.

You and yours.

Martinez spoke first.

'Now I'm calling it in, no arguments.'

Sam didn't speak.

'You OK, man?'

Sam nodded, took out his cell.

'Message from Grace,' he said quietly.

He listened.

'Damn it,' he said.

'What?'

Sam was still staring at the phone in his hand.

'She's gone out to an emergency,' he said. 'Alone.'

'Where is she?'

'She didn't say,' Sam said. 'Just that she was going to help out this mom and kid she's been treating and get them back to their place – which is near Claudia's house.'

'Should be OK then,' Martinez said.

'Get them back from where?' Sam said grimly.

He hit Grace's number, got voicemail.

'Grace, it's Sam. Call me straight back.'

'She'll be fine,' Martinez told him again.

Sam took a second, then nodded at him.

'Go ahead,' he said. 'Call it in.'

'He's over there,' Sara said, fighting back tears as Grace got out of the Toyota.

They were in the access road leading to a big parking lot, now closed.

No lighting where they stood, rows of palms and a wide stretch of grass between the narrow road and the highway over to their right. A thicker cluster of trees thirty or so yards ahead where the road curved to the right, leading back to the highway.

'I can't see him,' Grace said, peering into the gloom, and she'd left her headlights turned on, but the trees under which Pete had taken cover were well beyond the scope of their beam.

'He's right there, hunkered down.' Sara wiped her eyes with the back of her hand, then raised her voice to call: 'Pete, honey, Doc Lucca's here, like I told you.'

There was no movement, but suddenly Grace saw a smear of pale oval in the darkness, and her own nerves were blown away by a fierce pang of empathy with this boy and his confusion, *his* fears. And if this were another child, she might be wondering about an element of playing up his mom, perhaps to spite her because of the new boyfriend, but Grace had never detected a shred of meanness in young Pete.

'Where's your friend?' she asked, quietly.

'He drove his car around the bend somewhere, to get out of sight,' Sara said. 'We both figured if Pete couldn't see him anymore, he might relax a little, come back out and talk to me, but he hasn't budged.'

Grace looked again toward the pale oval, raised her right hand in greeting.

'What exactly happened to spark this off?' she asked.

'Nothing more than I told you. Something spooked him back at Jimbo's, and then on the drive back, the more Charlie tried calming him down, the worse Pete got.' Sara's right hand twisted strands of her hair, her agitation intense. 'Grace, if he won't talk to you, I don't know what's going to happen.'

'It'll be OK,' Grace said. 'I'm going to get closer, if he'll let me, and I want you to wait in my car because it's damned creepy out here.'

'Please be careful with him.'

'As if he were my own,' Grace said.

She began walking, very slowly, toward the boy, heard her phone ring, realized she had left it in its cradle on the dash in the car.

Sam.

She did not turn back.

'Goddamned voicemail,' Sam said.

'You said she's with a patient,' Martinez said, trying to sound reasonable, knowing that Sam didn't give a damn about any patient right now, just wanted Grace locked down safe and sound with the rest of the family.

'She promised she wouldn't do this kind of thing until Cooper was off the streets,' Sam said. 'She swore she'd be careful.'

'It's a patient,' Martinez said. 'One of her kids. I guess she couldn't say no, but it doesn't mean she isn't being careful.'

'Meantime, I don't know where she is.'

'Same for her,' Martinez said. 'She lives with that every single day, man.'

Sirens heading their way.

Job to do.

Killer to catch.

'I'm not going back with him.'

Pete's first words to Grace.

He hadn't spoken as she'd approached, had let her come, and she'd kept her movements slow and steady, hoping to maintain a calm front, though the dark shapes moving in the breeze all around her were spooky as hell, and Grace was horribly aware that putting one foot wrong, saying a single word out of place at this time could result in disaster . . .

At first, when she'd neared him, he'd looked like an animal poised for flight, but then she'd told him that all she cared about was keeping him safe, and she thought he'd relaxed just a little, though now he was still crouched low on the ground, his hazel eyes, huge with terror and resentment, on her face.

'No one's going to make you do that, Pete,' she told him.

His eyes darted away, checking around. 'My mom likes him.'

'Your mom won't be liking him any more if he's done anything to hurt you.'

'She thinks he's the bee's knees.'

Grace was still standing, her back to the Toyota, in which Sara now sat waiting for her son to be brought safely back to her.

'Would you mind if I got down with you?' she asked.

He shook his head, and she knelt in the dirt, glad she'd worn jeans, and somewhere overhead a barred owl hooted, eerie in the night.

She waited another moment, composing herself again, and then she asked, quietly and calmly:

'Has he done something to hurt you, Pete?'

'Not really,' Pete said. 'Only . . .'

'Only what?' she nudged him gently.

'He says things.'

'What kind of things?' Grace asked.

She felt hate start to blossom deep inside her, unjustly perhaps, this stranger being found guilty, sight unseen, and she ought to have known better, but she was sitting on the ground feet away from a terrified child, and unjust instincts thrived at moments like these.

'Not that kind,' Pete said, knowing what she might be thinking, because he was ten, not five, but there was defensiveness in his tone, as if he might be blamed if it *were* that kind.

'What kind then, Pete?'

'He likes it when I get scared,' Pete said. 'He has this smile, and I hate him.'

'What did he do today that upset you so much?' she asked. 'Do you think you can tell me that, Pete? Though it doesn't matter if you're not ready to. All that matters is getting you and your mom safely home.'

'But he'll come too.'

'I don't think he will,' Grace said. 'I'll drive you home.'

'Will you tell him to leave us alone?' Now Pete's eyes focused tight on hers. 'Please, Doc, please tell him.'

'I'm not sure I can do that, Pete,' Grace said. 'It's not my place.'

'Then I'm not going home.'

'But I will talk to your mom, and I will ask her to tell Charlie not to come by until you're ready to have him there.'

'I'll never be ready.'

'Then that's what you'll tell your mom.'

'She'll get mad.'

'Maybe, a little,' Grace said. 'Maybe a little sad, too.'

'Because she likes him.' Pete shook his head. 'She's wrong.'

'Maybe.' Grace put out her hand. 'Will you come back now?' She looked around, back through the darkness toward her car's headlights. 'Because I have to tell you, Pete, I'm really pretty scared out here myself.'

'I'm sorry,' he said.

'It's not your fault.'

For a moment, he fell silent, and then he said: 'If I come back now, in your car, can you at least make sure that Charlie doesn't come back to our place?'

Grace nodded. 'I'm sure I can do that.'

And Pete put his hand in hers.

Sam tried Grace's number again.

It rang twice, and then a woman answered.

'Hello?'

Not Grace.

'Who's this?' he said.

'Is that Sam?' the voice asked.

'I asked you first,' he said. 'That's my wife's phone.'

'It's OK,' she said. 'This is Sara Mankowitz. My son, Pete, is one of your wife's patients.'

'Right,' Sam said tersely. 'So please tell me why you're answering her phone?'

Some other time along the road, he might be friendlier, but right this minute he needed to know where Grace was and if she was safe.

'You sound upset.' Sara Mankowitz's voice trembled. 'I'm so sorry, it's all my fault, but I needed Grace's help and—'

'Where is my wife? Is she OK?'

'She's fine. She's talking to Pete.'

Sam told himself to breathe, because that was better, she was safe.

'I'd like to speak to her, please,' he said.

'I'll have to ask her to call you back.'

'I'd rather wait,' Sam said. 'Where do you live, Mrs Mankowitz?'

'We're not at my house,' she said. 'Please call me Sara.'

'So where are you?' Sam asked.

Getting one of his bad feelings.

'We're just off the highway,' Sara said, and started to cry. 'I'm sorry.'

A pulse throbbed in Sam's right temple. 'Don't be sorry, Sara,' he said. 'Just tell me what's going on.'

'What's going on is that Pete had a really bad panic attack and jumped out of my friend's car and we couldn't get him back, and the only person he listens to when he gets like this is Grace, and he's never been as bad as this before, and it was getting so dangerous.'

'Where are you exactly, Sara?' Sam asked.

'Just off Crandon Boulevard.'

'Where *exactly*?' he demanded.

'We're near the tennis centre—'

'And is this *consultation* happening in her car, or your friend's?' He was still on the towpath at Sadie's Boatyard, pacing up and down, his mind racing because, Jesus, it was dark out there, and . . .

'No, but—'

'Give me your exact location.'

'Oh, my God,' Sara Mankowitz said.

'What?' Sam said. 'What's happening?'

'It's OK.' Relief lit up her voice. 'She has him, they're coming. I have to go.'

Sam heard the call cut off.

He tried the number again.

Got no answer.

'What's happening, man?' Martinez asked.

'I wish I knew,' Sam said. 'But I need to go find Grace.'

They could see lights now, the sirens almost on them.

'Can't go now,' Martinez said.

'Going anyway,' Sam said.

It was, she thought afterwards, when she allowed herself to remember, like the worst kind of cliché, in that it felt like slow-motion and fast-forward all at once.

It began as they were emerging from the palms.

Pete gripping her hand tightly, his fear palpable, even though the only other person in sight was his mother, getting out of the Toyota at the far end of the road, her body language tentative at first as she waited for her son's reaction, then more hopeful, extending her arms to him.

'Ready for a big hug?' Grace asked Pete softly.

'Uh-huh,' he said, a little husky, wanting it badly.

He let go of Grace's hand, getting ready to run to Sara.

And then they both heard it.

A throaty engine sound.

Coming out of the darkness to their left.

And then, a VW Beetle convertible, top down, moving very slowly.

A man at the wheel.

'That's him,' Pete cried out and grabbed at Grace's T-shirt.

Seeing Charlie.

Grace saw the man, too.

Knew who he was.

Not Charles Duggan.

And in a tiny space of calm at the core of her own rising, swarming fear, she registered what she needed to do.

'Pete, go to your mom,' she told him.

She felt, rather than saw, his scared, questioning eyes.

She took a breath. 'Sara,' she called, 'I need you to take Pete and *run*.'

'What's wrong?' The other woman was just a few feet away.

'Sara, that is *not* Charlie, take my word for it.' She pushed Pete hard toward his mother. 'Pete, go straight to your mommy, and both of you *run*.'

The boy moved, ran, reached his mother, and Sara stared at Grace for one moment, then grabbed her son's hand and did as she'd been told, turned and started to run, past the Toyota, then hesitating, looking back—

'Just *run*,' Grace yelled. 'Get back to the highway, get to *people*!'

The VW stopped.

Fear soared to terror. Grace took off, reached her car, wrenched open the door, got in, heart hammering, slammed the door shut, felt for the ignition key.

He opened his door, got out.

Too far away, too shrouded in darkness, for her to see him clearly, but she knew who he was, oh Lord, she *knew*.

Jerome Cooper – Cal the Hater – Sara's 'friend' Charlie – engineering a relationship with Sara Mankowitz, terrorizing her vulnerable child, just to get to Grace, and the new, stinking proof of the man's wickedness filled her with pure horror and loathing.

Her car would not start.

And he was walking toward her.

Slowly, coming closer.

She locked her doors, turned the key for the second time, and the engine started.

He kept on coming, was just a few feet away now, and Grace stared up at her rear-view mirror, but it was inky black behind her, and now he was right in front of the Toyota, *right* in front, so she put the car into reverse – still too dark to see, but she put her foot down anyway and felt, almost instantly, a thud, heard a sickening crunch as she collided with something.

'Oh, dear God.'

She slammed the car back into neutral, but he was still just *standing* there, his face hardly visible because he was *so* close, his body blocking the glare of the Toyota's headlights, and there was no escaping him, this bastard who'd already done so much harm to so many, an evil man who would use a *child* to get to her and her family, and she would not let him hurt Pete any more, she would not let him go on killing . . .

'Get *away* from me!' she yelled.

He leaned in toward the windshield, and she revved the engine, but he seemed to lean even closer, growing bigger, even more menacing.

She shifted into forward gear.

It all flew back through her mind, memories and images she'd fought so hard to eradicate: Cooper stealing Joshua from his crib, *drugging* him . . . Seeing his boat exploding, believing their baby son was dead . . .

She would not allow him to do this new thing to her, to her family . . .

'I won't *let* you!'

Her foot went down hard on the gas pedal.

The Toyota powered forward.

The impact slammed her in her seat, forward, then back, shocking sounds reverberating through her skull, her head.

And then she realized she could not see him any more.

Knew she had *done* it.

She was unaware of her own shaking as she remained in her seat.

She turned off her engine.

And heard him.

Moaning.

She sat and waited for the sound to stop.

Waited for what seemed an interminable time.

And still it did not stop.

And the thought came to her that the real Grace would call 911 and get out of the car to go help the monster, because he was still a human being, making human sounds of pain.

And finally, she did pick up her phone and make a call.

To Sam.

Who picked up fast, as if he'd been waiting.

She didn't listen to what he was saying, because she had to tell him.

What she had done.

'I tried to finish it, but he's still alive.'

'Who?' Sam's voice sounded strange, afraid. 'Who's still alive?'

'Cooper,' she said. 'He came at me, and I ran him down, but he's still moaning.'

'OK,' Sam said. 'Grace, listen to me.'

'I'm listening,' she said.

'Are you in your car now?'

'Yes.'

'You need to stay there,' he told her. 'Are the doors locked?'

'Yes,' she said. 'Don't worry about me.'

'Where are you, Grace? Can you tell me exactly where you are? The boy's mother said you were near the tennis center on Crandon Boulevard.'

'That's right,' she said.

'Where *exactly*?'

'There's a pull-off,' she said, 'near a big parking lot.'

'OK,' Sam said. 'Grace, I'm calling for back-up, and I'm on my way, and you just stay put.'

'I will,' she said.

Too tired, suddenly, to move. Leaden, finished.

And then she saw that people were coming. Sara and Pete, clinging together, and two more people, strangers, a man and a woman, and Grace saw Sara push Pete toward the strangers, and the woman took him in her arms, holding him protectively as Sara came closer.

In the Toyota's headlights, Grace saw horror on Sara Mankowitz's face.

'What have you done?' she heard her cry. 'What have you *done*?'

Grace knew then that she had to move, had to find the strength to get out and speak to Sara and make her understand that this was not her friend, that this was a monster.

So she unlocked her door and got out of the car, and if *he* was still alive, if he could talk, who knew what he would be telling Sara, filling her mind with.

'Grace, what did you *do*?' Sara's voice was thin and high with distress.

'Sara,' Grace began. 'This man is not Charlie. This man—'

She stopped.

Looking down at the man on the ground.

The man she had run down with her car.

Not Cooper.

Not Cal.

And the strangest, *strangest* thing of all was that, lying there at her feet, this man did not even really look like him. His hair was the kind of silver that Cooper had dyed his when he was being Cal the Hater, and, lying there, she guessed he looked slim.

But it was not him.

Numbness struck, shut part of Grace down.

'But he was terrifying Pete,' she said, 'and then he came right at me, and I told him to get away, but he kept coming.'

Her voice still worked, and her heart was still beating.

'He was coming to *help*,' Sara said, weeping now.

And the man on the ground spoke to Sara.

'I was just trying to help,' he said, his voice faint, but distinct.

And then he died.

TWENTY-TWO

'Why aren't you saying it?' Grace asked Sam.

Later.

Fire and Rescue had come first, then the Key Biscayne police, and other strangers, too, in and out of uniform, all of them behaving kindly to her, calmly, the way trained emergency personnel behaved with someone on the edge.

She didn't know how much time had elapsed between *then* and now.

Since the moment she had ended everything that was good and decent.

'Why aren't I saying what?' Sam asked.

'I don't know,' she said. 'I guess, maybe "My God, Grace, what have you done?" Something like that.'

Sam knew shock when he saw it.

He could not begin to imagine how she was feeling, though he had killed, more than once, in the line of duty, and one time, a few years ago, acting out of jurisdiction, he had ended the life of someone close to Cathy, a killer, but nonetheless . . . Cops were, for the most part, pretty well taken care of on the psychological front after traumatic events, and sure, cops were human, too, but Grace . . .

Grace lived to take care of others.

And Grace had just killed.

Sam felt his own level of pain rising by the second.

She was still shut down.

'I thought it was him,' she said again.

She had told him that, had told everyone that, over and over.

'I know,' Sam said. 'He looked like him.'

Not enough like him, he thought, for others to see the resemblance and be convinced, though he hoped to God to be wrong about that.

Grace looked at him, saw raw wounds in his warm eyes.

'I feel like a china doll,' she said. 'I know I'm alive, and I know what I've done. I've killed a man in cold blood. But I can't seem to *feel* it yet, and I think I'm glad of that.'

They were sitting on the ground at the side of the narrow road, and Grace had a blanket around her shoulders, and Sam had one arm around her. The crime scene was illuminated now by headlights and lightbars from police cars, and flashlights lit up the dead man – Grace's victim – where he still lay in front of her car.

She was still shivering.

'Couldn't we sit in your car?' she asked.

Sam had already told her they could not sit in the Toyota because it was evidence for the time being, and in any event, she could not imagine ever being able to get into that car again.

'I don't think that's a good idea,' Sam said now. 'It might be misconstrued.'

'In case you're telling me what to say,' she said.

Her voice was lifeless.

'Something like that,' Sam said.

'But you could be doing that here, too,' she said.

He wished, on one level, that she were being less rational, grew more afraid for her with every moment that passed.

'I guess they're giving us a little time,' he said.

'Before they take me,' Grace said.

'I've called Jerry Wagner,' Sam said.

That pierced the china shield, an arrowhead getting through.

Jerry Wagner had become Cathy's defense lawyer when she was fourteen and had been unjustly arraigned for the murder of her parents and more besides.

'That bad?' she asked, softly.

'He's the best I could think of,' Sam said, 'and he knows you.'

Grace looked again into his wounded eyes, saw that he was breaking apart inside, knew that she would have done anything to spare him this.

Too late now.

'I really believed it was him,' she said.

'I know you did,' Sam said.

'Charlie.' She shook her head. 'I can't even remember his surname.'

'Duggan,' Sam said.

'Charlie Duggan,' she said.

The name spoken by her sounded remote, the way she felt. Dissociated. And even at the core of the dullness that had overtaken her, her psychologist's mind comprehended what was happening to her, because dissociation was a common response to trauma, and God knew she had experienced many shocks over the past several years.

But she had never killed before.

Once, years ago, she had contributed to a man's accidental death while she had been in fear for her life, and she had felt the repercussions of that for a long time – and she had *wanted* to kill, briefly but violently, after Cooper had stolen Joshua, when she'd believed their baby lost.

But this man, this Charlie Duggan, had been an innocent man.

'I was just trying to help.'

His last words, spoken before witnesses.

'I killed him,' she said again now. 'I killed a man, and I'm not feeling it yet, but I know enough to realize that it's going to hit soon.'

'I'm here for you,' Sam said.

He'd called Martinez a while back, had told him swiftly and carefully what had happened here, and his friend, deeply shocked, had told him that he would deal with the unfolding situation at Sadie's Boatyard, and that he would make a discreet call to Mike Alvarez – and the lieutenant had already called Sam, had told him to consider himself off-duty, had assured him that his thoughts were with him and Grace, and if there was anything they needed, he'd do his best to help.

'You need to go back to Claudia's,' Grace told him. 'Be with our children.'

'They're OK,' Sam said. 'I've talked to your sis.'

'But *he's* still out there,' she said. 'I didn't finish him.'

'I'm staying with you,' Sam said.

'Will they let you?'

'Not during questioning, but after.'

'Will they let me leave?'

'You'll get bail.'

'Tonight?'

'I don't know.'

'Not tonight,' she said, slowly.

'Don't be scared,' Sam said, and held her tighter.

'I'm not,' she said. 'Except of what I did. What I was capable of doing.' She paused. 'And of what this will do to Cathy and Joshua.'

'Joshua won't know anything about it,' Sam said. 'We'll all see to that.'

'He will some day,' she said. 'If I go to jail.'

'You won't go to jail, sweetheart.'

'How do you know?'

'I won't let that happen. Jerry Wagner won't let it. They'll hear the whole story and they'll understand.'

'Even I don't understand,' she said.

And then, suddenly, two men stood over them, blotting out the lights.

Two detectives from Miami-Dade Homicide.

Grace heard their names, but did not absorb them.

Just one name going around and around in her head.

Charlie Duggan.

Her victim.

'Grace.' Sam's voice, sharp and clear, penetrated. 'Grace, listen to me. You're probably going to be arrested, and they'll be taking you to Miami-Dade headquarters in Doral.' He saw her nod. 'But I don't want you to say *anything* till Jerry Wagner arrives. You can confirm your name and address, but that's all. Do you understand?'

'Of course,' she told him. 'Don't worry too much.'

He kissed her forehead, and helped her to her feet, and the detectives waited, did not prevent him.

Sam told her that he loved her, and Grace told him the same back.

And then, suddenly, she realized what she had not said until now.

'I'm so sorry,' she said.

'I know you are,' Sam said.

Inside the Fred Taylor Headquarters building on NW 25th Street in the city of Doral, west of Miami International Airport, two detectives from the Miami-Dade homicide bureau questioned her for what seemed an eternity.

She heard the Miranda warnings, comprehended them, but Jerry Wagner had arrived before her to identify himself as her representing attorney, and he did not allow a statement to be taken.

'Don't say anything,' he told her.

Her right to remain silent, as enshrined in the Fifth Amendment.

The charge, she already knew, was vehicular homicide.

Ugly, harsh, cold.

And accurate, it seemed to her.

'You need to tell me why you did it,' Wagner said to her before the interview.

'The whole story?' Grace asked.

'In time,' he answered, 'but tonight I'll take the edited version.'

'I thought he was someone else,' she said.

'Jerome Cooper,' Wagner said.

'Yes.' Grace paused. 'I thought he was going to . . .'

She stopped, abruptly uncertain of exactly what she *had* thought Cooper had been about to do, and a new sense of panic threatened to engulf her, one she knew she had to control for her family's sake more than for her own . . .

Yet the fact was she did not feel sure now what she'd thought out there in the dark. Maybe that he had been going to hurt her, maybe even kill her, and she had been terrified – but that was not what had been uppermost in the seconds leading up to Charles Duggan's death. What had been exploding in her head right then had been rage at the man because he had been using Pete to get to her, because he had terrified that vulnerable boy, and because once upon a time he had stolen her child, her baby . . .

Which meant, she thought now, that she had wanted to punish him.

And maybe Jerry Wagner was a mind-reader, because he decided not to wait for her to say any more in case she strengthened the case against her, so maybe this was *not* the moment for unvarnished truth out of the mouth of an honest woman who had never before, so far as he knew, harmed another human being.

Until she had mown a man down with her car.

'You thought a multiple killer was coming at you,' Wagner said.

'I guess,' Grace said.

'You guess?'

And she nodded, because she remembered now that it was true.

'That's what I thought,' she said. 'I told him to get away.'

She remembered that, too.

'But he didn't back off,' Wagner said.

'No,' Grace said. 'I thought he was Cooper.'

'That's all I need for now,' Wagner said.

They began questioning her, and she registered their questions, did as her lawyer had told her and said as little as good manners allowed, but her brain seemed too fogged now for any clear understanding of what the homicide detectives, or even Wagner, wanted of her.

She was, after all, guilty.

Guilty.

That was the only thought that occasionally dragged itself clear of the fog. Her awareness of that guilt, and the terrible ache in her heart.

For her victim. For Sam. For Joshua. For Cathy and Saul, and Claudia and David and Mildred, and Sara Mankowitz, and any other people she had irrevocably harmed.

No ache for herself.

But for the life she had thrown away.

TWENTY-THREE

May 7

Thursday night into Friday morning.

The longest, darkest of nights.

After the questioning in Doral, they had taken her first, for 'processing', to the Pretrial Detention Center on NW 13th Street in Miami, after which they had transferred her to the Women's Detention Center on NW 7th Avenue, where Jerry Wagner had come to see her for a second time.

Grace had scarcely noticed his appearance earlier, at Miami-Dade headquarters, but now, across a stained table, she looked at him with a greater degree of clarity and remembered him well, recalling the first time she had ever seen him, at the funeral of Cathy's aunt. She remembered thinking then that he looked every bit the distinguished lawyer, sturdy and prosperous, with well-cut curling hair, and he was little changed now, just older, with silver threads in the hair, his hands still beautifully manicured, his eyes still the same piercing blue.

He had taken as good care of Cathy as he'd been able.

Not the same. Cathy had been an innocent fourteen-year-old, while she was a forty-year-old psychologist married mother.

And she was not innocent.

Which was what she told Wagner. Again. In another room, another place.

A prison.

'Will they let me go home?' she asked.

'Not tonight,' the lawyer answered.

She thought she'd been prepared for that, but it felt like a body blow.

'But tomorrow,' Wagner continued steadily, 'you'll go before a judge, and hopefully you'll be released on your own recognizance or on the posting of a bond. Bail, in other words.'

'What if the judge won't grant either of those things?'

'He or she will grant it.' Wagner's smile was gentle. 'You have an unblemished record, you're a person of high standing in the community, you're not a flight risk, and you have a small child and patients who depend on you.'

'I'd say the last remains to be seen,' Grace said.

Wagner assembled his papers and notes, and rose.

'Tomorrow, Dr Lucca,' he said.

'I think they charged me as Mrs Becket,' she told him.

He smiled again. 'I know that.'

'What's in a name?' she said.

'That's the way,' Jerry Wagner said. 'Stay strong, Grace.'

She spent the long, dark night with four other women, each on their own metal-framed bunk bed bolted to a graffiti-covered wall and disquietingly stained floor, each prisoner with a mattress and blanket, united in their sharing of air and space and toilet facilities – the single, stinking steel lavatory and sink – but utterly disconnected in every other sense.

The detention center sat forty or fifty feet beneath the I-95-836 corridor of the expressway system, which meant that it was never quiet.

Traffic rumbling, roaring, pounding.

One of the women snored steadily through the night, while another – the youngest – wept for a while into her open hands until an older, hatchet-faced woman told her that if she didn't cut it out, she would do it for her. And Grace wished she possessed the courage to step up for the youngster, but found she was all out of that commodity, and was simply relieved when the weeping stopped.

She spoke only when addressed, which happened just once.

'You got any rollies?'

The question had come from the hard-faced prisoner, and Grace floundered for a moment, then realized that, of course, the woman was asking for cigarettes or marijuana or whatever.

'No,' she said. 'I'm sorry.'

And after that, thank God, she was of no interest to any of them.

For a while, as she lay still and silent in the dark, she thought about Cathy again, and then her thoughts flew to Joshua, but drawing him into this place, even in her thoughts, seemed an abomination. And each person that came to mind went the same way, ejected back into the outside world, the decent world where they belonged and she no longer did.

She was here, in jail, because she had killed a man.

An innocent man.

She had taken his life.

Don't, she told herself. *Not now.*

If she let herself go down that path now, in here, let herself believe it, really *feel* it, she feared she might lose herself deep inside the guilt.

And then how would she ever get out, go home, hold Joshua again?

But she was a killer now.

Killers had no rights.

Don't, she told herself again.

Not now.

Not yet.

Plenty of time for that later.

* * *

The longest, darkest night for Sam, too.

And for Cathy, who remembered what incarceration felt like.

Sam had come downstairs at four a.m., had found her in the kitchen, sitting over an untouched cup of herbal tea, had given her a hug, then poured himself a glass of water and sat down beside her.

He knew that she was remembering.

'It won't be the same for Grace,' he told her, trying to reassure himself, he realized, as much as their daughter. 'You were a child.'

And you were innocent.

The unspoken words hung in the air, both of them experiencing terrible guilt for the implications of their thoughts. Yet the facts were undeniable.

Because Grace had killed a man.

A man who had terrified her but who, it appeared, had meant her no harm.

Her patient's mother's friend.

Sam had seen Sara Mankowitz only briefly at the scene, had seen a distraught woman struggling with shock and the overriding need to take care of her son.

But he had heard what she'd said to the Key Biscayne officers.

'He was coming to help.'

Martinez had voiced it well enough in a phone call earlier.

'Oh, man, what a mess.'

Saul had been the most stoic, the staunchest of them all.

'It makes no sense,' he had said. 'Grace is all about *not* hurting anyone.'

And Claudia, shocked almost beyond speech, was presently doing the most valuable thing she could; sitting with Joshua, who'd woken a while ago and begun to cry, his distress only seeming to intensify when Sam had picked him up.

Little boy's antennae in fine working order.

Unlike their lives.

Jerry Wagner met with Sam in a corridor at the courthouse one hour before Grace's first court appearance.

They spoke fast, Wagner saying he needed everything Sam could tell him about what had led Grace to act in such a massively uncharacteristic way.

'It's abundantly plain,' the lawyer said, 'that violence is anathema to her, and yet there's no denying that she did what she's accused of. It was not an accident, in that the gas pedal did not jam, nor did she put her foot on that pedal instead of the brake, because she would have said so before anything else, and everyone who was at the scene knows she did not say that.'

'You push someone hard enough,' Sam began.

'But Charles Duggan did not push Grace,' Wagner said, cutting that line off. 'That's our problem. She ran him down, and she's admitted it. She told him to get away, because she thought he was someone else, but he was not. Mistaken identity won't wash with a car as a weapon any more than it would with a gun, you know that. Duggan was an innocent victim, and there seems no changing that.'

'There has to be,' Sam said.

'You have something?' Wagner's eyes were sharper than ever.

'No.' Sam shook his head. 'Not yet.'

'Then just give me what you do have.'

Sam outlined the Cooper story and their ordeals, along with Grace's unproven sightings of Cal-Cooper both last spring and more recently, consolidated them with the fact that the killer had written to Sam in March a year ago. After which he brought Wagner up to date with the new killings and the psychological onslaught by the 'heart killer' against their family.

'Enough for self-defense,' Wagner said.

'If Duggan were Cooper,' Sam said, his hopelessness growing.

'Probably more than enough for temporary insanity,' Wagner said, 'if that was the way we wanted to go.'

'Don't we?' Sam said.

'Statistically, it's a tough road,' Wagner said, 'and even if a judge or jury buys it, there's the worry of having to prove that the defendant – Grace – is no longer insane and does not, therefore, have to be remanded to an institution.' He paused. 'Worst case, Grace could be remanded to an institution until "recovery", and then transferred to jail to finish her sentence.'

He saw the horror in Sam's eyes, felt great pity for him.

'Fortunately,' he went on, 'as you know, we don't have to state our plea till the arraignment, so we have time to work out the best possible way to go.'

Arraignment. Jail. Sentence. Those words applying to Grace.

Unthinkable.

* * *

He had never seen her as pale and drawn as this.

Except maybe while Cal the Hater had had Joshua.

But she was holding up somehow, her bearing erect, her voice only a little shaky when she spoke.

He read the gladness in her eyes when she saw him.

Something very different when she saw Cathy and Saul.

Shame already eating away at her.

Bail was set, after argument between the state and defense, at one hundred thousand dollars. Sam paid ten per cent to the bondsman, and six hours later she was released.

She had thought, during the long night, that she would remember every single instant of that for the rest of her life. Yet by morning, with more unknown terrors to face, it had already begun to blur: the searching, the fingerprinting, the sampling of DNA, the transport, her first surge of panic in the cell, her fear of the other prisoners, the noises. Everything fading out except for the stench ingrained in her nostrils and throat and on her skin and in her hair, making her long, above all else, for hot water and soap.

She let them hug her, one at a time, but found she could not embrace them in return. 'I'm sorry,' she told them. 'I just feel so unclean.'

'I know,' Cathy said.

'We'll walk ahead,' Saul said.

Always tactful, Sam's young brother. As warm as their father, but David usually spoke candidly, whereas Saul generally took time to consider other people's feelings.

'I must sound very ungrateful,' Grace said to Sam, as they walked slowly behind the others, her need to hang back seeming bizarre, given how desperately she longed to leave, 'but I wish we were going home instead of to Claudia's.'

'No choice, sweetheart,' Sam said, the Key Biscayne address having been officially entered as her place of residence for the time being.

Not to mention that less than four days ago an excised human heart had been placed in their bathtub.

'I know,' Grace said. 'It just seems hard right now.'

Sam looked at her, understood her wish for privacy.

'In some ways, I guess it will be,' he said. 'But I'm going to be a whole lot happier knowing you're safe at Claudia's.' He was unsmiling. 'And staying there this time.'

'Am I under house arrest?' It was an effort to sound light.

He gripped her hand. 'I just mean no going out alone.'

No such stipulations had been made by the judge. Her passport and driver's license had been handed in, and she was to have no communication with any witnesses. And, of course, there was the bond.

'I'm just so sorry, Sam.'

She kept on saying that, but she knew already that there were no words to express the vastness of her regret.

The kind that a person might pray never to have to feel.

'Will you do something for me?' she said.

'Anything.'

'Call Magda, ask her to cancel all my appointments.'

'Till when?'

She had stopped walking. 'Indefinitely.'

He felt the implications of that word like another cut of foreboding.

'You're allowed to work,' he said.

'I can't,' she said. 'Not now.'

'Not yet, maybe.'

'Will you call her?' she said. 'Please, Sam.'

'Sure,' he said, and began to move, but she caught at his arm, stopped him.

'One more request,' she said. 'Bigger.'

He waited.

'I know better than to say that I need to speak to Charles Duggan's family – God knows I have no right to ask them for anything.' She continued quickly. 'But maybe you could talk to them, tell them how deeply sorry I am.'

'They may not want to talk to me either,' Sam said.

'No.' Grace looked at Cathy and Saul, waiting by the Saab. 'It hasn't begun to sink in yet, not really. Not for me, and I guess not for any of you either. What I've done.'

Sam saw her pain, and the knowledge that it was probably just a fraction of what lay ahead grabbed at his own heart, squeezed it hard.

'We'll get through it,' he said.

'I don't see how we can,' Grace said.

'Together,' Sam said. 'Like always.'

'I don't know,' she said.

Because some things were just too bad to get through.

And anyway, after her trial they might not be together.

* * *

A little after six thirty, with Grace sleeping and the family quietly on alert for anything she might need, Sam headed back to the station, where Martinez was waiting for him, the unit still busy with detectives catching up on paperwork at the end of a hard week.

Sadie T. Marshall's derelict boatyard – Martinez told Sam – had been gone over as well as was feasible by City of Miami officers working without individual search warrants for every one of the rust buckets languishing there.

'Nothing,' Martinez told him. 'And no prints on the handbill.'

No Sadie either, as yet.

'Ida called,' Martinez said. 'They got a match for the heart in your tub.'

Sanders still leaning hard on the lab, it seemed.

'Ricardo Torres?' Sam guessed.

The young man's mother having provided hair and a toothbrush.

'Afraid so,' Martinez confirmed.

Sam's heart sank.

He thought about Lilian Torres, about the dark-eyed young man.

'Broward have already seen his mom,' Martinez told him.

Their case, Sam supposed, since though Torres's heart had been dumped in Miami-Dade, it was just as feasible for now that the crime might have taken place closer to the victim's home.

Unless the Miami Beach detectives proved otherwise.

In the next half-hour or so, Sam's mood descended to the point where he was chewing out everyone who came near him, including Martinez when he tried telling him to take it easy. But it was only when Mike Alvarez told him to get the hell out of the office that Sam realized what he'd been doing, and apologized.

'It's OK,' the lieutenant told him. 'It's late on Friday and you've had twenty-four hours of hell, but you need to take some time out. Unless you can do the job, Sam, you're no use to anyone, least of all Grace.'

For the first time he could remember in a long while, Sam was not sure that he was fit for purpose, or was likely to be any time soon.

Rules, routines, methods, reports.

Everything could go hang so far as he was concerned, except for two things.

One: get Cooper.

Two: find some way to help Grace.

Nothing else mattered.

She saw her own face on the television news.

Robbie, sitting watching in one of the nooks, noticed her standing behind him and reached for the remote.

'It's OK,' Grace told him.

Uncertain if seeing the story on screen made it more or even less real.

No photographs yet of Charles Duggan, nor any relatives yet to weep or talk about their loss.

Robbie turned off the TV anyway, stood up, looked at her, thought he'd never seen her look fragile before.

'What can I do for you, Aunt Grace?'

'Just be you, Robbie,' she told him.

Woody came up behind her, tail wagging, looking for a walk, the spaniel not far behind.

'Not now, Woody,' Grace said.

'He's OK,' Robbie said. 'I took them both out a while back.'

And Claudia had given Joshua his dinner, bathed him and put him to bed, and already Grace felt surplus to requirements.

Better that way, perhaps.

If she was going to jail.

TWENTY-FOUR

May 8

She had not thought it possible for any night to seem longer or darker than the last, yet the hours spent in this big comfortable bed with Sam right beside her, seemed to her, if anything, even longer and more painful.

He was watching out for her, she was aware, all the time.

'You need to rest,' she told him some time around three. 'I'm OK.'

'Me too,' he said.

Liars, both.

'If you feel like talking,' he'd said earlier, 'I'm here.'

'I don't think I do,' she'd told him. 'I don't think I can.'

'You will.'

'I know,' she'd said.

Except that talking would not make this right, would not make any of it go away or not have happened.

She was a psychologist, and she understood the processes, knew what was needed to help her own long-term healing after the trauma of harming another human being, knew the 'symptoms' she could anticipate, knew, if anyone did, that there was treatment to be sought, aid to be had.

If she deserved it.

Which she surely did not.

Those thoughts, of course, were 'symptomatic', too, and suddenly as she lay there beside Sam, so helpless in his own grief and fear for her, she wanted to scream at herself, because what *use* was any of her psychology training now to anyone? No use to Sam nor to their son, nor Cathy . . .

Nor to Charlie Duggan.

The memory seared more vividly than the clearest flash photograph – she was there again, in the car again, seeing *him* again, her right foot slamming down hard on the gas pedal again.

Killing him again.

She slept for a short while, fitful, dream-filled sleep, and then woke to the bleak horror of fresh realization.

Sam was still with her, watching her again.

'Have you been doing that all night?' she asked him.

Something close to resentment in her tone, for which she could have cut out her tongue, and another rush of emotions took flight: pity for him, fresh shame, and another new realization, that she might have to learn to guard her thoughts, to be less open.

Their marriage, their partnership, had been built on openness.

Another casualty.

'I'm OK,' she told him.

'No, you're not,' he told her.

She thought she smiled at him.

He kissed her, and she managed not to pull away, though she wanted to, and she had no understanding of why that should be, unless it was more about her being undeserving of love . . .

More psycho garbage.

'Are you going to work?' she asked him, a moment later.

Knowing that she wanted him gone, at least for a while.

'I don't think so,' Sam said. 'It's Saturday.'

'You must need to, though,' she said. 'All that time out, and the case.'

Please, she heard in her head. *Please go.*

'I guess,' he said. 'But I don't want to leave you, not today.'

'Why not?' she said. 'Claudia will be here.'

'Cathy said she's going to be here, too,' Sam said.

Her guards, Grace thought, and felt another burst of anger against herself.

'That's nice,' she said. 'We can all hang out together, and you can go to work and do what you have to do.'

Sam looked at the woman who looked like his wife, but did not seem like her.

'You're not OK,' he said.

'No,' she said. 'Of course I'm not.'

'We'll get through this,' he said, as he had when they'd left the detention center yesterday.

Don't argue it, she told herself.

She kissed him instead, on the lips.

'Go to work, Sam,' she said.

'Something not right about this guy, Duggan,' Martinez told Sam as soon as he walked into the unit at nine twenty-five. 'Did they tell you he had no ID on him at the scene?'

Having worked long hours since the second heart had been found at the Fontainebleau, most of the detectives were taking the weekend, which meant the office was quiet, though Martinez, upset as all hell about Grace, had been there since before eight.

'They did not.' Sam sank into his chair, but the small hairs on the back of his neck were already lifting.

'Seems Mrs Mankowitz said Duggan told her he was working on Virginia Key at the university marine lab, but they never heard of him there.'

'Maybe she misunderstood.'

'I talked with her fifteen minutes ago. It's what he told her.' Martinez paused. 'And that's not all. His car isn't registered in his name either.' He glanced down at a Post-it sticker on his desk. 'The RO's a Bernice van Heusen in Savannah, Georgia.'

'Stolen?'

'Not reported.'

'Where does Duggan live?' Sam asked.

'No one seems to know,' Martinez said. 'No ID, no nothing on him, so no way of informing his family. There's a bunch of Duggans listed in South Florida who I'm sure Key Biscayne or Miami-Dade are calling, but I've started too.'

'Give me the list,' Sam said. 'I'll carry on.'

'How's about we share?' Martinez said.

Sam smiled. 'You can take off the kid gloves now. I'm not cracking up.'

'No point,' his partner said.

By ten fifteen, they'd spoken to two Charles Duggans, both very much alive.

No other people by that name.

Hard to say what it might mean if they and the official investigators did not find any trace of the Duggan who had been Sara Mankowitz's friend.

But it meant *something*, that was for sure.

'By the book, of course,' Martinez pointed out, 'we shouldn't be checking up on this guy.'

Sam was silent for a moment or two.

'Seems to me,' he said, 'Alvarez might be right about my taking some time.'

'You going to see Mrs Mankowitz?'

'Could be,' Sam said.

'Go carefully, man,' Martinez said.

Sam found Sara Mankowitz at home.

A one-storey single family dwelling, well maintained, the way most houses were on Key Biscayne.

He knew he ought not to have come, off-duty or not.

Grace had been forbidden from speaking to witnesses, though no such stipulation had been made so far as he was concerned.

It was still wrong, and he knew it.

Right now, he didn't give a damn.

'How did you know where I live?'

She was defensive rather than hostile. Her face was pale and her eyes were red from weeping or exhaustion, probably both.

'I knew you lived near my sister-in-law's home.'

'And you're a detective, after all.' She opened the front door more fully to let him in, then hesitated. 'I'm not sure I should be talking to you.'

'It's OK,' Sam said. 'This has nothing to do with what happened.'

'Really?' Still doubtful, Sara closed the door and walked ahead of him into her living room. 'Would you like to sit down?'

'Thank you.' Sam sat in a gray leather armchair.

'Coffee?'

'No, thank you,' he said. 'How are you and your son doing?'

'Pete's resting,' she said. 'He hasn't slept much since.'

'And you?'

'I'm as you might expect, in the circumstances.' Sara paused. 'What do you want from me, Detective Becket?'

'I was hoping you might have Charles Duggan's address.'

'I don't.' She was still standing. 'I've already told the police.'

'Do you know whereabouts he lived?'

'In Coral Gables, near the university.'

'Near UM?' Sam said. 'But you never visited him there?'

'Why are you asking me these questions?'

'Because we haven't been able to find an address for Mr Duggan.'

Sara sat down in the second armchair. 'That does seem strange.'

'It is,' Sam said. 'What can you tell me about him?'

'He was a nice man,' she said. 'I haven't known him very long.'

'How did you meet?'

For a moment, he thought she might refuse to answer, but then she leaned back, and Sam realized this was perhaps what she needed, to talk about her lost friend.

'We met one morning after I'd dropped Pete off at school.'

Her voice had dropped, as if she was afraid her son might overhear.

'You met at the school?'

She shook her head. 'In a coffee shop nearby. I needed a shot of caffeine, and Charlie was at the next table. He smiled at me, said something about the weather, then left me in peace, which I thought was polite.'

Sam waited, knew there would be more.

'A week or so later, I saw him in the post office and we chatted while we waited in line.' Sara stopped.

'And you became friends,' Sam said. 'I'm so sorry for your loss.'

He waited for her to go on, but she remained silent.

'I gather Pete wasn't so keen,' he said.

'That ought to be privileged information.' She was sharp, her cheeks flushed.

'I'm not sure it qualifies under patient confidentiality,' Sam said, 'which Grace takes very seriously, as I'm sure you know.' He leaned forward, keeping his manner gentle. 'But there were things she had to tell me when I got to the scene on Thursday evening.' He paused. 'Why, for example, you had felt it necessary to call her out to a potentially dangerous situation.'

'She was Pete's psychologist,' Sara said. 'He needed her help.'

The '*was*' bugged Sam. A lot.

'At the side of a busy highway?'

Her expression changed. 'I know.' She looked briefly close to tears. 'I wish I hadn't called, believe me, and I am sorrier than you could know.'

Again, he gave her a few moments.

'Why was Pete afraid of Mr Duggan?'

'I don't think it was Charlie he was afraid of,' Sara defended the dead man. 'Pete is easily scared, and he'd been spooked earlier.'

'At Jimbo's.'

'Yes.'

'Mr Duggan's choice, I believe.'

'Yes.'

'A curious choice for a nervous boy, don't you think?'

'I'd never been there before,' Sara said.

'But Mr Duggan probably had, since he'd been working at the marine lab.'

'Why are you interrogating me?'

'I'm just trying to get a picture of what happened.'

'Before your wife ran down an innocent man.' Her mouth trembled.

Sam's instincts were to stop and comfort her, to say how sorry Grace was, how sorry they both were for her pain, but he knew he might never have another shot at this kind of questioning.

'I am a little confused,' he said.

'About what?'

'No one at the lab on Virginia Key seems to have heard of Charles Duggan. He was not working there.'

'As I told another detective who phoned this morning, maybe he was just using their facilities,' Sara said. 'He was a researcher.'

'Who did he work for?'

'He was freelance, but he'd studied marine life at college, so I guess it would make sense if he was using their library.'

'Which college, do you know?'

'I don't know.'

'He didn't tell you?'

'It didn't come up.' Sara stood up. 'I think I've had enough of this.'

'Of course.' Sam got up too. 'Just one last thing?'

She sighed. 'What is it?'

'Do you have a photograph of Mr Duggan?' He thought it unlikely she'd hand it over if she did, since if she'd had one, she'd already have given it to Miami-Dade or Key Biscayne PD.

'Why?'

'Because it's proving hard to find his family, and it would be kinder if they don't have to use images from the scene, as you can imagine.'

'Of course.' For a moment, she seemed about to cry again. 'I told the police after it happened that Charlie said his mom lived in North Miami, so I don't understand why it should be so hard tracking her down.'

'What about his father?'

'Charlie said he died years ago.'

'That's why a photograph might help,' Sam persisted. 'We'd hate for his mother to find out from the TV or newspapers.'

'But the story's already out there,' Sara said.

'He hasn't been named,' Sam pointed out.

'As a matter of fact – ' she looked a little awkward – 'I forgot, when they asked me Thursday, that I did have one photo, on my cellphone. I was looking at it just this morning, and I figured that I should maybe call someone.'

'Would you mind forwarding it to my phone?' Sam asked, pushing his luck.

'I don't know how. Pete usually does stuff like that for me.'

'I could show you, if you don't mind.'

Her purse was on a sideboard beneath a painting of Greenwich Village, and she took out the phone, located the photo and handed the phone to Sam, and he itched to take the whole thing.

'Did you have a phone number for Mr Duggan?'

'Only a cellphone number,' she said. 'I've given it to the police.'

He didn't ask for her number, knew he'd be pushing his luck.

But he badly wanted the photograph, had been unable to take any shots of the dead man Thursday night.

He scrutinized the picture, set it up to send. 'He looked nice.'

'He was nice,' she said.

The photo was of the dead man seated on a white garden chair, a glass in one hand, smiling into the lens, and if Sam half-closed his eyes, he thought he could see how, in the darkness and confusion, Grace might have believed him to be Cooper.

'Your backyard?' he asked, and sent the shot.

Sara Mankowitz nodded, abruptly, close to tears again.

'Will you tell Grace I'm sorry?' she said. 'For getting her involved.'

'You know she was just trying to help, don't you?' He checked to make sure the photo had reached his own cell, then handed back her phone.

'I know,' she said. 'But so was Charlie.'

He asked his final question at the door.

'Did he ever mention a Bernice van Heusen to you?'

'No. Who is she?'

'I don't know,' said Sam.

His next stop was a photo lab on Crandon Boulevard, where he asked the technician and his assistant if either of them recognized Duggan while their software uploaded the dead man's photo and produced a number of prints.

No recognition, no big surprise.

Virginia Key his next port of call.

Jimbo Luznar's place on Duck Lake Road had been something of a South Florida institution for more than fifty years, a shrimp shack complete with bocce court, pretty much a dump, but popular with movie producers and fishermen alike.

Just a dump in Sam's book.

He decided against showing his badge, paid the five bucks entrance fee and drove along Arthur Lamb Road past the wastewater treatment plant, and, arriving at Jimbo's, seeing the mess of trucks and bikes, some dumped, others fit to be, he thought about Grace's instant suspicion of a man who'd thought this an appropriate place to bring a sensitive kid.

His wife's instincts so seldom off track, and faint pinpricks of hope were still buzzing through his veins as he parked the Saab.

Something *wrong* about Duggan, Martinez had said.

'Not right' – his exact words.

Translating to Sam as 'get the hell out the office and go dig up whatever you can because it just *might* help Grace'.

Alejandro Martinez loved Grace too.

A whole lot of people loved her.

No one more than himself.

And he would do anything.

Anything.

No help to be had at Jimbo's, though the people there this noontime knew that a man had been killed near Crandon Boulevard Thursday night.

'I heard a woman mowed him down,' one guy said.

Leather jacketed, despite the heat, tattoo on one cheek.

Sam wanted to punch him, maybe arrest him.

Couldn't arrest a guy for speaking the truth.

And punching his stupid face would not help Grace one bit.

So he moved on.

He sent Duggan's photo to Martinez's cellphone, then called him as he drove, told him he planned to show the picture around the Applied Physics building at the nearby Rosenstiel School of Marine and Atmospheric Science.

'It's Saturday,' Martinez reminded him. 'Won't be a full house.'

'So I'll come back another day,' Sam said. 'And I'll scoot around the other place while I'm here.' The 'other place' being the NOAA's Atlantic Oceanographic and Meteorological Laboratory, because what the hell, someone there might recognize Duggan. 'Might as well cover as many campuses as I can think of, since his girlfriend thinks he studied "marine life" someplace.'

'Cutter's coming in later,' Martinez said. 'I'll make a few copies of the photo, and maybe she and I can show them round a few places, too.' He paused. 'I found a Bernice van Heusen in Savannah, by the way – she passed away last year, aged seventy-one.'

'How did Duggan come to be driving her car, I wonder?'

Sam had already reached the Rosenstiel building.

'Me too,' Martinez said. 'How's Grace holding up?'

'Last time I called, Claudia said she was taking a nap.'

Grace rarely took naps in the daytime.

'Best thing, man.'

Sam found a parking spot and stared unseeing at the white building he was about to visit. 'Still think there's something wrong about Duggan?'

'If we can't find his life before death,' Martinez said, 'sure I do.'

'Could mean he wasn't who he claimed to be,' Sam said.

'Let's don't get ahead of ourselves,' his friend said.

Sam had to follow the thought through. 'Could mean Grace had real grounds to believe she was in danger.'

'She thought he was Cooper,' Martinez said flatly. 'We have to stay real. Even if Duggan turns out to be a grade-A sleazebag, it doesn't mean the judge is going to say it was OK for her to nail him with her car.'

'He might if she was under *real* threat,' Sam said. 'Self-defense.'

'We still gotta prove it,' Martinez said.

David and Mildred flew in to Miami International from New York City early that evening, Saul and Cathy dispatched to meet them.

And to break the news.

'Couldn't we keep it from them just a little longer?' Grace had asked Sam earlier. 'It seems so cruel to ruin their homecoming this way.'

'And if they heard it someplace else?' Sam had said gently.

And Grace had sagged a little and given way.

'Sam said we should take you home,' Saul told the newly-weds while they were still reeling with shock.

Cathy had tried to get them to sit, have some coffee or something stronger, but neither David nor Mildred were having that.

'We're not going home,' David said. 'We're coming with you to Claudia's.'

'I'm not sure that's what Grace wants,' Cathy said.

'I don't know what she wants,' David said, 'but what she's going to get is our love and support.'

'The unconditional kind,' Mildred said.

David grasped at her hand, and she gripped it firmly.

'Lousy homecoming,' Saul said.

'We've had the honeymoon,' Mildred said. 'Now comes the marriage.'

* * *

After the greetings, hugs and some tears, another family dinner, and then Sam drove them back to Golden Beach.

He had already checked on the house a few times, but he wanted to look around again to make sure all was secure. Daniel had tried persuading them to stay, though Névé was pretty much full, but neither of the senior Beckets had been prepared to countenance the idea.

'You'll be noticing the occasional patrol car,' Sam told them on the way, glancing sideways at his father, waiting for an argument. David's lips did tighten for a moment, but that was all, and Sam guessed he was remembering Mildred's suffering at the hands of Cal the Hater.

'One more thing, Dad,' Sam said.

This, he knew, would not be so easily received.

'I took the liberty of having an alarm installed,' he said.

He heard his father's sharp intake of breath, but then Mildred's weathered hand reached out from the back and patted her husband's shoulder, and again David restrained himself.

'I think that's a very kind idea,' Mildred said.

'Dad?' Sam said. 'Are you OK with it?'

'Do I have a choice?' David asked.

'It's been installed,' Sam said, 'so I guess not.'

'I can still choose not to use the damn thing,' David said.

'He'll use it,' Mildred said.

Grace thought, upstairs at Névé, waiting for Sam's return, that she would never have believed it possible to be surrounded by all her loved ones and yet feel so alone.

They had all been the same as they always were around her. Meaning every word of unqualified love, their smiles as warming as always.

Yet she was ice cold inside.

She felt, in spite of their kindness, like a pariah. Her crime seeming, with every passing day, more unforgivable.

She knew that Jerry Wagner intended to find some means of pleading not guilty, hoped to keep her out of prison or an institution. And she knew that, for the sake of her family, she had to do all she could to help him.

But she was not really certain that she could do that.

Because she deserved to be punished.

TWENTY-FIVE

May 9

The same photograph of Duggan that Sara Mankowitz had given Sam, appeared in the newspapers on Sunday, with an appeal to anyone who recognized the victim to come forward with further information.

Other photos too.

New ones of Grace. One of her with Sam, taken a few years back at a fundraiser for Miami General, laughing together, having fun. Another taken as they'd left the courthouse on Friday afternoon.

Coverage in the *Herald*, the *Sun-Sentinel*, and the *Key Biscayne News*.

Same thing on the local TV news stations.

'At least they didn't use her mug shot,' Robbie said to Mike.

'Shut up, man,' his brother told him.

Saul and Cathy just coming out on to the deck.

'It's OK,' Saul told them. 'We've seen the papers.'

'We've been trying to keep them from Grace,' Cathy said, 'but I heard the TV on in their room, so I guess it's a losing battle.'

'She's not doing so well, is she?' Mike said.

Saul slumped down on a lounger. 'I've never seen her like this.'

'It's eating her up.' Cathy sat beside him. 'I don't know what to do for her.'

'You're doing it,' Robbie said. 'Staying close.'

'Being yourself,' Mike agreed.

'I guess it's all any of us can do,' Saul said.

In Golden Beach, Mildred and David had seen the newspapers with a sense of growing bleakness, had set them aside and tried to find a little solace in some honeymoon photos that Mildred had taken with her cellphone.

Not for long. Their hearts not in it.

'I thought Joshua seemed to be feeling it too,' Mildred said. 'Like summer and winter for him all in one. His mom cuddling him, playing with him every second, then suddenly backing off.'

David had noticed that too. 'It's the way I've seen some terminal patients behave. Drawing close, then pushing loved ones away.'

'She thinks she's going to jail,' Mildred said.

Her husband shook his craggy head. 'It's unthinkable.'

'Too many bad things have happened to this family,' Mildred said. 'It isn't right.'

'I don't know what it'll do to Sam if she's found guilty.'

'Samuel's a strong man,' Mildred said.

'Everyone has a breaking point,' David said.

Sam had come to the station at lunchtime.

He'd woken before dawn after less than two hours' sleep with the clear conviction that the best way for him to help Grace now was to get back on the job.

Two jobs now.

Keep on digging into the apparently mysterious Charles Duggan. And focus harder than ever on apprehending Jerome Cooper, because whatever came to pass in Grace's case, if Cal the Hater was put behind bars once and for all, then at least their family as a whole could start feeling safe again, free to move on with their lives.

'Go to work,' Grace had told him.

Same as she'd told him yesterday, and he'd told her again this morning that he wanted to be with her, and she hadn't pulled away from him in a physical sense, but he'd felt her pushing him away nonetheless, and if he wasn't careful, there was a real risk she'd become even more withdrawn.

Bad for her, bad for Joshua, not great for him.

So he'd stuck around all morning, and then he'd left her with Claudia who was starting to put together brunch.

Martinez was in the office too, had brought in bagels with lox and fresh-squeezed juice from Markie's, one of their regular haunts, and Sam was surprised to find he was hungry.

'You got a message.' Martinez nodded toward his phone.

Sam picked up and listened.

'Tony and I heard what happened,' a familiar voice said. 'Anything we can do, just ask.'

Angie Carlino was an old pal and former colleague, now a mom of three working in the Pinella County Sheriff's Office over in

Tampa. She was tough, warm-hearted and always direct, and her tone in the message reflected that.

'Love to you and Grace, and hang in there, both of you.'

Same kind of encouragement he'd been getting from his colleagues here on Washington Avenue.

Blessings to be counted.

His phone rang.

'My, you're popular,' Martinez said.

'Dave Rowan,' a gruff voice said, 'with something you might want to check out.'

Detective Dave Rowan from Broward County Sheriff's homicide unit, was in charge of the Torres case now. They'd had some dealings with him a few years back, and Rowan was as aware as most local cops of Sam's history with Jerome Cooper, not to mention his family's present troubles.

'We've been checking party-related nuisance complaints and arrests for the night of April twenty-fourth – ' the night Lilian Torres had believed her son to be attending a party – 'and we've got nothing much our way, but it seems there was a pretty wild one at a vacant warehouse over in Wynwood.'

'OK,' Sam said, and waited for more.

'I'm sending you a link right now,' Rowan told him. 'Someone posted a YouTube video filmed at the party. There's quite a crowd, but a couple of people stood out for me.'

'Torres?'

'Oh, yes.'

'And Cooper?' Sam's pulse sped up.

'I think you'd better take a look for yourself,' Rowan said.

When Magda Shrike had an hour to spare, she liked to break off from her paperwork catch-up time on a Sunday for some late brunch and a trawl through the newspapers.

Her first response on seeing Grace's photos on the *Herald's* front page was dismay. She had spoken with her friend briefly last evening, had heard the welter of emotions in her voice – shame the clearest of all.

A lot for her to bear, too much, but as soon as Grace was ready to accept some professional support, Magda would do her utmost to help her through.

Not ready yet, though, not by a long shot, and experience had taught both women that some pain had to be endured, worked through or just plain survived before counseling could be of real use.

Grace's expression in the photo snapped outside the courthouse filled Magda with sorrow.

Yet the images of her friend were not all that had seized her attention when she'd first looked at the newspaper.

It was the photograph of the victim, Charles Duggan.

'*If you know this man, please call the helpline* . . .'

Magda did not believe that she knew him, but she was almost certain that she had seen him someplace before.

The problem was, she could not seem to remember where.

She leaned back now in her chair and shut her eyes, trying to filter out all the mental junk and pinpoint that memory . . .

Nothing specific.

Though it did vaguely seem to her that there might be a connection with one of the magazines to which she occasionally contributed. Her most recent article, titled 'Fear and Beyond', had been published in *Psychology 101 Magazine* a month ago, and had necessitated several meetings with an editor at their offices on Biscayne Boulevard.

The telephone on her desk rang, and she let it go to voicemail.

Heard that it was a patient. Sounding needy.

She picked up the phone. 'This is Dr Shrike.'

She folded up the newspaper with her left hand and set it aside.

Perhaps later, she might remember . . .

Tom O'Hagen had been calling Toy off and on for the best part of twenty-four hours.

Leaving voicemail some of the time.

Getting more and more wound up.

'Where the fuck are you?'

And then, this morning, over a late breakfast, he'd seen it.

The photograph.

Twice over. On the TV and in the newspaper.

So he had stopped calling Toy.

Goddamned idiot.

'Shit,' he said now.

Looked down at his half-eaten breakfast.

Appetite shot to pieces.
Fucking fool.

They were sitting in front of Sam's desktop PC, working their way through the YouTube video.

Both looking for Cooper.

Both tense as tightropes.

They saw Ricardo Torres.

Young and alive, eyes twinkling.

Talking to someone else.

Another man.

'What the . . .?'

Sam saw him about one-eighth of a second before Martinez.

Not Cooper.

Someone else altogether.

The man whose photograph they and their colleagues had begun showing around college campuses across Miami-Dade.

Charles Duggan.

Two ghosts in one hit.

Jerry Wagner had come to Key Biscayne for a meeting with Grace.

'I don't know if it's going to be a good time,' she'd said when he'd called ahead. 'Sam's working, but the others may be around.'

'I imagine we could find a quiet space somewhere,' he'd said.

'Couldn't we wait till tomorrow?'

'I'd rather we didn't,' Wagner had told her.

So she'd agreed, and the family had melted away so that attorney and client could sit out on the terrace and not be disturbed.

'I thought I remembered that you liked ice tea,' Grace said.

'You remembered correctly,' Wagner said, and nodded at the plate of cookies on the table between them. 'And those look tempting.'

'Cathy baked them last night,' Grace said. 'She couldn't sleep.'

'A lot of that going around, I'd imagine,' Wagner said.

She poured his tea, gave him a couple of cookies, waited till he was properly comfortable, and then went first.

'I have to plead guilty,' she said.

'No, you don't,' he said.

'Yes, I do,' Grace said, quiet but insistent. 'I do because I am guilty, and there's no getting away from that. But I'm not saying that I don't want you to help me reduce my punishment – my sentence – because I have a family to consider, and it would be selfish of me to say something like that.'

Wagner took a drink of tea.

'You need to listen to me,' he said.

'Of course,' she said.

'This isn't going to play out like some TV movie, Grace. We tell your tale of nightmares and a judge or jury want nothing more than to get the nice lady back home where she belongs, so the judge finds some way to suspend your sentence.' He paused. 'If you plead guilty to a charge of vehicular homicide, you will almost certainly serve ten to fifteen years in the state prison.'

Grace closed her eyes.

Pictured Joshua as a teenager, his future face indistinct to her because she would not be there to see him.

Better for him if she died than this.

'Grace.'

She opened her eyes.

'Are you OK?'

She nodded.

'Then can we please get to work to try to salvage some kind of workable life for you and your family.' His smile was kindly. 'Plenty of time later for you to work on your guilt. I daresay you can't counsel yourself, but you're bound to know a few half-decent therapists.'

Grace almost managed a smile. 'I do.'

'You look like hell,' he told her.

'I know.'

'So are you going to let me help you?'

She took a long moment before she answered.

Knowing there was no real choice.

'I am,' she said.

It was hard to take in.

These two unconnected cases overlapping this way.

'Not so unconnected, I guess,' Martinez said.

'Grace,' Sam said.

The connection. Plainly.

Though it made no sense.

'We need to talk to Rowan again,' Martinez said.

Jurisdictional niceties to be settled.

Sam's mind was reeling.

'Am I crazy,' Martinez said, 'or do we have ourselves a new suspect?'

'For the killings?' Sam said.

'Charles Duggan, deceased,' Martinez said.

Killed by Grace.

'I don't think I buy that,' Sam said.

Cal-Cooper still right at the top of his suspect list. The handwritten extract of the *Epistle* left in Sadie's Boatyard having added weight to that, the preliminary comparison with the original *Epistles* pointing to the writing being genuine.

Though maybe nothing in this case was exactly as it appeared.

Except Jerome Cooper's undying malevolence towards Sam.

All at your door, Samuel Lincoln Becket.
You and yours.

'One thing's for sure now,' Sam said. 'You were right about Duggan.'

'If that's even who he was,' Martinez said.

They both sat for a moment, staring at the frozen screen on Sam's PC.

'I guess,' Martinez said, slowly, 'this might just help Grace.'

Sam shook his head. 'All we have right now is a guy at a party.'

'Talking to a murder victim, man.'

'Two dead men,' Sam said.

'But it's something,' Martinez said.

One of Jerry Wagner's gifts, he liked to think, was for persuading his clients to think productively for themselves.

And the fact was that, as they sat sipping ice tea, a little more clarity had begun to return to Grace, most of it painful. But something else had accompanied the torment: a greater degree of comprehension of what had led to the catastrophic events of Thursday evening.

The culmination of other events, forebodings and small panics . . .

And, she was only just becoming properly aware, the key element that had been present in two of those alarms *before* the disaster.

The red convertible VW Beetle.

The single most important thing that she'd forgotten to tell Sam about while they'd been waiting for the police to arrest her.

'I can't be sure if I forgot it exactly,' she told Wagner now. 'It was so uppermost in my mind when I saw that car coming toward us – I think I was still holding Pete's hand at that moment. He was ready to go back to Sara, but then everything seemed to happen so fast, and all that's seemed to count since then is that it wasn't – *he* wasn't Jerome Cooper – which meant I'd killed an innocent man.'

Wagner had been jotting down notes as she spoke.

Now he laid down his gold and black Mont Blanc pen.

'You may have killed him,' he said, 'but I'd say there seems a little more reasonable doubt over whether he was innocent.'

'You still can't kill a man for driving a red VW,' Grace said.

'Maybe not,' Wagner said, 'and we may not be any farther down the road just yet to learning more about Mr Duggan, but I'd say it's high time I see if we can get a good close look at his car.'

Sunday evening felt hardly any better than the morning had.

Grace had told Sam about her meeting with Wagner, about her memory jolt regarding the red VW, and for a while he had felt positive about that – one more ingredient to stir around the pot as he tried to figure out who Duggan might have been . . .

Yet Grace appeared to feel no positivity. She was going through the motions, but she was listless.

'She's very depressed,' Claudia said to him in the kitchen.

'Of course she is,' Sam said.

Feeling much the same.

He had not yet told Grace about the YouTube video, because all it would do was add another layer to the confusion she was already feeling, and Martinez had questioned that decision, but Sam had told him he thought it was too soon.

Not that he was sure about anything.

They watched TV together for a while in the big family nook, and the others came and went but said they all had stuff to do.

'They're giving us space,' Sam said.

'They're relieved not to have to babysit me,' Grace said.

He looked at her.

'Don't look at me that way,' she said.

'What way?' he asked.

'Sharply,' she said. 'Analytically.'

He half laughed. 'I wasn't.'

'You were. You do it all the time.'

'Since when?' he said, and wanted to kick himself for his stupidity.

He was saved by Woody, who appeared, wanting to be picked up, and Grace set him on her lap for a while and stroked his head and fondled his ears, but Sam could tell that her heart wasn't in that either.

'I think I'll go to bed,' she said, shortly after ten.

'Me too,' Sam said.

'You don't have to,' she said.

'Gracie, I'm tired,' he said. 'I want to come to bed with you.'

They looked in on Joshua, who was sound asleep, and they put the TV on in their room, and she got undressed and took off what little make-up she'd put on that morning, and brushed her hair and put on a nightdress.

'I never get tired of that,' Sam said.

'Of what?'

'Watching you do those things.'

She smiled at him, but it seemed an intensely sad smile, and soon after that she got into bed and turned out the light on her side.

'Goodnight,' she said.

'I love you, Gracie,' he told her, and kissed her.

'I love you too,' she said.

She was asleep within minutes, and Sam was glad for her temporary escape, wished he could switch himself off the same way, but Charles Duggan was on his mind, and first thing tomorrow he was going to talk to Mike Alvarez, try getting the lieutenant on side.

He left the bed quietly just after eleven and went back downstairs, watched some more TV, felt something niggling at him but couldn't nail it, and after a while, he fell asleep on the couch.

When he woke, someone had put a rug over him, and he wondered if it was Grace, wished she'd woken him instead, so he could have gone back to bed with her, but it was after five now, and he needed an early start.

He went upstairs, wanting to go look at Joshua, but he couldn't do that because he was sleeping in Robbie's room, and suddenly he missed their home, their real *life*, with such violence that he had to stop himself from punching the wall.

'Easy,' he told himself softly.

He opened the door of their room.

She was sleeping, hair spread on the pillow.

He wanted to get back into bed with her, hold her, kiss her awake.

But he knew that would be selfish.

He sighed, went into the bathroom and shut the door quietly behind him.

TWENTY-SIX

May 10

With no patients before eleven fifteen on Monday morning, Magda drove her Lexus Hybrid to the offices of Shrinkwrap Publications, the company on Biscayne Boulevard that published, among other medical and self-help titles, *Psychology 101 Magazine*.

Her editor was out, but a copy of Sunday's *Herald* was on the reception desk, Grace's and Charles Duggan's photographs face-up. The young woman on duty looked vaguely familiar, but had no ID pin.

Magda took a chance.

'I see you were looking at that, too,' she said in her most affable tone.

'Sure.' The other woman's eyes seemed almost to sparkle with excitement. 'I was going to call the number in the article, but one of the editors said she would do it.'

'I thought I recognized him,' Magda said, 'but I couldn't quite place him.'

'It's Richard Bianchi,' the receptionist said. 'He's – he was – a freelance copy editor. He was in and out of here all the time just a little while back.'

Back in the Lexus, about to phone Grace, Magda changed her mind.

She didn't have Sam's cellphone number, but she certainly knew where he worked.

She got the number and put through a call.

'Surely,' Sam said to Lieutenant Alvarez, 'if Charles Duggan, aka Richard Bianchi, is now a person of interest in the murder of Ricardo

Torres, that also makes him a person of interest in the killing of Andrew Victor and, therefore, part of a Miami Beach case?'

He'd been in Alvarez's office for almost ten minutes, would have been there much earlier had the lieutenant not been in a meeting with Captain Kennedy. But since then Magda Shrike had called, and Sam had talked with Dave Rowan, who'd received two calls from Shrinkwrap Publications and had been willing to share with Sam a few basic starting points about the dead man.

Born in Fort Myers, Florida, twenty-eight years ago. A mostly unsuccessful writer, a few features and two short stories published, supplementing his income as a copy editor.

Pretty much all that the publishers had on file about Richard Bianchi.

No rap sheet.

But a *name.*

And now, thanks to the Broward detective's cooperation, Sam also had his address on NW North River Drive.

Not a million miles from Sadie's Boatyard.

'We need a search warrant,' Sam said. 'Or consent.'

'That's not going to happen,' Alvarez told him.

'The guy used a false identity.'

'No fake ID was found on him.'

'No ID found on him, period,' Sam said. 'He told Sara Mankowitz and her son that his name was Charles Duggan. He told her on that last day that he'd been working at the university marine lab on Virginia Key.'

'Hearsay,' the lieutenant said.

'I'd guess it's in her statement,' Sam persisted. 'And given that she's a possible witness for the prosecution against Grace, mightn't that help with a warrant?'

'It's still hearsay,' Alvarez said. 'Bianchi's parents have been informed. They're on their way over from Fort Myers to make the ID.'

'Bianchi as Charles Duggan told Sara Mankowitz his father was dead and his mother lived in North Miami,' Sam said.

'Hearsay again,' the lieutenant said. 'Though if Mr Bianchi's parents weren't coming to ID him, we might have applied for a warrant to help us obtain further information to confirm his identity, but . . .' He shook his head.

'What about the YouTube video?' Sam said. 'We could subpoena YouTube to determine who posted it, then subpoena that individual, make their testimony probable cause for the warrant.'

'In the Torres case, maybe,' Alvarez said.

'Which is Broward's,' Sam said. 'Damn it.'

'Take it easy, Sam.'

'I'm trying, believe me.'

'I know.' Alvarez had come up through the ranks, had been a violent crimes detective, understood the work and its frustrations, and he sympathized with Sam on a personal level too, but his hands were tied.

'The guy was probably following Grace,' Sam said doggedly, 'for weeks before that night.'

'Probably,' Alvarez stressed. 'Grace noticed a red VW Beetle convertible a couple of times.'

'And he just *happened* to be talking to Ricardo Torres the night Torres disappeared and was murdered.' Frustration was building to anger. 'I mean, come *on*, we have to take a look at his place.'

'Not going to happen, Sam.' Alvarez was kind, but implacable. 'Richard Bianchi is, for the time being, a victim. To all intents and purposes, he made a living as a freelance copy editor, and all you have to the contrary is that he attended the same party as a homicide victim. And he *may* have told a woman he picked up at a coffee shop that he had a different name. He's a writer – maybe that's how he used to get his inspiration.'

'He picked up this particular woman because Grace was treating her son.'

'You have no proof of that.'

'The average age at that party was nineteen. Bianchi was twenty-eight.'

'Can't arrest a guy for that,' Alvarez said. 'Let alone a dead guy.'

'Jesus,' Sam said.

'I'm sorry, Sam. Believe me.'

'And meantime, Grace has to go on living this hell.'

'Until you find something solid enough for a judge.' Alvarez was seeing way too much emotion in the other man's eyes. 'You have to separate these cases, Sam. The Victor homicide is yours, and I'm sure there's hope for cooperation with Broward on the Torres case. But Grace's case is something else altogether, and unless you find some hard evidence to prove Bianchi's involvement in those homicides, you plainly need to keep a long way from anything or anyone connected with him.'

Sam did not answer.

'Go find Martinez, Sam, and do what you're best at.'

Sam stood up slowly.

'Are we at least allowed to look into Bianchi's life?'

'If you guys really believe he might be hooked up in these killings, I'd be concerned if you didn't.' Alvarez paused. 'But if anyone is going to be speaking to any members of Mr Bianchi's family, Sam, it cannot be you.'

'I know it,' Sam said.

'Just be careful,' the lieutenant told him. 'Remember, if you put a foot wrong with those people, it's Grace who's going to take the hit.'

'We need to take a good close look at that VW,' Sam said to Martinez.

'Didn't you say Grace's lawyer was on to that?'

'Maybe,' Sam said. 'Who knows?'

Afternoon now. Basic checks already completed on Bianchi and his family.

Father a teacher, mother a doctor's receptionist, one sister, a charity fundraiser, and Bianchi himself appeared to have led a blameless existence. Nothing else new, except that it seemed he'd also boosted his income and experience by editing articles for an Internet newspaper. A couple of rejected novels under his belt – neither of them thrillers nor crime fiction – and no rap sheet.

But Sam still itched to look at his car.

The car that had been registered to a woman, now deceased, in Savannah, Georgia.

'Probably impounded,' Martinez said.

'Maybe not,' Sam said. 'It wasn't involved in the accident.'

'Still, it had to have been taken someplace.'

'Not necessarily,' Sam said. 'It wasn't blocking the road.'

'It'll have been towed,' Martinez insisted.

Plenty of towing companies in Miami, even just on Key Biscayne.

'I'm going to take a look on my way back,' Sam said.

'Coming with you,' Martinez said.

'You don't need to do that.'

'Two pairs of eyes in case it is there,' his partner said. 'Plus I need to make sure you don't do anything dumb.'

The Beetle was long gone.

'Sorry I wasted your time,' Sam told Martinez.

They were standing in the narrow road off the highway, close to where Sam had waited with Grace for the cops to come for her.

Close, too, to where she had described the VW crawling slowly toward her and the boy in her care.

Where Duggan-Bianchi had come at her, and she had driven at him.

'Why the hell did he do that?' Sam said. 'Why didn't he get out of the way?'

He'd asked himself the same question repeatedly since Thursday night.

'Too busy taunting Grace, I guess,' Martinez said. 'Threatening her.'

'But he must have known it was dangerous, even crazy,' Sam said.

'Maybe not,' Martinez said. 'If he was a bully, he'd have figured he'd win.'

'Pete told Grace he thought Charlie liked him being frightened.'

'Bet he was surprised then,' Martinez said. 'When Grace . . .'

Sam was silent.

'Anyway,' Martinez said. 'No chance of getting to the car any time soon.'

'And even if we do,' Sam said.

'Any evidence will be inadmissible.'

'I'd still like to get a look.'

'You'll have to wait.'

'Is there anything we don't have to wait for?'

His friend saw his frustration.

'Go back to your wife and son,' he told him.

No one waiting for Martinez.

'I know I'm a lucky bastard,' Sam said.

'You just hold on to that,' Martinez said

'Doing my best,' Sam said.

'This has to be good news,' Daniel said after Sam had told them about Bianchi. 'Doesn't it?'

They were all outside on the terrace after dinner.

'I'm hoping so,' Sam said.

'If Duggan was a phony identity,' Claudia said, 'that surely proves he had something to hide.'

'Don't get your hopes up, sis,' Grace told her.

'Sounds to me like the guy was a weirdo,' Robbie said.

'He scared the hell out of that poor kid,' Mike said.

'It's going to be OK,' Saul said, positively.

'I blame his mother,' Cathy said.

'Can we stop this, please?' Grace said sharply.

'But it's good news,' Robbie said. 'Like Dad said.'

'The man's still dead,' Grace said. 'Whatever his name was.'

Claudia reached for her hand, but Grace pulled away and stood up.

'I'm going to check on Joshua, and then I'm going to bed.'

'I'll come with you,' Sam said.

'No need,' Grace said.

She bent to kiss his cheek, turned and went into the house.

They all sat in silence for several moments.

'She keeps doing that, Sam,' Claudia said. 'Wanting to be alone.'

'Except for Joshua,' Cathy said. 'Which is something, I guess.'

Sam said nothing.

'She's scared,' Daniel said. 'And being cooped up is getting on her nerves.'

'Dad's right,' Mike said. 'The rest of us get to go out every day.'

'Grace could go out too, to see patients or with one of us,' Cathy said. 'She doesn't want to.'

Sam stood up. 'I'm heading up, guys.'

'You're what she needs,' Cathy told him.

'This to be over is what she needs,' Saul said.

'I'm sorry,' Grace said, fifteen minutes later, joining Sam in the bedroom.

'No need.'

'I think I'm getting a little stir crazy.' She smiled. 'Not the best phrase, in the circumstances.'

'At least you smiled,' Sam said.

She sat down beside him on the edge of the bed, let him take her hand.

'Any word from Wagner?' he asked.

She shook her head. 'I guess he has his investigators looking for the VW.'

'Looks like he'll get to it faster than we could,' Sam said.

'Less constraints,' Grace said.

Sam looked sideways at her.

'Don't,' she said.

'I'm not "analyzing",' he said, remembering last night's conversation.

'I know,' she said. 'But still, please don't.'

'Why not?'

'Because that's one of the looks that says you love me.'

'And?'

'And it doesn't seem right,' she said.

'It's always right,' he said. 'It always will be.'

'Even now I'm a murderer?'

'You are not a murderer,' Sam said, 'and you know that.'

'I fit the definition, so far as I know.' Her voice was quiet, but hard. 'I certainly committed unlawful homicide. What else does that make me?'

'Stop it.'

'Easier said.'

'Please, Grace.'

'What?' She turned to him, hearing his pain. 'Tell me what I can do for you. I'll do anything.'

'For now, just let me hold you.'

She came silently into his arms, and he waited for her to cry, but there was no such release for her, though a while later, after they'd got under the covers, she fell asleep.

And then he didn't dare to cry, either, in case he woke her.

TWENTY-SEVEN

May 11

It was two in the morning when it came to him.

The thing that had been bugging him off and on. The niggle he'd been unable to get a handle on last night.

But right now, Grace was asleep, looking almost peaceful, and he was wide awake.

Thinking about a name.

That was what had been jabbing at him.

Something about the name Charles Duggan.

Something familiar about it.

He got carefully out of bed, and Grace stirred, moaned softly, then settled again.

He went downstairs.

Someone else was up, he saw as he padded barefoot across the cool floor, someone in the kitchen, and Sam had half a mind to go back upstairs, because what he needed was time alone, undisturbed.

'Hi.'

Mike was pouring milk into a frothing jug.

Not just a handsome young man, Sam had come to realize, but nice as hell with it.

'Hi,' Sam said.

'Can't sleep either?'

'Uh-uh.'

'Feel like joining me for some hot chocolate?'

Sam couldn't remember the last time he'd had hot chocolate, especially not in South Florida. 'Sure,' he said. 'Why not? Thanks, Mike.'

The dogs were in their baskets in the corner, side by side, but as Sam sat down at the table and Grace's nephew added more milk and plugged in the jug, Woody got up, stretched languidly, then came to him, tail wagging.

'Hi, guy,' Sam said, and leaned down to fondle his ears.

'Ludo never moves this time of night,' Mike said, 'for anything less than a cookie.'

'Smart dog,' Sam said.

'What's up?' Mike asked, then grimaced. 'Dumb question.'

'Not really.' Sam watched the young man mix the chocolate and add froth and cocoa powder. 'Looks good,' he said.

Mike brought over two mugs and sat down. 'Enjoy.'

'I will.' Sam waited a moment. 'Mike, did you ever hear the name Charles Duggan before?'

'You mean before this past week?'

'Only the name's been bugging me.'

'OK.' Mike nodded. 'You ever see *Day of the Jackal*?'

'Sure,' Sam said. 'The original. And I read the book.'

'Could be you're remembering something from that,' Mike said. 'It's like a fusion of two names, but the same character.'

Sam was already halfway there. 'The Jackal's alias?'

'Two aliases.' Mike grinned. 'Something I share with my dad. We're both movie buffs.' He went on. 'The Jackal used a dead kid's name when he applied for a passport. Paul Duggan. And his other alias was Charles Calthrop – first three letters of each, "Cha" and "Cal", spelt jackal in French – *chacal*.'

'Now I'm getting chills,' Sam said.

'Can you tell me what this is about?' Mike asked.

What it was about, Sam was suddenly as certain as he could be, was Jerome Cooper playing name games, maybe even sending a message hidden in the name Bianchi had used with Sara Mankowitz.

He looked at Mike, saw his dark eyes alive with intrigue, wished he'd kept his mouth shut.

'Could be nothing,' he said.

'Oh, boy,' Mike said, getting it suddenly. 'Nothing to do with the Jackal at all. Just Cal.'

'Like I said,' Sam replied. 'Could be nothing at all.'

'So what do we think?' Martinez's bleary voice asked on the phone. 'That Bianchi was maybe copycatting Cal?'

Sam having called him before six to fill him in.

No one else up yet in Névé this Tuesday morning.

'I don't know,' Sam said. 'If the handwriting on the *Epistle* extract isn't Cooper's, it's a damned good forgery.' He paused. 'Bianchi working for Cal seems more likely to me.'

'That implies payment,' Martinez said. 'Last we knew, Cooper barely had a pot to piss in.'

'That could have changed,' Sam said. 'And besides, there's more than one kind of payment.'

'We need to get inside Bianchi's place,' Martinez said.

'This Jackal thing isn't going to impress a judge.'

'And there's no way Bianchi's family are going to let you in.' Martinez paused. 'But you really think this is something, right?'

'I think it's one coincidence too many,' Sam said. 'And think about it. Cooper's always prided himself on his writing. This creep's a writer, a copy editor, a man of *words*, right?'

'Maybe he figured Bianchi could edit his *Epistles*,' Martinez said wryly.

'Except Cal would probably kill anyone who messed with his writing.'

'I take it we're not planning to share any of this with Detective Rowan?'

'You take it right.'

'So what do we do with it?' Martinez asked.

'Beats the hell out of me,' Sam said.

They drove over to the warehouse where the party had taken place. Where young Ricardo Torres had met with Richard Bianchi probably just hours before his death. All boarded up now. No hope of entering without breaking in.

No hope of forensics. No chance of a guest list any time soon, if ever. Even if YouTube came up with the individual who had posted the video, it had not been the kind of party to which invitations would have been sent out. Notification presumably by word of mouth and on the Internet.

'Goddamned Twitter,' Martinez said sourly.

New technology one of his pet gripes.

No residential neighbors for them to call on. Business premises only, all of which would have been closed that Saturday night.

They showed the cashier in a nearby garage their badges and a couple of photos of Cooper, and Martinez addressed the man in Spanish, asked if he'd been working on the night of Saturday, April 24, and he shook his head too quickly.

Shook it again when he looked at the photos.

'Damn waste of time,' Sam said, back in the Chevy.

The district not really Cal the Hater's kind of hunting ground.

Except it was not Cal-Cooper who'd hooked up with Torres that night.

Not necessarily he who'd hunted that young man down, strangled him to death and cut out his heart.

At ten minutes after three that afternoon, Grace's cellphone rang while she was out on the deck grooming the dogs, both eager for her attention, cool wet noses pushing at her, tails beating time.

'Sorry, guys,' she said and answered her phone.

And saw Pete Mankowitz's name in the display.

Grace stared at the phone.

No contact with witnesses.

She took the call.

'Doc?' His voice was quavering, uncertain.

She knew that tone too well.

'Hello, Pete. What's up?'

'I need to see you.'

'I'm afraid that isn't possible, Pete,' she told him. 'I'm so sorry.'

'I'm feeling so bad, Doc.'

'Where are you, Pete? Are you in school?'

'I mean I'm feeling *really* bad, like I might die.'

'OK, Pete.' They'd been down this route several times. 'You know this is a panic attack, and you know what to do.'

'I don't want to breathe,' he said. 'And I don't want to calm down, and I'm not at school, I'm never going back there, and I don't want to see another shrink – you're the only one who *gets* me, and if you don't let me see you, I'll kill myself. I mean it, Doc. I took a bottle of my mom's pills.'

'What do you mean?' Horror made it hard for her to breathe. 'You swallowed them?'

'Not yet, but I have them with me, and I'll do it.'

Grace's mind raced. If she called 911 right now – if she even knew where to find him – then Lord only knew what fresh traumas that would open up for him.

Not going to happen, not on her watch.

'OK, Pete, here's what we're going to do.' She toughened her tone. 'And it's the only way you're going to get to see me, so you have to listen, OK?'

He didn't answer.

'I'm going to come and meet you, but I won't be alone.'

'No *way*.'

'Hear me out, please, Pete. I have a good friend. She's the same kind of doctor as I am.'

'I told you, I'm not going to see another shrink.'

'You don't have to. This is just so you and I can get to talk today. So I don't get into more trouble.'

'You shouldn't *be* in trouble.'

'That isn't true, Pete. I did a very bad thing.'

'He was the bad one. Charlie was really bad.'

Jerry Wagner would want to hear about that, but there was no way she would ever let him put Pete on the witness stand.

'Will you let me bring my friend? Just so I don't get in trouble.'

He was still crying.

'There's no other way, Pete.'

'You have to promise not to tell my mom.'

'She's going to be so worried.'

'You call her and I'll run away and—'

'I won't call her.'

'Swear it,' Pete said.

'I swear,' Grace said.

'I'm going to be watching, and if there's anyone else except this lady, I'll run away and I'll take the pills and—'

'There won't be anyone else.'

'OK,' he said.

* * *

Something else had been needling Sam.

The registered owner of Bianchi's VW.

Bernice van Heusen.

The kind of name that might possibly have a story behind it.

Deceased last year, and at least a dozen ways he could think of that her car might have made its way down to South Florida from Savannah, but . . .

Even if Angie Carlino had not called yesterday offering help, Sam would still have thought of her now. With a zillion contacts all over, and an ability to suck secrets out of most people, if anyone could short cut the system without making waves of the kind he'd risk churning up if he did this himself, it was Angie.

'Hey, *bellissima*, how's it going?'

'All the better for hearing your voice, handsome.'

'Not as glad as I was to get your message,' Sam told her.

'What do you need?' Angie asked.

'Two things.'

'I already checked out this Bianchi character,' she said, 'and his family.'

The grapevine clearly working.

'Father: Robert Bianchi, a second-generation Italian teacher,' Angie told him. 'Mother: Josephine – known as Josie – doctor's receptionist with French blood on her mom's side. One sibling, a sister, Gina Bianchi, who lives in Naples, and works for a children's charity there.'

Little they didn't already have.

'Both clean, right?' he said.

'As fresh-bathed babes, Richard included,' she said. 'Sorry.'

'Any chance you could check into his school record?' Sam asked. 'History of bullying, anything of that nature. I know I'm pushing it, Angie.'

'Hey,' she said. 'I asked you what you needed.'

'God bless you,' he said. 'You have any pals in Savannah, Georgia?'

'Shoot,' Angie said.

Pete's phone was going straight to voicemail.

'Just to say my friend and I are on our way,' Grace told him. 'So the next time I call, you can take a look and check us out, OK?'

She had feared Magda's reaction, but her friend had simply listened, then made herself available. 'I'll leave now, pick you up.'

'That'll take time,' Grace had said.

'You've sworn to Sam you're not going anywhere alone, so take it or leave it.'

'I'll take it,' Grace said gratefully.

'And you have to call Pete's mother.'

'I know,' Grace had said.

Almost there now.

The Lexus felt smooth and calming, and there was a comfort in having this wise woman by her side, and at least she had not had to lie to Claudia when she'd left, and that was something.

Not that she'd told her the exact truth.

A patient, she'd said.

Not a *witness*.

'So where is it exactly?' Magda asked. 'This playground.'

'I'm not sure,' Grace said.

Pete had directed her to sit on a bench near the slides in Village Green Park, had said he'd come find her.

'There are a bunch of blue and green slides for little kids,' he had said.

She spotted the playground just as Magda found a parking spot.

No sign of Pete.

Time to confess.

'I haven't called his mom yet,' she said. 'And I know that seems wrong, but I gave Pete my word, and this is her number for you to call as soon as I've gone to talk to him.'

'This will end in tears.' Magda took the note with the number.

'So long as they're mine, not his,' Grace said. 'And do you think you could call from here, please, so Pete doesn't see?'

'Anything else?' Magda was dry.

'I'm sorry,' Grace said.

'Don't be sorry,' Magda said. 'Just be careful.'

'I'll do my best,' Grace said.

Detective Rowan called Sam.

'Just a courtesy call,' he said. 'To let you know Bianchi's parents let us take a look around their son's apartment.'

'I appreciate it, Mike.' Sam sounded calm. 'Find anything?'

'Nothing to tell you,' Rowan said, 'except the place was clean.'

'Too clean?' Sam jumped on the word.

'I raised that with his folks,' the Broward detective said, 'and his mom said she wished he'd been as tidy when he'd lived at home.'

'Think someone could have been there since he died?' Sam asked.
'No evidence of that,' Rowan said.

The boy seemed to come from nowhere after Grace had been sitting on one of the benches for three, maybe four minutes.

The little kids and their parents had gone for the day, but a few older boys and girls were fooling around near the slides.

Pete's face was a little grimy, and his eyes were red, but otherwise he looked physically fine.

'Hey,' he said.

'Hey,' Grace said back.

'Where's your friend?'

'Parking her car.'

'She parked the car before you got out,' Pete said.

Grace smiled. 'I asked her to wait a few moments. Then she's going to come and say hi, and then she'll go sit a little way away.'

'Why can't she just stay in the car?'

'That was our deal, remember?' Grace said. 'I have to have someone else here while we talk, so the judge doesn't get mad at me.'

On cue, Magda appeared, walking slowly, taking her time.

'Here she comes,' Grace said. 'Magda's very nice.'

'She has a weird name.'

'It's a little unusual, maybe, but she isn't weird at all.'

Grace smiled as her friend approached.

'Pete, this is Magda,' Grace said. 'Magda, this is Pete.'

Magda put out her hand, and Pete took it.

'Good strong handshake.' Magda smiled. 'Says a lot about a guy.'

'Thanks.' Pete looked uncertainly at Grace.

'It's OK,' Magda said. 'I'll sit over there, shall I?' She nodded toward another bench a decent distance away.

'Please,' Pete said.

'No problem,' Magda said, headed right over and sat down.

'I'm sorry,' Pete said.

'It's fine,' Grace told him.

Pete took another long look around and then, cautiously, he sat beside her.

'I'm doing better now,' he said.

'I can see that,' Grace said. 'I knew you could calm yourself down.'

'I wasn't as bad as I made out,' Pete said. 'I just wanted to get you here.'

'You know,' Grace said quietly, 'you shouldn't have gone anywhere without telling your mom.'

'I know,' he said. 'She's going to be mad as hell.'

'I guess she will,' Grace agreed. 'But you know why.'

'I know she loves me,' Pete said. 'But she wasn't going to let me see you.'

'Because of what happened. What I did to her friend.'

'He wasn't a good friend,' Pete said. 'He was a liar. He didn't even tell her his real name.'

Grace felt no great surprise that he knew that, since even if Sara had banned TV news, he'd have checked it out on Google or heard about it at school.

'No,' she said. 'That's true.'

'I'm ready to tell you now,' Pete said. 'About what he did.'

She felt a stab of pain, because this was the kind of breakthrough she worked toward with children like Pete, yet here, today, she was going to have stop him from going on, and who could say if she would ever be permitted to do her work again, to help troubled children?

'You can't tell me, Pete,' she said. 'I'm not allowed to speak to you for the present. Because you're a witness to what I did.'

'That's baloney,' he said. 'Anyway, I won't tell anyone except you.'

The fear was there again now, in those expressive eyes, in no way a pretense, and she was not convinced that his phone call had been a ruse to get her here, and there was no way she was prepared to take chances now.

'Where are the pills, Pete?'

'I don't have them,' he said. 'I made it up.'

'I'm not sure I believe that,' she said carefully.

'You want to search me?' he asked.

'Of course not.' Grace met his gaze evenly. 'I trust you.'

'I don't want to kill myself,' Pete told her.

'I'm very glad to hear that.' She paused. 'But you have had those kinds of thoughts before, haven't you? Wanting it all to stop.'

'Uh-huh.' His eyes veered away, downward.

'It's OK.' Grace knew now that she could not turn him away. 'You can tell me, if you like, about what he did.'

'Are you sure?' He was anxious. 'I don't want to get you in worse trouble.'

'I'm sure,' she said.

'Only it's weird,' he said, 'because I thought I'd feel better with him gone.'

'But you don't?'

He shook his head.

'That seems logical to me,' Grace told him. 'After all, you felt bad sometimes before he met your mom, didn't you?'

'I guess.'

She waited a moment.

'So,' she said. 'About him. Let's call him Charlie, OK?'

'He hurt me,' Pete said. 'I know I said he didn't when you asked me that night, before . . .'

'It's OK. Go on.'

'You know what a Hertz doughnut is, Doc?'

'I'm not sure,' Grace said, though she did know.

'Guy comes up to you with a box of doughnuts and says "Do you want a doughnut?" and you say sure, and then the guy punches you and says "Hurts, don't it?" Don't-it, like doughnut.'

Grace nodded. 'Charlie did that to you?'

Pranksters, she had always felt, were bullies.

'He did Indian burns on my arm, too.'

'Pete, why didn't you tell your mom?' The horror was in her tone, and probably in her face, but she couldn't help it.

There were tears in his eyes now. 'One time, he pushed me when we were out in our backyard at home, and I fell down and hit my knee on the table, and my mom came out and he helped me up, pretended he was helping me, you know, but he whispered in my ear that if I told, he'd come and get me.'

'Pete, I'm so sorry,' Grace said.

'He knew I was scared of stuff,' Pete went on, 'because Mom told him, and he said I was a wuss and laughed at me, but never when she was around.'

Grace remembered how she'd felt that evening when he'd started to tell her about what 'Charlie' had said to him, remembered the anger blossoming in her, and then *it* had happened, and that man had lain dying at her feet . . .

But now, right now, she could hear sirens, coming closer.

Stopping.

And then two uniformed Key Biscayne police officers, one male, one female, were coming their way, moving rapidly over the grass.

'Doc?' New fear in Pete's eyes.

'It's OK,' Grace told him calmly. 'I think it's me they want to talk to.'

'No!' He jumped up. 'They'll take you to *jail*!'

Magda was up on her feet.

Grace stood up slowly, saw another woman behind the officers, hurrying.

Sara Mankowitz.

'Mom!' Pete cried, fury in his voice.

He took off, running, but he didn't get far, the policewoman reaching him easily, taking hold of him by one arm.

'Don't hurt him!' Grace cried out.

Pete was yelling and kicking out, and Sara was weeping and the male officer had to go join the melee, and Grace's impulse was to go and help.

'No, Grace.' Magda was at her side. 'You can't do anything.'

'Oh, God,' Grace said. 'I've made it worse for him.'

'No, you haven't,' Magda told her. 'You did the only thing you could.'

'He was telling me what Duggan – Bianchi – did to him.'

'Careful,' Magda warned her. 'Not now.'

'Oh, God,' Grace said again.

'She didn't tell you where she was going?' Sam asked Claudia on the phone.

He was trying not to yell at her, but it was hard.

'She went out with Dr Shrike,' Claudia said. 'I figured that had to be OK.'

'What exactly did Grace say before they left?'

'I told you. She said they had something to do, that Magda was picking her up. And she did, I saw her car pull up, I checked that Dr Shrike was driving, and I felt like I sometimes do with the boys, making sure their friends aren't crazy drivers or going to drink. Grace is not a fool, Sam, as you know.'

'Did she say they were going to Magda's?'

'No, but I guess they might have.' Claudia's anxiety level suddenly rose. 'Sam, has something happened?'

'Nothing new,' Sam said. 'Other than that there's a multiple killer out there who hates our family and, oh, yes, Grace is out of jail on bail.'

'Hey,' Claudia said. 'Take it easy.'

Sam took a breath. 'I'm sorry.'

'It's all getting to you,' she said. 'Me, too. Though I know it's different. All the pressure on you to make it go away, make it better.'

'You're not wrong there,' Sam said.

'I'd offer to go looking for her, but with Joshua here . . .'

'You stay put,' Sam told her. 'I'm sure she's OK.'

'Me too.'

'Thank you.' He paused. 'I haven't been saying that enough. Thank you, all of you, the boys too. You've all been better than great.'

'We love you,' Claudia said simply.

'If you hear from Grace, have her call me, please.'

'Likewise,' Claudia said.

It could have been far worse for her.

She knew that.

Though it was bad enough as it was.

The Key Biscayne police were courteous with her, listened to what little she was able to tell them – since to her mind Pete was still her patient – and told her they would be making a report.

Then Magda, who had waited throughout, took her back to Névé.

Sam opened the door immediately.

He'd received a courtesy call an hour ago.

'Are you OK?' he asked her.

'Yes,' she said. 'Thank you.'

She heard the Lexus departing through the gates, wanted to turn and wave, but thought better of it, felt too much like an errant child.

'I've talked with Jerry Wagner,' Sam said. 'I expect you have too.'

He closed the front door.

The first floor was quiet, empty. The family cars were outside, but tact, she guessed, had driven them all into retreat.

'I know you're mad at me,' she said. 'And I'm mad at myself, too, but I still don't see what choice I had in the circumstances.'

Sam shook his head. 'How can you *not* see?'

'Magda was watching me at all times.'

'Does Magda carry a gun?' Sam asked.

'I doubt it,' Grace said, 'and I doubt you'd be happy if the answer was yes.'

Woody appeared, tail wagging, approached, then stopped, sensing a mood. 'I'd be happy,' Sam said, 'if I could trust you to behave like a sane person.'

'And ignore a child threatening to kill himself?' Grace felt her own anger mounting. 'And I don't care if he was a witness, or I didn't care at the time, and I'm betting that if you were me, you'd have done pretty much the same thing.'

'With one notable difference,' Sam said.

'You'd have called me first,' Grace said.

'You got that right,' Sam said, and walked away.

Sam seldom walked away from her.

It was much later before they talked about it again.

Family having intervened, time with their son, dinner, *safe* conversation, no one asking too many questions – though Claudia had tackled her briefly in the kitchen, had said that though she understood, she still objected to having been deceived.

'I'm sorry,' Grace had said.

'It must have been terrible for you,' Claudia had said.

'Much, much worse for Pete,' Grace had said.

She and Sam went up early, checked on Joshua, then went into their room and closed the door.

'Did Jerry tell you what to expect?' Grace asked.

'I'm not his client,' Sam said.

'He didn't know much yet,' she said. 'He said he thinks the prosecutor will be made aware and they may try to have the bond revoked.' The impact of that struck her suddenly. 'My God, Sam, what would that do to you financially?'

'I don't think it'll happen,' he said. 'But thank you for considering it.'

'A little late,' Grace said.

'Just a little,' he said.

'I wish you'd yell at me.'

'I don't want to.'

'Do you hate me?' she asked.

'What are you suddenly, sixteen?'

She sat on the bed. 'I'm sorry,' she said. 'I keep screwing up, but things keep happening when I least expect them to, and maybe my decision-making skills aren't at their best.'

'But if Pete called you again tomorrow, you'd probably go to him.'

'Not without checking with you first,' Grace said.

Sam sat down beside her.

'I don't think you realize how scared for you I am,' he said.

'I wish you wouldn't be.'

'All the time,' he said. 'Not just when you're off doing crazy things, but even when I know you're here, and I should believe you're safe, but I don't, not the way things are, and that's more my fault than yours.'

'Of course it isn't,' Grace said.

'My fault for not having gotten the job done yet,' Sam said.

'Oh, Sam,' she said, and leaned against him. 'I thought, for a while, I was going back to jail tonight.'

'What else did Jerry say?'

'That they might bring everyone back into court, and because I had contact with one of the state witnesses, the prosecution might try— I already said that . . .'

'You did,' Sam said.

'So what now?' Grace said.

'We wait.'

TWENTY-EIGHT

May 12

In the dream, she was in a cell, but there was only one other prisoner.

Joshua was there, too, chained up, too far away for her to hold him, but she could feel his warmth, hear his breathing . . .

'Joshua,' she said softly, so no one would hear and come to hurt them. 'Joshua, sweetheart, everything's going to be OK. Isn't it, Daddy?'

Except Sam didn't answer, because of course he wasn't there.

'I've left you,' his voice said suddenly.

'Sam?' she said. 'Where are you?

'I've left you because you never listen,' his voice told her. 'Because you lie.'

'I don't,' Grace said.

'You're a liar, and you're a murderer,' Sam's voice went on, 'and look what's happened to our little boy because of you, Gracie, just look at Joshua now.'

She turned her head, saw their little son in chains.

And then she saw that *he* was there too.

Cooper.

On his knees beside Joshua, a knife in his hand.

Pointing at his heart.

Grace screamed.

And woke up.

Alone in the big bed.

Only four in the morning, but Sam wasn't with her, though logic told her, even as her heart still pounded in her chest, that he had not left her, just the bed, because he hardly slept these nights and got up so as not to disturb her.

'Oh, God,' she said.

And lay back again, wondering, for the thousandth time since that night, what was going to become of them all.

'*Murderer*,' Sam's voice from the dream accused her again.

'You're right,' she said, into the dark.

'It looks like yesterday's going to go away,' Jerry Wagner told her when he called just after ten.

'Are you sure?' Grace asked.

She was in her sister's kitchen, and Claudia was standing by the big steel fridge, watching and listening, and Grace supposed this was how it would be now, one of them standing guard, making sure she didn't break out or do anything more to bring the wrath of the law down on her head.

'I have it on good authority,' Wagner went on, 'that Mrs Mankowitz got quite upset when she thought you'd been arrested, because she knew you were only trying to help her son, who was in real danger.'

'That's good of Sara,' Grace said.

'I guess so,' Wagner said, 'though maybe it's the least she can do if she can't take proper care of him herself.'

'That's a little unfair.' Grace sat down, weak with relief.

'Can we talk about you now, please?'

'Yes,' she said.

'About the fact that if you do get away with this, it's the very last time.'

'I know,' she said again.

'I'm not sure you do.' He spelt it out. 'You can*not* have any more contact with state witnesses. There will be no more chances. And then you'll all lose. You, Sam, Joshua, Cathy, the whole of your family.' Wagner paused. 'Are we clear? Or do I have to start thinking you might be safer with an electronic monitoring device around your ankle?'

'No,' Grace said. 'You don't.'

'I don't want to see you back in that place,' he said. 'And I plan to do every last thing I can to stop that happening.'

'I know,' she said. 'I'm very grateful.'

'Don't be grateful,' Wagner said. 'Just keep to the rules.'

Angie Carlino called Sam just after noon.

'No bullying history for Bianchi that I could dig up, though it doesn't mean he might not have been a nasty or even a troubled kid.' Angie paused. 'Bernice van Heusen aka Blossom van Heusen, aka at least three other married names. George van Heusen, a big property guy, having been her last husband.'

'Dead or alive?' Sam asked.

'All dead,' Angie said. 'But nothing suspicious, unless maybe Blossom excited them to death. From what I can make out, she used to make a good living out of prostitution.'

'Hooker or madam?'

'Both,' Angie said. 'Though she seems to have given it up for George, who died ten years ago – cancer – and left her a small fortune.'

Sam tried to conjure up the widow, then sixty-one.

'If she had money,' he asked, 'how come she drove an old Beetle?'

'Maybe she liked it,' Angie said. 'Sounds like she was a fun broad. Or maybe it was just one of a string of cars.'

'Where was she living at the end?'

'At home, in her house. Mr van Heusen's nice, big house, I guess.'

'She have staff looking after her?'

'I don't know,' Angie said. 'That's all I could get, Sam.'

'It's good,' he said. 'I owe you one.'

'No problem,' she said. 'How's Grace doing?'

'Doing OK,' Sam lied.

No sense adding to the worry pool, he figured.

Enough people swimming around in there already.

He waited till halfway through the afternoon, when all the other detectives were out of the office, before he shared his new thoughts with Martinez.

'I'm getting a definite feeling about Mrs van Heusen and Cooper,' he said. 'I know it's a leap, but the lady used to be a madam.'

'You're thinking Savannah's where Cooper holed up after he escaped?'

Sam shrugged. 'We know her car made its way to Miami.'

'Last driver Richard Bianchi,' Martinez said.

'If Cooper knew "Blossom",' Sam went on, 'if, say, he did hook up with her some time after he disappeared off our radar, I'm not sure it makes a bean of difference to the homicide investigations, but it might just make a hell of a difference when it comes to proving Grace's self-defense.'

'So what, you think Bianchi was hooked up with this Blossom broad too?'

Sam shook his head. 'I guess I'm saying that I'd like Bianchi to have been driving Mrs van Heusen's car because Cooper gave it to him.'

'Long shot,' Martinez said.

'I know it,' Sam said. 'Except if Bianchi's alias was given him by Cooper along with his car . . .' He paused. 'Think about it. Cooper stays away for as long as he can stand it, or maybe till he has to leave wherever he's been hiding out.'

'Maybe with Mrs van Heusen,' Martinez said. 'Until she dies.'

'So then he comes back down to Miami, ready to move his act along a little, change the MO, maybe because he has this new burning need to cut the hearts out of black, preferably gay men, maybe to keep his game with us alive.'

'Maybe just getting his jollies.'

'But he knows he can't risk hitting the clubs or streets anymore—'

'Unless he's changed his appearance.'

'Easier to find someone else to do it for him,' Sam said.

'So you're thinking Bianchi was maybe pimping guys for Cooper?'

'Could be,' Sam said.

Martinez shook his head. 'Hell of a long shot, man.'

'I know it,' Sam said again.

Jerry Wagner called just before five to tell Sam that according to his investigator, the VW was being kept under wraps by the Bianchi family.

'Just being protective, you think?' Sam asked. 'Or something more sinister?'

'Almost certainly simple grief and anger, I'd say. Parents wanting to keep their dead son's name intact.'

'Can't blame them for that,' Sam said.

'I don't,' Wagner said, 'but even if you got hold of the car now, nothing in there would be admissible, so I'd understand if you did blame them.'

'I'm going to stay around South Beach late tonight,' he told Martinez. 'Another unofficial stake-out.'

'The clubs again?' Martinez looked dubious.

'And the sidewalks, and the promenade,' Sam said. 'If there's anything to my Bianchi theory, then with his little helper gone, the Joy Boy's going to have to come out to play again soon if he wants another heart.'

'Pick up a couple of tamales first,' Martinez said, 'and I'm with you.'

'You got a deal,' Sam said.

The tamales tasted fine.

As did the company of his partner and good friend.

They'd almost lost him last year.

Quite a year.

No dice with the stake-out.

If the Joy Boy was out tonight, they couldn't see him.

Didn't mean he wasn't there.

They hung around till after two.

'Go home, man,' Martinez said.

'Wish I could,' Sam said.

'You got Grace and Joshua waiting for you,' Martinez said. 'Sounds enough like home to me.'

The rebuke was gentle, but deserved.

'I'm on my way,' Sam said.

TWENTY-NINE

May 13

Sam's cellphone started ringing at six thirty-five, while he was in the kitchen with Daniel, who was making French toast.

'Beth Riley just called me,' Martinez told him. 'Seems some tourists spotted something bad in the water near Dinner Key Marina.'

'What kind of bad?'

Over at the stove, Dan turned from his griddle, eyes interested.

'Blood,' Martinez answered. 'They said it looked like it was leaking from a boat moored out there.'

'What kind of boat?'

Sam's flesh had started to creep.

'Houseboat named *Aggie*.'

Cooper's last known boat, *Baby*, had been a battered old cruiser.

'We have a registered owner?' Sam asked.

'Not yet,' Martinez said.

'Anyone on their way?'

'Riley says Miami Police are sending a boat to take a look.'

'We need to stop them,' Sam said.

'You think it's him?'

'It could be anyone, any damned thing,' Sam said, 'but hell, yes, I think it could be Cooper, which is why we need to mount surveillance, not go storming in.'

'I'll make some calls,' Martinez said, 'and meet you where?'

'City Hall,' Sam said.

He ended the call, looked up at Daniel, knew he'd heard enough.

'Chances are,' he said quietly, 'it's nothing to do with Cooper.'

'What's nothing to do with Cooper?'

Grace was in the doorway, wearing a long white T-shirt, feet bare. She looked tired and fragile. Sam debated for an instant, knew he had to tell her.

'Someone's reported seeing what might be blood leaking out of a boat at a marina,' he said. 'There's absolutely no further information.'

'But you think it might be Cooper?'

'We're going to take a look,' Sam said.

Her eyes were wary.

'Please,' she said. 'Be careful.'

'You bet,' Sam said.

The *Aggie* was a white thirty-four foot Wavelength houseboat whose registered owner was one Tom O'Hagen.

Not Thomas, just Tom.

No rap sheet for anyone with that name.

Just a guy with a houseboat.

Maybe.

There had been no way of preventing Miami's marine patrol from taking a preliminary look at the water surrounding the boat, though Sam understood that an assurance of caution and discretion had been given to Lieutenant Alvarez.

Confirmation that what was in the water did look like blood and there was a dinghy tied up to the boat.

Anything more on hold for now.

The guys who had first called in the report were a couple of British tourists, name of Philip Hamblin and Terence Reed. Back on shore now and, having answered all Miami Police's questions, the two men were waiting for Sam and Martinez in the back of a patrol car in the parking lot of the white and blue building that had, in the thirties, been Pan Am's seaplane terminal, but was now, for better or worse, City Hall.

'Anything else you can tell us?' Sam asked them.

Mid to late twenties, both sporting deep sailing tans and a shared, ill-concealed look of excitement.

'Nothing more than we already did,' Hamblin said.

'You were what, moored near the *Aggie*?' Sam said.

'We'd been out in the Bay overnight,' Reed said. 'It was bloody dark out there, and we were both tired, so we decided to anchor and wait till it was light.'

'And then, on our way in this morning,' Hamblin said, 'we passed this houseboat and saw the blood in the water.'

'At least, that's what we thought it was,' Reed said.

'Did you see anyone on board?' Martinez asked.

Both Brits shook their heads.

'Anything special you can tell us about the boat?' Sam asked.

'Not really,' Reed said. 'It's just a houseboat.'

'It's the kind of boat a person could really live on, I suppose,' Hamblin said. 'Spend real time on.'

'So long as they're not in a rush to get anywhere,' Reed added.

'So you still think this could be him?' Martinez asked Sam, out of earshot of the Englishmen, walking back around the side of City Hall to the marina. 'Like the man said, houseboats are not exactly built for speedy getaways.'

'Maybe not,' Sam said, 'but plenty of space inside.'

For killing, not to mention mutilation.

They were both silent for a moment.

'The name O'Hagen ring any bells with you?' Martinez asked.

'Uh-uh,' Sam said. 'But there's an outside chance the *Aggie* might.'

He stopped walking, took out his PDA and keyed in a search.

'OK,' he said after a moment. 'Remember why Cal the Hater said he renamed his mom Jewel?'

Martinez nodded, too damned much of the killer's so-called *Epistles* still etched on his memory. 'After Caligula's mother, right?'

'Right,' Sam said. 'Julia Agrippina.'

'Shit,' Martinez said. 'Except Cooper hated his mom.'

With good reason, as they both knew.

'After killing her, though,' Sam said, 'maybe he wanted a tribute to her?'

'He sure loved his old boat,' Martinez said.

'More than he loved any person we know of,' Sam agreed.

'So what now? We board the *Aggie*, see if he's down below?'

'That's one option,' Sam said. 'Though if he's not on board and he sees or hears about it, we've blown our chances of catching him.'

'He could be anyplace,' Martinez said.

'Except Bianchi's apartment.'

'You think that's where he might have been holed up?'

'I don't have a clue,' Sam said. 'But it comes to mind. Whatever deal they may have had going on between them – unless I've been totally wrong about the connection – Cooper might have been living part-time at Bianchi's and the rest on the houseboat.' He shrugged. 'And right this minute, he could have taken another dinghy out to sea or he could be on shore picking up supplies.'

'Or another victim,' Martinez said flatly.

'Not his time of day,' Sam said. 'Unless that's another MO change.'

'Or maybe this has nothing to do with Cooper at all,' Martinez said. 'Maybe we got ourselves another killer with this O'Hagen.'

'Maybe we do.'

'Or O'Hagen could be an innocent man with a houseboat named after his Aunt Agatha.' Martinez shook his head, frustrated. 'Man, I wish we had something *real*.'

'How's about a houseboat with blood leaking out of its keel?' Sam said.

'I'm impressed,' Martinez said. 'I would've said butt.'

They settled, after a brief meeting with two marine patrol officers, on a stake-out position on a sailboat in range for their 10/50 binoculars. Miami Police and the Coast Guard standing by to assist, if and when.

Eleven a.m. and counting.

All the family were waiting at Névé.

Neither Daniel nor Grace, it seemed, had been capable of keeping their tension from the others.

'No way I'm going to college now,' Cathy had said, after she'd squeezed the news out of Grace, and Saul had said much the same.

And then Saul had answered the phone when his dad had called and had let the news slip out, which was why David and Mildred had driven right over. And now they were playing with Joshua, and Claudia and Cathy were half-heartedly making brunch, and though Sam had stressed the slimness of a possibility of a breakthrough, they all felt poised on the edge of something big.

'You OK?' Daniel found Grace on the terrace, sitting with the dogs.

'Sure,' she said.

'Getting a little crowded in there for you?' he said.

'I'll be in soon,' she said.

He left her to her thoughts, from which all optimism seemed absent.

She was, no matter what Sam and the others found, a killer out on bail.

Interested in only two things right now: hearing that her husband was safe and Cooper in custody. And the *safe* part was something she and Sam would have to talk about soon, because if she went to jail, then Joshua would need his father safe and sound and present in his life, not taking risks with brutal killers, monsters.

Sam loved his work, tough as it sometimes was.

Another thing she might end up taking away from him.

Just after one p.m., it became apparent that word had gotten out that the cops were keeping the *Aggie* under surveillance, because a keen-eyed woman on a yacht moored a few hundred yards away had phoned Miami PD to say that she had seen the guy who'd been living on the houseboat come aboard in the early hours of this morning.

'She claims she'd have noticed if he'd gotten off again,' reported one of the officers staking out the *Aggie* with the Miami Beach detectives.

'She give a description, by any chance?' Sam asked.

'"Tall, blond, otherwise nondescript," was what she told the dispatcher.'

That last word got to Sam more than the rest.

First time he'd ever set eyes on Jerome Cooper, he'd found him just that, a nondescript man with mean little stoat's eyes. Though in this case, if they were talking early hours, it would have been dark, which made him wonder how she even knew this guy had been blond.

'I need to talk to her,' he said.

No way of knowing if the dispatcher had asked enough questions.

Five minutes later, the lady, one Marilyn Segal, resident of Boca Raton, was answering Sam's questions on his cellphone.

'I don't suppose you got a close look at his face, ma'am?'

'If you mean did I take a look with my binoculars,' she said, 'I'm not in the habit of spying on my neighbors, either at home or on the yacht.'

More was the pity, Sam thought.

'You described him in your first call as "nondescript",' he said.

'I did,' Marilyn Segal confirmed, 'though that was probably the wrong word to use, because it was dark and he was too far away for me to see.'

'But you saw that his hair was blond?' Sam asked.

'Actually, it looked kind of silvery, but his movements were nimble, too youthful for him to have gray hair, which is why I said blond.' She paused. 'He boarded from a dinghy, and then he turned on some lights on board – which was when I saw him – and he stayed out on deck for a few minutes, then went inside.'

'And he was alone?' Sam asked.

'So far as I could tell.'

'Anything else you can add?' Sam asked.

'Only that I suffer from insomnia, which is why I said I'd noticed him leaving again.'

He thanked her, ended the call.

Martinez gave him a minute.

'So?' he asked, quietly.

Sam took a few moments more, knowing he had to temper his gut response with professional commonsense.

Instinct overcame all the other arguments in his head.
'We go in,' he said.

Boarding the *Aggie* was smooth as silk.
So easy, they kept waiting for all kinds of other shoes to drop – anything from a marine ambush to a booby trap explosive device.
Two Miami PD boats. Six officers, plus Sam and Martinez, all wearing life jackets, all armed.
No warnings given.
No resistance offered.
No bomb.
No one on board.

Someone had been there though.
An unspeakable stench was coming from someplace on the houseboat.
All the officers and the Miami Beach detectives, their .40 calibers drawn, ransacked the *Aggie* with their eyes, cautiously checking every hidey-hole, every closet, locker, *every* nook and cranny.
A number of quality shirts and pants hung on a rail in the master bedroom, and the rumpled sheets on the bed looked and felt expensive.
'Still warm,' Sam said quietly.
In a second cabin, and in a cuddy, they found sights far worse than the stink.
Human remains.
But Jerome Cooper was not *there.*
Sam was back on deck before the others, edging, as fast as caution allowed, around the perimeter of the boat, leaning over the side every few feet, keeping a double grip on his weapon, all his senses on high alert, scanning the water . . .
There.
Naked, face down.
'Suspect overboard,' he yelled.
He holstered his gun, pulled off his shoes.
'Sam, wait!'
He heard Martinez, other voices besides his, but he was already over the guard rail, and no way was he letting this happen, no *way* was he letting this monster drown when Grace needed him *alive*.

'Cover me!' he yelled.

And dove.

Cooper was limp when Sam reached him.

Lifeless.

The black snouts of seven weapons trained on him.

Seven men yelling warnings.

Sam grabbed the man by his hair, his left hand snaking under his slippery body to flip him over – knew, even before he saw Cooper's face, that he'd blown it, that it was a trick, a goddamned gamble, but a *trick*.

The killer opened his eyes and took a big breath.

And smiled.

'I knew you'd come,' he said.

Sam saw what was in his hand just before it struck.

A goddamned *hypodermic*.

Cooper jammed it in, hard.

'Jesus,' Sam said, gasping.

He heard the bullets exploding out of the guns at the same instant that Cooper brought up his other hand and landed a hard blow to his right temple.

And then the killer went limp again, folded down into the water.

Dizzy as hell, Sam yanked the hypodermic out of his body.

Keep hold of it, he ordered himself.

But it had already slipped from his fingers.

And he was going under.

THIRTY

It was Martinez – who *hated* to swim more than almost anything – who'd plunged right in with one of the Miami PD guys and helped fish him out, same time as the others were retrieving Cooper.

The killer not dead, though he ought to have been, with three of the police bullets having struck him, but one bullet had passed right through, missing vital organs, another had grazed his head, and he was presently being prepped for surgery at City Hospital for the removal of the third bullet from his left arm.

Lucky as hell, considering.

Under guard, under arrest.

And demanding to see Sam.

Who wanted nothing more than to oblige, who wanted Cooper alive and coherent for as long as it took to prove Bianchi's connection with him, to give Grace her self-defense plea.

Then the bastard could die.

But Sam was marooned in the ER at Miami General, with nothing much apparently wrong with him, apart from some bruising to his head and the after-effects of swallowing some ocean.

Some discomfort, too, from the puncture in his left shoulder, where the hollow needle – estimated to have been a large diameter eighteen gauge – of Jerome Cooper's hypodermic syringe had pierced him. And it remained to be seen what damage the needle might have done to nerves, tendons or ligaments, but Sam's trapezius muscles were well-developed, and in any event, he knew he'd been lucky as hell too, because if Cooper had stuck it in a little way across his chest, he'd have had a punctured lung at the very least.

'No prizes for guessing it was my heart he was aiming for,' Sam said.

Martinez the only one with him at that moment, Grace on her way.

His friend in dry clothes, but still shocked and still mad at Sam for his recklessness – and that happened too damned often for *his* goddamned sanity – and sure he understood, but Jesus . . . He'd still been on the *Aggie* when he'd seen Sam turn Cooper face up, had seen the sonofabitch's hand move, had seen him stab *something* into Sam, had presumed a blade of some kind, and his initial relief at the absence of a major wound had been immense.

'So what are we thinking?' he said now, because the scenario still made no sense to him. 'That he let the blood leak out of the boat, that he wanted to get caught, or was it supposed to be "suicide by cop"?'

'With a twist,' Sam said.

'So he jumps overboard naked, holding a fucking hypodermic, and then he turns over to play dead just in *case* you show up?'

'I'm guessing he saw us coming,' Sam said.

Seemed clear to him, since Cooper-Cal was crazy, always had been.

'And if someone else had jumped in after him?' Martinez said.

'I guess he'd have stuck them with the needle,' Sam said.

'But Miami PD are saying there were scalpels on the *Aggie*, so if he wanted your heart, why use a fucking hypodermic?'

'I'd like to think it was just the first thing that came to hand,' Sam said.

'Yeah,' Martinez said. 'Me too.'

'Except I saw the syringe,' Sam said quietly. 'And it was full.'

Martinez did not speak.

'It looked a lot like blood,' Sam said.

Grace arrived moments later, and Sam shut down those thoughts, focused on making her believe that he was fine and that Jerome Cooper was in custody.

'Hard to take in,' he said. 'But we have him.'

'He could have killed you,' she said.

'Not easily,' Sam said. 'Too many guns trained on him.'

'Piece of cake, right?' she said.

He looked at her white face and still frightened eyes.

'You holding up, Gracie?'

'They said something about a syringe,' she said.

'He tried to stick me with it,' Sam said.

She was looking at the dressing on his shoulder. 'Apparently he did more than try.'

'It's not much,' he said.

Her eyes met his, held steady. 'Did he inject you with something?'

'I don't think so,' he said.

'But you're not sure,' she said.

'Main thing,' Sam said, 'we have him.'

'Yes,' she said.

'Worth celebrating, I'd say,' Sam said.

'Are they doing blood tests?' Grace asked.

No diverting her.

'Sure,' he said. 'Taking all precautions. Just in case.'

She chose to leave it, leaned in, stroked his forehead, his hair.

'I'm glad you got him,' she said, gently. 'Thank you, for us all.'

Cathy and Saul came by the ER to see him, and he thought he did a better job of convincing them that he was better than OK, and for a while he had himself believing it too.

And then his father showed up.

Man of few words when David Becket was scared to death, but everything he said and asked, however calmly, led back to the thing Sam was trying not to think about.

'You know what they're concerned about, son,' he said.

'Sure I know,' Sam said. 'BBV.'

Blood borne viruses – BBV – the doctors' most likely concern. Anything from hepatitis B to HIV.

Cops, like hospital personnel, knew all about the dangers of needlestick injuries. An ordinary needlestick could introduce contaminants into the body, both from the outside of the needle and from the bore itself, and whatever Cooper had used that hypodermic for prior to stabbing it into Sam could define what he might be up against now. And that was without knowing what might have been loaded inside the syringe.

Blood, bodily fluids, who the hell knew?

'They're getting a search warrant for Cooper's blood,' Sam said. 'Officer exposed, so no problem there.'

So long as it had been Cooper's blood and not a sample he'd taken from one of his victims – though for all Sam knew, the bastard might have sucked up the red stuff from a bottle of Chianti.

But in that instant, it had looked more like blood than wine.

'They'll be giving you a lot of medication,' David said.

'I know,' Sam said.

Antibiotics, antiviral, immunoglobulins.

All of which might make him feel sick by themselves, plus, whether or not Cooper tested positive for HIV or any other disease, Sam knew he would still have to come for regular testing for months to come. All kinds of mental trauma that neither he nor Grace, nor the rest of their family needed.

'And you have no idea if he pushed the plunger home?' David asked.

'No,' Sam said. 'I'd say I wish I did know, but I'm not sure that's true.'

And chances were they would never know, because he had dropped the hypodermic in the ocean, though so long as nothing showed up positive in his blood tests, and so long as he didn't get sick, it might not matter too much.

Except that it was another crime committed by Cooper – maybe just GBH, maybe attempted murder – and the syringe was evidence.

All other answers to be drawn out of Cal the Hater.

Along with things even more important to Sam right now.

'I need to get out of here,' he told the doctor who'd just said she wanted to keep him overnight for observation.

'You need to rest,' she said. 'And I'd like to monitor you for any ill-effects.'

'I can rest at home,' he told her.

Lying through his teeth, because though he knew the docs over at City were unlikely to let Cooper be questioned until tomorrow at the earliest, he wanted to get back over to Dinner Key, wanted to see the *Aggie* again before Crime Scene started taking her apart.

'My wife will monitor me for ill-effects,' he said.

'Still,' the doctor said, 'I'd be happier keeping you here.'

She was young – God, they were all so *young* – and pretty, but stern.

'How's about I go home now,' Sam said, 'and come back tomorrow?'

'I'd advise against it,' she said.

'And I do appreciate your advice, Doc,' he told her, 'but I'm going to have to discharge myself.'

'You'll need to wait for some of your drugs to be ready,' she said.

'Can I come back for them later?' he asked.

'You're certainly in a great hurry to *rest*, Detective,' she said dryly.

THIRTY-ONE

Still Thursday, May the thirteenth.

After six p.m. when Sam and Martinez got back to Dinner Key.

On the way, Sam had called Gail Tewkesbury and Anne Dover, Andrew Victor's sister, to tell them about the arrest of the prime suspect in Andy's killing.

'Slow progress from here,' he told them both, 'but we have him.'

Gail had wept on the phone. Anne Dover had been reserved and subdued. Both women had thanked Sam for the capture.

Which had felt good.

As long as it lasted.

Elliot Sanders had been and gone, though his work and Crime Scene's would run and run in this case.

The on-call Assistant State Attorney had been there too, called to join the party at the outset as a matter of urgency because of the complex totality of circumstances. Everyone had known they had to back off while City of Miami sought a warrant to search the *Aggie*, based on the fact that a fugitive had been on board, and that during the arrest of that fugitive – in the course of which he had injured a police detective – evidence of new crimes had been in plain sight on the houseboat. Warrants already existed for Cooper's past crimes, but here was a load of new stuff in another jurisdiction, and the investigators needed all the expert legal help they could get with the construction of the search and arrest warrants and any other legal aspects of the case, for which the State Attorney would be responsible in court.

No one concerned was willing to risk a single mistake.

Everything – photography, crime scene sketches, evidence collection and preservation – was on hold until the arrival of the warrant.

A forensic cornucopia awaited Crime Scene and the Medical Examiner.

More than enough – sickening enough – to Sam and Martinez now.

A bathtub stood in one of two cuddies, partially cleaned, but with blood, flesh and bone fragments still clinging to the sides and splashed over the walls and floor around the tub.

DNA everywhere.

Prints, too, though Sam was already taking grim bets with himself that even if Richard Bianchi – whose blood and fingerprints were on file at the morgue – had been on the *Aggie*, Cooper would have taken pains to eradicate every trace.

Sanders would be photographing every square inch of the houseboat from every angle, and if feasible, the Miami Beach detectives guessed that he would want the bathtub extricated from the cabin, then raised by a forklift on to a flatbed tractor trailer and taken back to his office.

Sam and Martinez had caught preliminary glimpses of more than the tub.

In the second small cuddy cabin.

Cooper's very own operating room.

No table, but another blood-splattered floor.

Other things, too, in plain view.

An anatomy textbook.

A large plastic container holding the collection of surgical instruments and tools about which Martinez had been told. Some of it makeshift, some the real McCoy: two pairs of common kitchen scissors and some tongs, two scalpels and a rib spreader.

'Holy Mary,' Martinez said, looking at the instruments. 'I am going to get under the hottest shower when I get home tonight and I may never get out of it again.'

Sam felt sick.

'You shouldn't be here, man,' Martinez said.

'Where the hell else should I be?' Sam said.

Pushing away the memory of the hypodermic.

The New Epistles of Cal the Hater stood in what seemed pride of place on a table in the sitting area.

Not written in the cheap notebooks Cooper had used in the old days.

Leather-bound now.

No expense spared.

And as soon as Crime Scene released them, Sam and Martinez would pore over every single word. Both with the same deep-down, off the record motivation.

Finding the link with Bianchi.

Proving Grace's self-defense plea.

Not yet though.

Cooper was out of surgery.

No visitors. Certainly no interviews.

He had been placed under arrest when they'd hauled him back on to the *Aggie*, had been read his rights, but had been in no shape for anyone to be sure he'd comprehended them.

No one was going to take chances.

He'd been asking to see Sam, but word had come down from Captain Kennedy. No visit.

Martinez drove Sam to City Hospital.

They did not set foot inside the room.

Sam stood outside, looked through the glass window.

Shackled to his hospital bed, left arm bandaged, a dressing on the right side of his head, Jerome Cooper, aka Cal the Hater – most probably aka Tom O'Hagen too – was sleeping.

He looked peaceful, Sam thought, for a depraved, damned man.

Cooper's eyes flicked open.
He looked straight at Sam through the glass.
Smiled again. Then waved.
'Easy,' Martinez said, softly.
Sam felt it pass through him.
The urge to kill.
He let it go.
Not a feeling he liked.

THIRTY-TWO

May 18

They'd kept Cooper in City Hospital for three days, had moved him late Monday to the prison ward at Jackson Memorial. Too soon after surgery to move him into the prison population.

Tests so far concluded that the killer did not have HIV, hepatitis or STDs.

Sam remembered, from his first *Epistles*, Cooper declaring himself a Trojan ('American's Most Trusted') guy.

Safe sex for the monster.

It hadn't prevented Sam from having to spend the weekend shuttling back and forth between Key Biscayne and Miami General. Grace doing her best, when he let her, to take care of him, make sure he rested.

And then, this Tuesday morning, she'd seen him off at the big steel front door, same as she often did at home on the island.

She knew what lay ahead for him.

'Try not to let him get to you,' she said.

'I'll do my best,' Sam said. 'It won't just be me, so don't worry.'

'I love you, Sam,' she said.

'Me too, Gracie,' he told her.

Five of them present at the first interview.

Sam and Martinez. Detective Peter Collins from City of Miami. Dave Rowan from Broward. And FDLE Special Agent Joe Duval – who'd assisted Miami Beach during the Couples case last year, and who was with them today to help smooth the way in respect of the multiple jurisdictions. Any more might have made the interview non-consensual in the eyes of a lawyer.

No one leaving a single goddamned thing to chance.

There was no lawyer. Cooper, secured to his bed rail, left arm now in a sling, a smaller dressing on the side of his head, had been pronounced fit for questioning, and had waived his rights to an attorney and to silence.

The killer having undergone anesthesia and surgery since his arrest, Sam had begun by reading him his Miranda rights again to ensure that he fully understood them.

Cooper understood OK.

There were just too many things he wanted to talk about.

Things of which he seemed proud.

Like the creation of Tom O'Hagen.

That had always been one of his *things*, he reminded Sam: creating personae, for himself and others.

'O'Hagen was the new me,' Cooper said. 'The one with the whacky houseboat and cool clothes.'

Five of them there, but the killer had, thus far, spoken only to Sam.

'Tom O'Hagen is an anagram of the name of a Nazi who liked taking potshots at Jews. Amon Goeth. I read that Schindler book and saw the movie.' Cooper smiled. 'I figured we might have had something in common, and though I looked him up and the real bastard was ugly and fat, the actor who played him in the movie was just the kind of guy I'd always wanted to be – lean and gorgeous.'

The notion rang true to Sam. Cal the Hater had always prided himself on his liking for reading, and the name-play was not new, and Sam wondered how far Cooper planned to go with his confession, if there was any hope that he was to be speedily proven right about the killer having renamed Richard Bianchi using the Jackal's aliases.

As to appearance, Cooper had never been gorgeous, so far as Sam knew, but he had certainly been leaner than he now was. And what was more than a little strange – and damned important, from Sam's personal standpoint – was that the late Richard Bianchi had, in some ways, looked almost more like the old Cal-Cooper than the killer did now.

'You've put on a little weight,' Sam said, 'since the last time we met.'

'I've been eating well,' Cooper said. 'Or I was till your pals shot me.' He smiled again. 'How're you feeling, after your swim?'

'Got yourself a nice new boat too,' Sam said.

Not planning on being drawn to the ocean ambush till he was damned well ready.

'Glad you like it.'

'Is that where you live?' Detective Collins asked.

Cooper didn't answer.

'Where have you been living since you left Miami Beach almost two years ago?' Dave Rowan asked.

'Here and there.' Cooper directed his answer to Sam.

'Here and there in Florida, or elsewhere?' Joe Duval asked.

Cooper ignored him too.

Likewise when Martinez questioned him about Andrew Victor.

Same deal when Rowan asked him about Ricardo Torres.

Sam felt their anger and empathized.

'Tell us about the *Aggie*,' he said. 'Did you name her?'

'Details in the *New Epistles*,' Cooper said.

'We got better things to do than read your diary,' Martinez said.

'Somehow I doubt that.' Cooper looked at Sam as he responded. 'Especially considering how much information the original *Epistles* must have given you.'

'You're not wrong there,' Sam said.

More than enough in those writings for Cooper to have been charged with the murders of Sanjiv Adani, Tobias Graham – his first two known victims – the attempted murder of Mildred Bleeker, and the kidnapping of Joshua Becket.

They, and everyone else involved in the investigation, would be reading every single word of the *New Epistles*. Balm to this man's ego.

Meantime, plenty more things and people he was refusing to talk about, or was flat-out denying.

Like having known Richard Bianchi.

'What about Charles Duggan?' Sam asked.

'I never heard of him,' Cooper said.

'But you got his name out of a movie, too, didn't you?' Martinez said. 'A little like O'Hagen.'

'Or was it the book?' Sam asked.

'I told you,' Cooper said. 'I never heard the name.'

'But reading's still your big thing, isn't it?' Sam said. 'And writing, of course.'

'I like reading.' Cooper shrugged. 'I like – and hate – all kinds of things.'

'What do you hate?' Dave Rowan asked him.

'I hate you,' Cooper said to Sam.

'Tell me something I didn't know,' Sam said.

'All in good time,' Cooper said.

'What was in the hypodermic you stuck Detective Becket with last Wednesday the thirteenth of May?' Detective Collins asked.

Miami's case, after all.

Cooper did not look at him.

'I was beginning to think you might not get there in time,' he said to Sam.

'I'm glad I didn't disappoint you,' Sam said.

'I might have drowned, waiting,' Cooper said. 'Imagine that.'

Sam said nothing, not rising to it.

'I presume you guessed I was aiming for your black heart?' Cooper said.

No one reacted.

'What was in the hypodermic?' Collins persisted.

Cooper smiled at Sam.

'Like I said, all in good time.'

'I'm thinking the game-playing means Bianchi was his, for sure, and he knows we know it,' Martinez said, later. 'He's just not going to help us prove it until he maybe wants something from us.'

'Or it could mean he knows damned well I need a lot more than something from *him*,' Sam said, 'so he's just making out he has something to hide.'

'You don't really believe that,' Martinez said.

'No,' Sam said.

What this was about, they both knew, was Cooper trying to play his endgame his way, and maybe he might have gone on living and killing if the Brits hadn't spotted the blood in the water, or maybe Cooper had felt it was all over after Bianchi's death, and had deliberately leaked the blood.

But at least they had him, and that was good in itself, that was fine, and they were going to keep him, too, which was even better. The task on and around the *Aggie* gigantic, but the wealth of evidence patently of the kind that ought ultimately to be enough to send Cooper to death row.

Meantime, Grace's life – their world – was still on hold.

THIRTY-THREE

May 19

The Crime Scene work would last for many days, perhaps weeks. Technicians taking apart every piece of the *Aggie* that could be taken apart, examining, gathering, preserving, analyzing the discernible evidence – the blood, the prints, the human remnants – and hunting down the hidden, the invisible. Assembling conclusive proof of Cooper's guilt, seeking evidence of the presence, prior to their deaths, of Andrew Victor and Ricardo Torres and whichever poor soul or souls had come Cal the Hater's way more recently; because the remains on board had been relatively fresh. Which meant that he had probably taken, murdered, mutilated and disposed of another victim too recently for the killer to have finished cleaning up with the pressure washer and Clorox – Cooper's old favorite brand – found on board.

No sign of Andy Victor's red pushbike or iPod, or his cellphone. Or any other victims' belongings.

No new body had yet washed up anyplace.

No new heart in a toy dinghy or anywhere else.

No proof yet that Richard Bianchi had ever stepped on to the *Aggie*, though even if such proof was never found, what Sam wanted badly was hard evidence that Torres had been on board, since that might help serve to make Bianchi, by association, a suspect of at least conspiracy to commit murder.

Nothing so simple.

A little more solid information was starting to flow their way.

The anatomy textbook contained illustrations relating to heart excision prior to transplantation, and a sheaf of downloaded printed material appeared to cover the same subject. No computer, however, had been found on board the houseboat, and there was no way of identifying from the printouts themselves which or *whose* computer they might have been downloaded from.

No likelihood yet – if ever – of obtaining a warrant to search any computers owned or used by Richard Bianchi.

And, by the by, confirmation had finally arrived from Elliot Sanders's office that the first heart found – the one that had come tucked inside two Tupperware containers in the kiddie dinghy tied up outside the Becket home – had belonged to Andrew Victor.

Plenty of useful stuff for Sam Becket, the investigator.

None of it enough for Sam, the husband.

The man of the moment – the center of massive media attention focusing on the comings and goings at Dinner Key – was still being held on a no bail warrant in the prison ward at Jackson Memorial. Only six days since they had boarded the *Aggie*, and already Sam was painfully conscious of his anger levels rising ever higher. And he *thought* he was sure he could keep that under control, had learned how to deal with scum and frustration over the years, but still, he was beginning to admit to himself – and *only* himself – that this was one case from which he ought, by rights, to be considering withdrawing.

But Cooper had made it personal, had repeatedly endangered his family – and Sam was doing his damnedest to block out the assault on himself with the hypodermic. But he was now as sure as any man could be that Cooper was also to blame for everything bad that was happening to Grace right now.

Which meant, right or wrong, that of all the violent crime cases currently under investigation in the entire state of Florida, this was the very *last* case from which he would ever withdraw.

Mike Alvarez called Sam and Martinez to his office halfway through Wednesday morning, asked them to sit.

'I know how tough this has been on you already,' he said. 'And we all know it's going to get tougher.'

No fool, the lieutenant, addressing this to the pair of them, aware that what hurt one impacted fiercely on the other.

'Worth it,' Sam said, 'if we can nail Cooper for all his crimes.'

'Except no one's forgetting,' Alvarez said, 'that some of those have been crimes against you, Sam, and members of your family. Which is why I need to tell you again – both of you – to be *damned* careful with this suspect. Make sure all the warrant issues are covered, tell him his rights again, every interview, even when you don't need to.'

'No question,' Sam said.

'Applies to you, too,' the lieutenant said to Martinez.

'Of course,' Martinez said.

'The very last thing I want is to have to pull you off the case, OK?'

'We don't want that either,' Martinez said.

'Sam? Are you sure you're up to this?' Alvarez persisted.

Sam thought about the pleasure that Cooper had appeared to derive from their first interview, thought about the confrontations still to come, and felt his own sick rage heighten just a little more.

Last chance.

'Never more sure of anything,' he said.

They holed up in the office Wednesday afternoon, and read their copy of the *New Epistles of Cal the Hater* from cover to cover.

Two days to go till Grace's arraignment, and Sam and Martinez were doing their jobs, poring over every word for evidence in the heart homicides and earlier crimes, but both men were also ransacking every page for something, *anything*, that might give Sam the magic wand needed to prove Grace's self-defense.

Jerry Wagner called at noon.

'Anything?' he asked.

Knowing full well that Sam could not disclose to him if there was.

Equally certain that if Sam found even a scrap of something he could use, he'd find a way of letting his wife's lawyer know about it.

'Not yet,' Sam said.

And went on reading.

In many ways, these were the same screwed up, self-indulgent, semi-tragic garbage as the earlier writings had been. Except that as they turned these pages, they found that the killer was describing a period during which he had – if he wrote with any semblance of honesty – been given new chances. At a kind of love, perhaps even a fresh start.

Blossom van Heusen, apparently unaware of his true evil, had thought she'd seen something worthwhile in Cooper. And he seemed, perhaps, to have found in her the kind of mother he'd been deprived of.

'Didn't stop him screwing her,' Martinez said.

'And I guess the hate still won,' Sam said.

'Doesn't it always with the sickest fucks?' Martinez said.

A point which, in other circumstances, Sam might have felt like debating, but in this case, truth to tell, he didn't give a damn.

Except, Blossom aside, there was something else in the *New Epistles*.

Some*one*.

Mentioned just once.

They both spotted it almost simultaneously.

'Think he slipped up?' Martinez asked.

'I don't know,' Sam said.

Because the Jerome Cooper he had first met had been a messed-up nobody with a wicked, whacko mom, a real liking for the written word, a far greater love of bestowing and receiving pain, and pure evil for brains.

This man had learned a thing or several.

Sam was no longer certain if he ever made mistakes.

> Toy came to see me today and brought me some meat from his very own Fresh Market. I wonder sometimes how I'd manage without him.

Grace called him at four o'clock.

'I was thinking,' she said tentatively, 'that maybe we could go out, just the two of us, maybe to a restaurant.'

He felt startled, gladdened and ashamed in one hit, because it had not occurred to him that she wanted, perhaps needed, to do something so *normal*.

'I'd love to.' He paused, wanting to get it right. 'Someplace near Claudia's, someplace new?'

'I thought La Terrazza,' Grace said.

One of their favorite places, up in Sunny Isles, a restaurant where they were well known.

'I've done too much hiding away,' she said.

'It's a great idea,' Sam said.

'And we're not going to talk about it,' she said.

He wondered if she meant the impending arraignment, or Cooper, or the needlestick.

'Any of it,' she said.

In a way, they both knew they were acting out. Not the romance of it, nor the pleasure of walking into a pretty local restaurant where they'd enjoyed so many happy evenings in the past. It was simply that they had contrived to find a way, perhaps for one night only, to carve out a piece of private pleasure, a slice of their real selves, Sam and Grace, the way they'd been for so many years.

They ate with appetite, surprising themselves, and they talked about many things, mostly happy, good memories, and about the family; Saul's growing success and his relationship with Mel and their gladness for him; their hopes that JWU would help take Cathy forward into the kind of career she longed for; Joshua's blessedly easy nature, the way the upheaval seemed to have stimulated rather than disrupted his continuing development – though that was the only time they referred to the 'upheaval', because that was the kind of dangerous terrain they had agreed to refrain from discussing.

And then, as they neared the end of their meal:

'We haven't talked about going home,' Grace said.

'I thought you didn't want to talk about it,' Sam said.

'Just this part,' she said. 'Cooper's locked up now, so I guess it's something we need to discuss.'

'Do you want to go back?' Sam shook his head. 'Of course you do, and so do I, but I meant—'

'With Friday coming,' she said.

Sadness filled him because the ease of the evening was gone.

'And my bail conditions,' she said.

'I'm sure that could be changed,' Sam said. 'We can talk to Jerry before the hearing.'

'No,' she said. 'It might irritate the judge.'

'I doubt that, in the circumstances.'

Grace shook her head. 'After the arraignment, maybe.'

Sam looked at her for a long moment, knew she wasn't ready.

'Would it hurt too much if we went to visit our house?' he asked.

'Honestly?'

'Sure,' he said.

'I think it would hurt to visit,' she said. 'But we could go look at it, if you'd like.'

They sat outside in the Saab, and gazed at it.

'It looks lonely,' she said.

Sam said nothing, just held her hand.

Grace managed a smile. 'This feels strange, sitting out here. Like teenagers, not going inside because of our parents.'

'If that's how it feels to you,' Sam said, 'maybe we should make out?'

'Maybe we should,' she said. 'Though maybe we should just wait till we get back to that nice big bed.'

'It is a great bed,' Sam agreed.

'But it's not home,' Grace said.

'We'll be back here soon,' he said.

'You will,' she said.

'We both will,' Sam said.

She didn't answer.

'Believe it,' he said. 'Please believe it.'

'I'll try,' she said.

THIRTY-FOUR

May 20

'You didn't come yesterday.'

Cooper seemed put out.

He had made it known to everyone who came within earshot that he wanted to talk to Sam every day, that he didn't care who else came along for the ride but that there was only one detective he was interested in speaking to.

Almost having it his way this morning, with only Sam and Martinez here to see him. Not that anyone wanted to appease him, but they'd all agreed at a meeting Tuesday evening that it was way too crowded with every jurisdiction represented – not to mention too much *fun* for Cooper – so the plan was, for the moment, to take it in shifts, partly in hopes of wrong-footing the bastard.

His attorney, Albert Singer, was with him today.

Middle-aged, silvering dark hair, Gucci glasses.

Appointed by his client, not the court, and Sam knew a little about Singer, knew that the guy had been reprimanded by the Bar a few times for 'inappropriate' behavior. Which made him the right type of lawyer for Cooper, Sam supposed, in more ways than one. No court-appointed public defender they'd come across would have been likely to allow the killer to talk to them this way, waiving his rights, even if that was what he wanted. Singer didn't look exactly happy about it either, but he was, at least, letting them make a start on his client's terms.

Better for the prosecution case, perhaps, though only time would tell.

One thing was for sure: nothing Jerome Cooper was doing was for Sam Becket's benefit.

The tape was running.

'For the record,' Sam said, 'we've discussed your Miranda warnings and you're still waiving them and speaking to us.'

Albert Singer's small mouth pursed a little.

'I was worried,' Cooper said. 'I thought you might be sick.'

'Never better,' Sam said.

Detective Collins and his colleague Mike Lopez had questioned the killer again yesterday about the contents of the syringe, had gotten nowhere.

'We've been reading.' Sam started the proceedings.

'I thought you might have been,' Cooper said.

'So now we know where you got the money to buy the *Aggie*.'

'And some other stuff,' Cooper said.

'I can't imagine that Blossom had that in mind as a way for you to spend her hard-earned cash,' Sam said.

'Don't presume to know anything about what she wanted,' Cooper said.

Real anger in his mean little eyes.

'She gave you money, and she gave you her car,' Sam said.

'She must have liked you a lot,' Martinez said.

'She didn't give me a car,' Cooper said to Sam.

'Maybe you just took it then,' Sam said.

'I'm not a thief.'

'That's not true,' Sam said. 'You wrote in your earlier *Epistles* about taking money from your victims.'

'My client's not here to answer to theft,' Albert Singer said.

'That's OK,' Cooper told him.

Singer's headshake was minimally disapproving.

'In the past,' Cooper said, 'a couple of times, I took what I had to.'

'You kidnapped a baby.' Martinez said it so Sam wouldn't have to, kept his gaze on the killer's face. 'A car's small fry by comparison.'

'I didn't take a car.'

'So you're saying Mrs van Heusen gave it to you?' Sam said.

'I don't know anything about a car,' Cooper said, and glanced at Singer.

'Moving on,' Sam said.

'I think it's time we took a break,' the attorney said, 'so I can consult with my client.'

'I'm happy to keep moving,' Cooper said.

'Who's Toy?' Sam asked.

The killer blinked, though his expression did not alter.

'You mentioned him in your new *Epistle*,' Martinez said.

'So who is Toy?' Sam asked again.

'Beats me,' Cooper said.

Martinez unfolded a sheet of copy paper, glanced at Sam, who nodded.

'"Toy came to see me today and brought me some meat from his very own Fresh Market,"' he read.

'Straight out of your handsome leather-bound notebook,' Sam said.

'I don't remember writing that,' Cooper said.

Martinez continued. 'You went on: "I wonder sometimes how I'd manage without him."'

'I remember now,' Cooper said, smoothly. 'He was a guy who used to do my shopping sometimes.'

The touch of evasiveness had already gone, his confidence restored – or maybe the momentary uncertainty had been a part of the act.

'What's his real name?' Martinez asked.

'I don't know.' Same as the last session, Cooper responded to Martinez's question, but directed the answer at Sam. 'I called him Toy because he was cute.'

'How are these questions relevant?' Singer enquired.

Sam turned to him. 'In view of the words "brought me some meat", in the circumstances, I'd say they're highly relevant.'

'It's OK,' Cooper told the attorney, his manner easy.

'When was the last time Toy did your *shopping*?' Martinez asked.

'I don't recall,' Cooper said. 'Isn't there a date in the *Epistle*?'

'I don't recall,' Martinez said.

'Me neither,' Sam said.

'That's a shame,' Cooper said.

'What does Toy look like?' Martinez asked.

'Cute. Like I said.'

'Cute blonde and blue-eyed?' asked Sam. 'Or dark?'

'More your type,' Martinez said.

'I must insist on time to speak to my client,' Albert Singer said.

'Speaking of blonde and blue-eyed,' Cooper said, 'how is Grace?'

Sam had been anticipating it, yet the intensity of his surge of fury still took him by surprise.

'Looks like we could be heading for the same destination, give or take,' Cooper said. 'Who'd have thought it? Me and stepsister Grace, both in jail.'

'Shut your mouth,' Martinez said.

'I'm sure I'll be making a few pals,' the killer went on. 'People who'll know people where she's going, you know?'

The fury in Sam's head turned white-hot.

'Was that a threat?' His voice was quiet.

'Detective Becket,' Singer began.

'Shut up,' Sam said.

He felt Martinez's hand touch his right arm, restraining, remembered Alvarez's warnings.

'I'm sorry,' he said to the attorney.

'I should think so,' Singer said.

'Detective Samuel Becket has a temper,' Cooper said to the lawyer. 'He kicked me one time in the street outside his house, pushed me right over.'

'Gee,' Martinez said.

'One more thing,' Cooper said to Sam, 'before we finish—'

'This guy thinks he's Hannibal-fucking-Lecter holding court,' Martinez said.

'Maybe you'd like to remind your client – ' Sam's tone was measured now – 'that he's here to answer our questions.'

'I was only being polite,' Cooper said. 'And I just realized I've forgotten to ask how Grace's dad is doing?' He smiled again. 'Is the old bastard still alive?'

'Mr Cooper,' Albert Singer admonished his client.

Sam got to his feet.

'Interview terminated,' he said, and added the time.

The rest of the day went downhill after that for Sam.

It had started out OK, all things considered, with Grace telling him at six a.m. that she was taking Joshua and a picnic to the beach, and Claudia was coming along, so Sam didn't have to worry, but no one else was invited, Grace said, because they all deserved a break from her.

'No one wants a break from you,' Sam told her.

'If they don't,' she said, 'they're crazy.'

'If I wasn't working,' Sam asked, 'would I be invited?'

'If you weren't working,' Grace said, 'I'd probably dump our kid and run away with you to Hawaii.'

'I never knew you wanted to go to Hawaii.'

'I don't especially,' she said.

'You doing OK, Gracie?' Sam asked.

'So long as you don't ask me that,' she said.

Downhill all the way after that.

First the interview, then a virtual slap-down by the lieutenant.

With the contents of the *New Epistles* logged as evidence, Sam had hoped to convince Alvarez to allow him to swear an affidavit for a warrant to examine any computers used by the late Richard Bianchi in the hope that they would further prove the connection between Bianchi and Cooper. Probable cause for the warrant being the relationship between Cooper and the late Bernice van Heusen of Savannah, Georgia, whose Volkswagen car had been driven by Bianchi up until his death.

'It's a no go,' Alvarez told him. 'No one would cheer louder than me if you could prove that the material found on the *Aggie* was downloaded by Bianchi. But there's insufficient probable cause for the search, and you know it.'

'I'd bet a year's pay the proof is there,' Sam said, tense to his fingertips.

'And you might win,' Alvarez said. 'But we both know that the Internet material could have been downloaded by Cooper or anyone else via any computer any*where*, and so far as the Beetle goes, there isn't a shred of conclusive evidence that the car was ever connected with any crime committed by Cooper.'

'Not to mention,' Sam said to Martinez back in their office, 'the affidavit would go down a whole lot better if it weren't being sworn by the husband of the woman accused of running Bianchi down.'

'I'm sorry, man,' Martinez said.

'Yeah,' Sam said. 'Me too.'

Martinez had more bad news.

Searches for any bank accounts in the names of Jerome Cooper or Tom O'Hagen, along with the broader search undertaken courtesy of the Financial Crimes Enforcement Network, had been fruitless. Cash presumably being the killer's method of payment for the *Aggie* and most daily requirements. No credit cards had been found on the houseboat and, aside from three hundred and forty-eight dollars and some cents, no cash stash had been located to date.

It could, of course, be anywhere, and even if they did ever gain access to Bianchi's home, it wouldn't mean two beans if nothing was found there either.

Didn't stop Sam wanting to get in there.

Meantime, no warrant and no help from FinCEN.

And a quiet desperation was grinding its way through the man whose wife's arraignment was happening next morning.

'I'm heading out,' Sam told Martinez just after two. 'I won't blame you if you don't want to join me.'

Martinez picked up his jacket and asked no questions until they were in his Chevy, motor running.

'So?' he said.

'Shrinkwrap Publications,' Sam said, checking for the zip code.

The outfit that had employed Bianchi as a freelance copy editor.

'You sure about this?' Martinez asked.

'Not sure of anything,' Sam said.

The young man at the reception desk was friendly at the outset, but as soon as Sam asked if he knew whether Richard Bianchi had ever used a computer in their offices, the guy, whose name tag identified him as Mark Curtiz, became wary.

'I'm going to have to ask my manager.'

'No problem,' Sam said.

The woman who showed up three minutes later was middle-aged, sharply dressed and patently hostile.

She introduced herself as Ana Garcia, double-checked their IDs, then turned to the receptionist.

'I guess you don't know who this detective is.' She was frosty. 'His name is Samuel Becket. His wife is the person who killed Richard Bianchi.'

'Oh, my God,' Mark Curtiz said.

'We're Miami Beach Police Department detectives, ma'am.' Martinez stepped in. 'Working on a homicide investigation.'

'That's as may be.' Ana Garcia was crisp. 'But Mr Bianchi was a friend, and his parents, who are understandably grieving, have asked us to be cautious about who we speak to about their son.'

'And we're very sorry for their loss,' Sam said.

Feeling awkward as hell.

Ms Garcia's dark eyes were cold. 'Mr Curtiz tells me you believe Mr Bianchi might have used computer equipment at these offices.'

'We asked Mr Curtiz if that was the case,' Martinez said.

'Mr Curtiz wouldn't know if it was,' the manager said. 'But whether Mr Bianchi did or did not use computers here, I can't imagine it's appropriate for Detective Becket to be here asking these questions.'

'Are you refusing to answer our questions, ma'am?' Martinez asked.

'I'm refusing to answer your questions because you're here with this man.'

Sam caught Martinez's eye, then looked back at Ana Garcia. 'I understand your position, ma'am.'

'I'm sure you do,' she said.

Not a good day for Sam.

Alvarez called him back into his office at around five, did not invite him to sit.

'There's been a complaint made against you. I doubt that's a surprise.'

'Ms Garcia,' Sam said. 'Shrinkwrap Publications.'

'And I guess you're going to assure me that your visit was in the course of the homicide investigation.'

'Yes, it was.'

'Ms Garcia says she felt it inappropriate for you to be questioning Mr Bianchi's colleagues.'

'Last time I looked, I was lead investigator on the case, and *Mr* Bianchi –' Sam could not keep the edge out of his voice – 'is a person of interest in that case, as I thought you agreed.'

'Sit down, Sam.'

'I'm good, Lieutenant,' Sam said.

'Sit down.' The tone was sharp for Alvarez. 'The Captain is concerned, as is Sergeant Riley, and so am I. You're working to your own agenda, Sam, and God knows I can understand why you might be tempted to do that, but it is not acceptable and you know it. It isn't fair to the victims.'

That stung like hell.

'Finding out what happened to the victims is what I'm trying to do here, Lieutenant. Richard Bianchi is a part of the investigation.'

'Maybe.' Alvarez stuck to his guns. 'But Bianchi is dead, and Jerome Cooper is in custody, and what you need to be doing, *all* you need to be doing as a detective in this unit, is helping to build the case against him.'

'Yes, sir,' Sam said.

'The Captain doesn't want any more complaints, Sam.' Alvarez paused. 'You're much too close to this one, we all know that. I don't want to even consider taking you off the case, but I will if I have to.'

'Is that what the Captain wants?'

Sam was unaccustomed to feeling hostility toward this good man, but the anger that he'd been managing to keep damped down because he had a job to do, and because Grace and Joshua needed him to stay in control, was burning a little more fiercely again.

'Do you think it might be better for you?' Alvarez asked.

Sam took a second. 'In no way would it be better, Lieutenant,' he said.

'Then you need to be very careful,' Alvarez said.

'I will,' Sam said.

'I mean it, Sam,' Alvarez said.

A warning.

Bad day for Sam.

Worse day for Grace.

Jerry Wagner had come to see her.

He had been waiting for her on her return from the beach, had seen her face fall as she saw him, had seen how tousled and happy her little son looked after his day out with his mommy and his aunt, and had felt sad for them.

'We need to prepare for tomorrow,' he said.

'I know,' Grace said. 'Just give me five minutes to sort this guy out.'

'I can do that,' Claudia said.

Her ever-present sister, or that was how it felt, and Grace knew her flash of resentment was wholly unjustifiable, yet there it was, and she knew that Claudia had seen it, but appeared to understand and forgive it, which made it even worse.

'It seems I don't need five minutes,' Grace said.

They went out on to the terrace, where most significant meetings these days, with lawyer or family, seemed to be held, and she wondered if she would ever feel able to relax out here in this lovely setting again.

Lucky still to be here at all, she reminded herself.

She offered to fetch ice tea.

'Only if you want some,' Wagner said.

'Not really.'

His smile was kindly. 'It won't be so bad,' he said. 'It's not a trial, and not a time when anyone can present evidence.'

'I know,' Grace said. 'Still.'

Wagner reached over and patted her hand like a gentle uncle. 'The charge will be read to you, and you will be required to enter a plea. Which I will do for you.' He paused. 'It is vital that you say nothing that could be in any way self-incriminating, Grace. No matter how you feel about it. The arraignment is not the time for explaining your actions, or for apology. The judge will ask if we will waive reading of the full charging document, and then he will ask you to rise, and ask for your plea.'

Grace was silent.

'Do you understand?' Wagner asked.

'Yes, I do,' she said. 'You've been very clear. It's just—' She stopped, looked away, felt abruptly close to tears.

'Take your time.'

She took a breath, found control again. 'I guess it's just that this is really going to happen, and of course I knew that, intellectually, but . . .'

'It's hard,' the attorney said. 'And I won't insult you by saying that tomorrow is nothing, because for you that must seem impossible to believe. But you will get through it.'

Grace nodded. 'And what is my plea?'

'As we discussed.'

She said nothing, needing to hear him say it.

The two words that felt to her like perjury, but which she knew she had to utter for the sake of Joshua and Sam and Cathy.

Wagner understood.

'Not guilty,' he said, 'is your plea.'

'Yes,' Grace said.

'And then you leave the rest to me,' he said.

'Thank you,' Grace said.

They made love that night.

It had been a long time. They had lain together each night, had been physically close for comfort, had been loving, been *together*, but since the evening when she had changed everything, full sexual intimacy had seemed impossible.

Tonight, it was unanticipated, spontaneous, starting out with a desperate need for solace, turning swiftly into desire, fueled by fear as well as love.

Afterwards, they both shed tears, then fell asleep still embracing, but all too soon they were awake again, lying sleepless, neither wanting to leave the bed, leave the other.

'What if they revoke my bail?' Grace said softly, at around three.

'They won't,' Sam said.

'But it could happen,' she said.

'Jerry won't let it happen.'

'If it does, I think you should all go home.' Grace's mind spun off into an imagined and horrific future of jail cells, purgatory, loveless hell, but then she felt Sam's arms tighten around her, and she stopped the spiral, grabbed back on to that first thought. 'Better for you all to go on with your lives.'

'It's not going to happen,' Sam said.

'But if it does,' she insisted.

'Not going there, Gracie,' he said. 'You can't make me.'

'OK,' she said.

And went on holding on.

THIRTY-FIVE

May 21

The arraignment was scheduled for ten a.m.

Magda had called to ask if Grace would mind if she attended, and the others had all, at different times, expressed their own need to come and support her, but Grace had been crystal clear with them all.

No one to attend except Sam.

'When it comes to the trial, I'm sure I'll be depending on you all.'

'I don't think it'll come to that,' Claudia had said.

'Me neither,' Saul had agreed.

Cathy's silence had spoken volumes. She, of all of them, knowing that bad, crazy things sometimes happened in courts of law.

'I just love you, Grace,' was what she had finally said.

'Those really are the best words in the world,' Grace said.

'I can think of two I'd rather hear right now,' Claudia said.

'Not guilty,' said Saul.

So just Sam at the courthouse with her and Wagner.

The Richard E. Gerstein Justice Building. 1351 NW 12th Street. So close to the jail, she'd heard, that prisoners were brought to court over a catwalk so they didn't have to be taken outside.

Not that way for her today. She and Sam walked up the steps and through the metal detectors, same as all the other free citizens.

Sam held her tightly before the attorney led her away.

Felt her trembling.

'Stay strong, Gracie,' he told her.

'I'm so sorry,' she told him.

'You have to stop that,' he said.

'I won't stop being honest with you,' she said.

He knew what she meant, wished with all his soul he could find a way to make her stop feeling so *guilty*, but he had a bleak and terrible feeling that was one gift he might never be able to give her back.

Her innocence.

Wagner asked her, before it began, if she would like to go back home now that Cooper was behind bars and it was safe again for her and the family.

'I don't know,' Grace said.

'Because of what happened there?' the lawyer asked.

She nodded. 'And, I guess, because I'm nervous about rocking the boat.'

'Are you sure?' Wagner was gentle, suspecting that was not her real reason. 'Because I think the judge would allow it.'

The truth was she wasn't sure she could bear to go home. Not just because she was afraid of the memory of that thing in the tub. It was also that she didn't think she could stand to go home with Sam and Joshua, to begin to feel a kind of sham normality and then have it ripped away again.

'I'm sure,' she said.

If she had been asked, later, for a description of the courtroom, she would have found it impossible to give one. For a time, her own heartbeat exercised her more than her surroundings, so alarmingly loud and rapid, pounding in her ears, that she thought she might pass out, but then she looked around and found Sam, kept her eyes on his face for as long as she could, anchored herself, steadied her breathing, remained conscious.

It went as Wagner had told her it would.

Except that he had not warned her about the press or TV cameras which she could almost feel zooming in on her face.

Hoping, perhaps, for tears, but not getting them. Not because of any sense of courage, but because she was too frozen inside.

The conditions of her release were the same as before.

She found it hard to speak, to thank Wagner for that, though he seemed to know how she felt, held her hand for a moment, was supportive, strong.

Her trial was scheduled for November 8.

Pretrial hearing set for June 11 – sooner than it might have been, Wagner said, because of free space on the judge's calendar.

Judge Arthur Brazen presiding, a man Grace could remember little about afterwards, except that he had white hair and wore spectacles.

She didn't know if an early pretrial hearing was a good or bad thing.

Didn't remember what Wagner said about it.

Still too frozen.

THIRTY-SIX

May 23

It had been a long time since David and Sam Becket had taken a day trip together, just the two of them.

When Sam had called his father after the arraignment to give him the news and ask if he would accompany him to Fort Myers on Sunday, to call on Richard Bianchi's parents, David had at first said no.

'It's a mistake,' he'd said. 'If it backfires, you risk too much.'

It was less than two weeks since Alvarez had ordered Sam not to speak to Bianchi's family, and even if this was 'off-duty', if it got back to the department, he preferred not to contemplate the possible consequences.

He put the department out of his mind.

'The Bianchis already hate Grace for killing their son,' he said. 'How much worse can I make it?'

'What does Grace think?' David had asked.

'She's not keen,' Sam said. 'I told her that together you and I would be gentle and respectful, but she said how "gentle" could we be trying to convince parents whose son just died that he was in league with a serial killer?'

'Don't you think she makes a good point, son?'

'What I think,' Sam said, 'is I don't have any real choice.'

Having no prior arrangement, there was no guarantee the Bianchis would be home. Being Sunday, they were unlikely to be working, but they might, of course, be at church or out shopping, or anyplace. Though Sam's worst scenario was that they might be in the midst of finalizing plans for their son's funeral, scheduled for Thursday.

The closer they got to Fort Myers, the worse he felt.

The house was a modest suburban one-storey, small, white-painted with a red-tile roof and well-cared for yard.

Robert Bianchi answered the door.

He wore a dark-blue polo shirt over navy trousers, was clean-shaven and his dark-brown eyes were enquiring and friendly.

Until he learned who his callers were.

Shock and incredulity transformed his face, and it was impossible to know how much the man might have aged in the last two weeks, but he looked old beyond his fifty-three years.

'We have nothing to say to you,' he said to Sam, then turned to David. 'I'm sorry you've had a wasted trip, sir.'

'Not wasted, I hope, Mr Bianchi,' David said.

'I assure you it has been,' the other man said.

A woman appeared behind him.

'Who is it, Robbie?'

'No one,' her husband told her.

Josephine Bianchi wore a black T-shirt and pants, her wavy blonde hair tied roughly off her face, her blue eyes red-rimmed and shadowed.

'You,' she said, looking at Sam.

Sam remembered the photograph in the *Sun-Sentinel* of him and Grace at the hospital fundraiser, laughing, and fresh awareness of his own insensitivity stabbed harder at his conscience.

'They're leaving,' Robert Bianchi told her.

'No.' She recovered quickly, took her husband's arm. 'You've come this far for a reason,' she said. 'You may as well come in.'

'We could come back later,' Sam said.

'Why would you want to do that?' Josephine Bianchi asked harshly.

'We know we're intruding,' David said.

'Of course you know,' she said, 'since I'm sure neither of you is an idiot.'

'I've come—'

'To plead for your wife,' she cut Sam off. 'Our son's killer.'

'In a sense,' Sam said.

'For the love of God,' Robert Bianchi said, 'come in and let's get this over with.'

In their living room, small but homely, with a couple of watercolor beach scenes on the walls, a fully laden bookcase and several old family group photos (no way for Sam to peer closely to check out Richard as a youngster, not today), they all stood, stiffly, the atmosphere hostile.

Sam came directly to it.

'I'm here,' he said, 'because I believe there's a strong possibility that your son may, perhaps unwittingly, have been used by a known criminal.'

'You're talking about this murderer,' Josephine Bianchi said.

Unsurprisingly, since they were presumably being kept in touch by their own attorney, perhaps even by the Key Biscayne police.

'Jerome Cooper,' Sam confirmed.

Josephine Bianchi's eyes were hard as stone. 'You dare to come to our house while we are mourning our son, and you accuse him.'

'That isn't what he said, Mrs Bianchi,' David pointed out gently.

'It's what he implied,' Robert Bianchi said. 'He's been implying as much all over Miami, so far as we can tell, and getting nowhere, which is where his inquiries will remain.'

'There's already been one complaint made against you,' his wife said. 'I'm stunned by your nerve, let alone your callousness.'

'My son is not a callous man,' David said. 'And I assure you he would not be here today if he felt he had any choice.'

'He had a choice,' Bianchi said grimly.

'I understand that this must feel like a terrible intrusion,' Sam said.

'We don't need your understanding,' Josephine Bianchi said. 'Our son is dead because of your wife.'

David glanced at a chair behind him. 'May I?'

'Of course.' Robert Bianchi gestured. 'Would you like some water? Josie, please fetch a glass of—'

'No, thank you.' David sat down. 'I'm fine.'

'You OK?' Sam looked at his father.

David nodded, gave a small sigh, then asked: 'How much do you know about my daughter-in-law?'

'All we need to know.' Robert Bianchi's tone was bitter.

'Perhaps not,' David went on. 'Grace was a colleague of mine long before she met my son, when I was still a pediatrician, and she is one of the most remarkable people I know.'

'With respect, Dr Becket,' Bianchi said, 'you're somewhat biased.'

'I've lost count of the number of children she's helped.'

'That's her job,' Josephine Bianchi said. 'And I'd like to point out that one of the prosecution witnesses is the mother of the child she was supposedly "helping" when she drove her car at our son.'

They were in danger of running out of time, Sam realized.

'I truly believe,' he tried again, 'that your son might have got himself into something he didn't bargain—'

'Our son was a writer.' Bianchi's voice shook as he cut in. 'He had short stories published, and he took other work to supplement his income. As a copy editor, not as some killer's accomplice.'

'I know you have his car,' Sam said.

'We certainly do,' Josephine Bianchi said.

'Do you have his computer, too?' Sam asked.

There was a moment's silence, and then, from outside the room, came the sound of the front door opening and closing.

'Gina,' Josie said quietly.

'I'll tell her.' Robert left the room, closed the door behind him.

'Our daughter,' his wife explained.

The voices out in the hallway were muted for a moment, and then the door opened and a tall, slim, dark-haired woman dressed in black came in.

She strode straight across the room to Sam.

'Bastard,' she said.

Richard Bianchi's sister, the charity worker, did not resemble her late brother. Sam saw, too late, her right hand swing back, though even if there had been time, he doubted he would have tried to stop her.

The sound of the slap resounded in the room.

Gina Bianchi began to weep.

'Gina,' her father said, in shock. 'You shouldn't have done that.'

'Why shouldn't she?' Josephine went to their daughter, put an arm around her, led her to the sofa, and gently pushed her down.

David got to his feet. 'I think we should go.'

Sam's face stung, but his need to achieve *something* for Grace was overpowering. 'I'm sorry, but I have to ask if you have your son's computer?'

'I'm sorry my daughter slapped you,' her father said.

'I'm not sorry,' Gina Bianchi told Sam. 'Though I'd sooner slap your wife.'

'Gina,' Robert Bianchi said again, rebuking.

'What's wrong with you?' Now Josephine Bianchi's anger was directed at her husband. 'I wouldn't give this man the spit out of my mouth.'

'I would do almost anything,' Bianchi said quietly, 'if it would help stop this disgusting nonsense about our son once and for all.'

'You think it would stop there?' Gina's voice was tinny, sharp, her dark eyes venomous. 'Give this man the computer, he'd still want to search Richard's home, Richard's trash.'

'They already looked at his apartment,' Josephine said.

'That's right,' Sam said. 'I believe you remarked that it was unusually clean, Mrs Bianchi.' 'Tidy' was what Detective Rowan had reported she had said, but that scarcely mattered now. 'Did you feel that someone might have been there to clean up?'

'Bastard,' Gina Bianchi said again.

But at least this time she did not slap him.

Neither David nor Sam spoke for the first few miles of the return journey, the Saab devouring the road, heading back towards I-75.

'You OK?' David asked, finally.

'I've been better,' Sam said.

'Me too,' his father said.

'I'm sorry,' Sam said. 'I shouldn't have put you through that.'

'It's not me you caused pain,' David said.

His father seldom expressed disapproval of him, and it hurt far worse than Gina Bianchi's slap.

'I understand why,' David said, 'but it was still wrong.'

'I know it,' Sam said.

'But you'd do it again, wouldn't you?'
'That, and more,' Sam said.

'I want you and Saul to go home,' Grace told Cathy on Sunday evening out on the deck. 'Tomorrow.'

Another companionable evening lay ahead, with Daniel and Mike barbecuing, Saul and Robbie fooling around in the pool, only Sam feeling very drained, the tension from the earlier part of the day still lingering.

'I don't think so,' Cathy said.

'I do,' Grace said, emphatically. 'With that man safely locked away, it's high time some of us got back to some kind of normality. And I know you won't go home without me,' she added to Sam, 'but I would like it if you could get the house opened up and ready to move back into.'

'That sounds good and positive.' Claudia walked past, carrying two salad bowls, Cathy taking one from her and setting it on the big table.

'I still can't believe the judge wouldn't let you go home,' Cathy said.

'I'm glad he didn't,' Claudia said, warmly.

'I think Mike and Robbie might be glad to have their space back,' Sam said.

Grace had told him she'd chosen not to request a change in her bail conditions, and she knew Sam had understood that she felt anything but positive about ever getting back home for keeps, but she felt guilty about that too, was beginning to feel she had an infinite supply of guilt, her own personal well.

Saul hauled himself out of the water, came over to towel off.

'What's up?'

'Grace says you and I should go home,' Cathy told him. 'I think it's too soon, and they can't go back yet because of her bail.'

'Maybe we could stay here another week or so?' Saul suggested.

'I know you're thinking about Richard Bianchi's funeral,' Grace said. 'And I know you just want to help me, but truthfully, the best way you two can help me right now is to get back to your lives.'

Dan left the barbecue and came over with a bottle of Becks. 'So long as you know we're happy for everyone to stay.'

'I'm afraid you're still stuck with three of us,' Grace said.

'Though we do think it's time Joshua slept in our room,' Sam added.
'I love having him share with me,' Robbie said.
'We know you do,' Sam said.
'To be honest,' Grace said, 'we're being selfish, wanting him with us.'
'OK,' Robbie said. 'I get that.'
'So do we get a say about going home?' Cathy asked.
'Not really,' Grace said.
'I guess a little normality would be good for you guys,' Claudia said.
'Saul?' Sam said.
Saul shrugged. 'OK with me.'
'How come he gets asked?' Cathy enquired.
'He's your uncle,' Grace said. 'Show some respect.'
'Give me a break,' Cathy said.
Sounding more normal already, Grace thought, and felt that in this one thing, at least, she had been right.

THIRTY-SEVEN

May 24

Normality ended again, abruptly, on Monday morning.
Sam woke with a sore throat and a slight fever.
'I'm calling your father,' Grace said.
'I'll call him later, if I need to,' Sam said. 'I'm sure it's just a cold.'
'I'll be checking up on you,' she said.
'There's a surprise,' he said.

His health went to the back of the line once he reached the office.
Robert Bianchi had called Chief Hernandez.
No surprise there either.
'You're off the case, Sam,' Lieutenant Alvarez told him. 'Order of the Chief.' Martinez, he said, would go on working it with Mary Cutter, but Sam was on desk duties until further notice.
'I warned you,' Alvarez said. 'I told you not to speak to his family.'
'I know you did,' Sam said. 'And for what it's worth, I'm sorry.'

He remembered too, sick at heart, the other thing Alvarez had said to him that day. That if he messed up with the Bianchi family, it was Grace who might suffer.

'Take the hit.' Alvarez's exact words.

David had tried telling him too, but he wouldn't listen.

He must have been out of his goddamned mind.

The captain called him into his office to issue an official warning.

'You're a good detective,' Tom Kennedy told him, 'and you've been under enormous strain, and I don't want to suspend you, but if you pull any more stunts like that one, I will not have a choice.'

Not Sam Becket's first tangle with the department.

Oh, man.

THIRTY-EIGHT

May 25

'We got a problem,' Martinez alerted Sam Tuesday morning.

Sam was feeling a little better, physically, than he had yesterday, but he was far from OK and, truth to tell, it no longer felt like a cold. He had not called his father yesterday, for which Grace had gotten mad at him, but it was only when she'd said that she didn't feel he should go near Joshua that he'd allowed himself to take the issue seriously.

A blood test later, at Miami General.

Shades of things to come after the needlestick.

'Cooper won't talk to anyone but you,' Martinez told him now.

'I guess he'd better take that up with the Chief,' Sam said.

'That's pretty much what's going on,' Martinez said.

Albert Singer had, it seemed, passed on his client's instructions to tell the cops that if they wanted to know what had happened to the other victims, then Sam Becket was going to have to see him, whether he was on the case or not. And as much as Broward and City of Miami wanted to tell Cooper to go straight to hell, Special Agent Duval was presently discussing the matter with Alvarez.

'No one's going to let this happen,' Sam said.

'I wouldn't be so sure,' Martinez said.

Sam didn't know how he felt about it. The notion of dancing to Cooper's tune was as sickening to him as it had to be infuriating to the others – but Lord knew he wanted, *needed*, to be back on the case . . .

The problem was, even if the captain allowed him to go back in there, Sam was going to have to find a way of cutting through the killer's taunting. A bargaining chip. Something Cooper wanted.

No deals.

No *way*.

But something.

Tom Kennedy called Sam to his office.

Second time in two days. A regular rollercoaster ride.

'I'm sure you know what's going on, Detective.'

'All I know is that Cooper wants to talk to me.'

'His lawyer seems to think he has something to share, but you're the only one he'll talk to.' Kennedy's gaze was sharp. 'I guess you can imagine how thrilled I am by that.'

'Yes, sir.'

'And that's not the only issue,' the captain continued. 'He's also stated again that he doesn't want his attorney present.'

'That's not good,' Sam said.

'It's not out of the question, though, if we play it strictly by the book. Detective Martinez to be with you. The interview to be taped. The defendant to be Mirandized again – and you ask him loud and clear if he wishes to be interviewed on tape without his attorney present – and you get his answer even louder and clearer.'

'No question about that,' Sam said.

'It goes without saying that the only reason I'm prepared even to consider this is that we want justice for as many of Cooper's victims as we can get.'

'I understand that, sir.'

'So is this an interview you feel confident to undertake, Sam?'

'I feel confident to undertake it, Captain, but not as confident as I'd like to be about what we'll get out of it.' Sam paused. 'Are the other departments in agreement with this? From a jurisdictional standpoint?'

'You can leave that with me,' Kennedy said. 'I think it's safe to assume Cooper's wanting to play games.'

'No question.'

'That's games with *you*, specifically, I'd guess.'

'No doubt about that either.'

Tom Kennedy wasn't finished making his points.

'Do you feel you have your priorities sorted now, Detective? That is, the case against Jerome Cooper as opposed to any possible case against the late Richard Bianchi?'

Sam took a moment. 'Is it acceptable to you that Bianchi's name may come up during the interview?'

'So long as it's in the best interests of the case against Cooper, yes.'

'Then yes, sir, my priorities are sorted.'

Kennedy stood up.

'Just don't screw this up, Becket.'

Sam was on his feet too.

'I'll do my best, sir.'

Cooper had been moved to the Pretrial Detention Center.

Same place Grace had been taken nineteen days ago.

Grace in the same place as that *filth*.

Not there today. They had checked him out of there and brought him to the State Attorney's office for questioning.

'I wish I felt good about this,' Martinez said before the interview.

'Me too,' Sam said.

He did not feel the way he ought to before a confrontation of this kind. The way he usually felt prior to an interview with a known evil-doer. He was never overconfident, always felt a strong kick of nervous tension and the wariness necessary to get the job done properly.

But this was different on so many fronts. The fact was he ought not to be walking into this room, not with the super-high personal stakes that he knew were, for the first time in his career, overshadowing the task at hand. Lord knew he'd been distracted by intense personal issues before, and Kennedy and Alvarez – and Martinez most of all – knew damned well his propensity for taking somewhat rash chances when his loved ones were at risk.

This was *so* different.

'You wanna call it off, man?' Martinez asked.

'Oh, yes,' Sam said. 'But there's no way on earth we're going to do that.'

'Are you sure that you wish to speak to us now without an attorney present?'

'I've told you.'

'Please confirm it now, for the record.'

'I, Jerome Cooper, confirm for the record that I wish to speak to Detective Samuel Lincoln Becket without an attorney present.' A pause. 'Does he have to be here?'

'For the record, the defendant is looking at Detective Martinez,' Sam said. 'Yes, he does.'

'For the record,' Martinez said, 'the defendant shrugged.'

'OK,' Cooper said. 'If he has to be here, he has to be here.'

Like a host snubbing an unexpected guest.

Sam was already getting a headache.

'If at any time during the interview,' he said, 'you wish to have an attorney present, please state it and the interview will be ceased until an attorney is available.'

'Yes.' A pause. 'That's fine. Can we get started?'

'Yes, we can.'

Sam double-checked the tape.

'You wanted to speak to me,' he said.

'Because I figured you'd want to speak to me too,' Cooper said.

'No other reason?'

'You want things from me,' Cooper said.

'Yes,' Sam said.

'Tell me what you want.'

'Further information regarding the allegations against you,' Sam said. 'Any further details you wish to give us regarding the unlawful killings of Sanjiv Adani, Tobias Graham—'

'I never knew that was his name at the time,' Cooper interrupted. 'He told me his friends called him Tabby, which I liked. Who knows, if he'd told me his real name, I might not have killed him.'

'Is that an admission that you unlawfully killed Tobias Graham?'

'I guess.' Cooper paused. 'You were starting a list of names.'

'I'll continue,' Sam said. 'Sanjiv Adani, Tobias Graham, Andrew Victor, Ricardo Torres.' He paused. 'And Roxanne Lucca.' Cooper's mother. Not a glimmer of reaction from the killer. 'Also any further details you wish to give us at this time regarding the attempted murder of Mildred Bleeker, and the kidnapping of Joshua Becket.'

'Your son,' Cooper said. 'And your step-mom now, I guess.'

'That is correct.'

'That stinky old bag lady and the old doc.' Cooper shook his head.

'Watch your mouth,' Martinez said.

'All makes it a little personal, doesn't it?' Cooper said.

'Would you like to end the interview?' Sam asked.

'No.'

'Are you sure?' Martinez checked.

'I'm only answering Sam's – excuse me, Detective Becket's – questions.'

'That's your prerogative,' Sam said.

'I've always liked that word,' Cooper said.

'You enjoy words,' Sam said. 'You wrote about that in your *Epistles*.'

'Many times.'

'Back to the interview,' Sam said.

'What kind of details would you be looking for, Detective?'

'You tell us.'

'Confessions?'

'If you wish.'

'Names, maybe,' Cooper suggested, 'of any victims you might not know about yet?'

'If you wish.'

'I wish for many things,' Cooper said. 'I guess you'd like to know the whereabouts of any missing bodies.' He paused. 'Or body parts, maybe?'

'It would be helpful,' Sam said.

'Anything else that would be helpful, Detective?' Another pause. 'How about the names of any accomplices?'

'Of course,' Sam said.

He was conscious of Martinez's increased tension, sitting beside him.

'So what's in it for me?' Cooper asked.

Finally.

'Truth,' Sam said.

'Anything else?'

'How about salvation?'

'Little late for that, wouldn't you say?'

'Not my place to guess,' Sam said.

'Come on, Sam, there has to be something you can give me.'

Sam leaned forward slightly. 'Call me Detective Becket, and I'll think about it.'

'OK. *Detective* Becket.'

'That's better,' Martinez said.

'Did someone speak?' Cooper asked.

'Don't get smart,' Martinez said, 'or we'll wrap this up.'

Cooper ignored him, kept on looking at Sam.

'I seem to remember,' Sam said, 'from your *Epistles*, you were pretty scared of places like this. Jail. Even juvey.'

'It's not so scary now,' Cooper said. 'I got my old tattoo removed a while back.'

He'd had a racist symbol tattooed on his chest, a white cross in a red circle with a blood drop in the middle. According to one of his old *Epistles*, he'd done it to try and please his mother, but she'd told him that all he'd done was turn himself into target practice for 'them'.

Them being anyone not Caucasian. Roxanne – Frank Lucca's second wife – having been a bigger racist than her son. And perhaps an even more evil human being: a mother who had abused and tormented her son, who had taught him to hate himself and others, and who had gone on to torture Grace and Claudia's father.

'Jewel, the white witch-bitch,' Cooper had called her in his writings.

A major part of why he'd turned himself into Cal the Hater.

'Still,' Sam said now, 'tattoo or not, there's the death penalty to consider.'

A ripple passed across Cooper's light-brown eyes.

Fear, maybe, though Sam could not be sure.

The guy being crazy, after all.

'What?' Cooper said. 'You offering me protection, or a deal, maybe?'

'No deal,' Sam said.

'Protection then.'

Something, in fact, that Sam thought he could feasibly have offered a man he felt deserving of protection.

To say that Sam did *not* want that was an understatement.

Martinez cleared his throat.

Wasting time.

'Going back to your friend "Toy".'

'You mean the guy who did my shopping,' Cooper said.

'Among other things,' Sam said.

'Toy's real name is Richard Bianchi, isn't it?' Martinez asked.

Maybe so Sam didn't have to.

'I never heard of Richard Bianchi,' Cooper said to Sam.

'I think you have,' Sam said. 'I think "Toy" was Bianchi. I think you used him to help you lure Ricardo Torres from a party to your houseboat, the *Aggie*, on the night of the twenty-fourth of April.'

'You think?'

'I think you gave him the red VW Beetle that you were given by, or took from, the late Bernice van Heusen, and I think he ran *errands* for you using that car.'

'What kind of errands?' Cooper asked. 'I'm fascinated.'

'What was the name of your final victim?' Sam changed tack. 'The person whose remains were found on the *Aggie*?'

'Final?' Cooper said. 'I wouldn't be too sure.'

'I'm very sure,' Sam said.

The low-burn of anger was starting to heat up now, along with his headache.

Not doing his job well enough, not just here and now, but not since the little dinghy with the first heart had been tied up outside their house.

Not up to the job.

'OK?' Martinez was as discreet as he could be.

Sensing Sam's distraction, or maybe his anger.

'How is wifey doing now?' Cooper asked, sensing it too.

Easy, Sam told himself.

Get back to the last question or end it now.

He took a breath.

'How did you choose your last victim?' he asked.

'Last as in "most recent",' Cooper said. 'Better.'

'Answer the question,' Martinez said.

'Not talking to you,' Cooper said, looking at Sam. 'You didn't answer my question about dear Grace.'

'Shut up,' Sam said.

'Who knew she and I had so much in common?' Cooper said.

'I told you to shut up.'

Beside him, Martinez braced.

'I guess the waiting must be hard on her, even out there.' Cooper smiled. 'Even in that nice big safe house.'

Sam froze.

'I wouldn't bet on the *safe* part,' Cooper said.

Sam was out of his chair, one hand shutting off the tape machine, the other grabbing the neck of the dirtbag's prison jumpsuit, before Martinez could stop him. 'Don't you even *think* about threatening my wife again, you piece of filth!'

'Sam!' Martinez was dragging him off. 'Jesus, Sam!'

'I told my lawyer you have a temper, didn't I?'

Biggest smile Sam had ever seen on Cooper's face.

Martinez was fighting to hold it together. He leaned over the table, veins standing out on his temples as he started the tape again, waited for it to be ready.

'Interview suspended,' he said.

'Due to police brutality,' Cooper said.

Just before Martinez could add the time.

'Holy man, did you ever screw that up.'

Sam could not remember the last time his partner had spoken to him with such heartfelt reproach.

Not nearly enough.

What the *hell* had he thought he was doing? Not just losing it, but agreeing to the interview in the first place? He had achieved nothing, either for the investigation or for Grace.

Worse than that, he had almost certainly done them all harm.

'Hey,' Martinez said, already softer.

Sam was sitting on a bench, slumped over, pounding head in his hands, still shaking inside.

'You OK?' Martinez asked, anxious.

Sam couldn't speak.

Uncertain who he hated more, Cooper or himself.

No contest.

He had never felt such shame in his life.

Telling Grace was tough.

He'd put it off by going to the hospital first, for his blood test.

The needle stung a little, a whole lot less than he deserved.

He drove to Key Biscayne, found Grace, left the house with her and went to the beach, walking slowly while he described what had happened, exactly what he had done.

She was gentle with him. Said things to him that almost made sense, that might *almost* have helped him forgive himself. She said she thought they had both lost their direction, some of their fundamental self-control, after what had befallen them last year. That they should, as they'd talked about a few times, have gotten some good, prolonged therapy instead of staying strong and believing they could manage life that way.

'I guess now we're paying the price for that,' she said.

He stopped, looked at her. 'You're being kinder than you ought to be,' he said. 'If it's because you're worried about me getting sick, there's no need.'

'You can't stop me worrying,' she said. 'Though if I am being kind, it's because I doubt if I'd have reacted any better if I'd been in your shoes.'

'I had a chance in there to get something out of him,' Sam said. 'Something that might have made a difference. To the case, to you, to us all.'

'He's grown smarter, more confident,' Grace said. 'More evil.'

Sam said nothing.

They walked on a little way, their shoes in their hands.

'If you really want to help me now,' she said after a while, 'please stop beating yourself up.' She stopped walking, looked up at him. 'Because what's happening to me is all my own doing, and if you do get suspended, it'll only be because you were so desperate to help me.'

'It'll be because I lost control,' Sam said.

'You're human,' she said. 'You reacted.'

'I'm trained not to,' he said.

He saw then, exposed in her eyes for just an instant, the awful pain she was still in, the guilt and fear and shame. Yet she was fighting not to let him see it. Right now, Grace was shelving all that to support him, because that was how she'd always operated when it came to him.

So talking to her on the beach was nowhere near as tough as it ought to have been.

Not nearly as tough as looking at himself in the mirror later that night.

He was going to be suspended, no two ways about it. Probably two to five days without pay. Another stain on his record.

And no way of using any time out to help prove that Grace had acted in self-defense, because he couldn't think of one other person left to talk to.

Bernice van Heusen, last registered owner of the VW, dead and gone.

The Bianchi family probably willing the judge to send Grace down for life.

Bianchi himself – Cooper's 'Toy' – not yet in his grave, but long gone.

Nowhere left to turn.

God help them all.

THIRTY-NINE

May 26

The captain was grim, but not unkind.

'Why the hell did you turn off the tape?'

The implication being that if Sam had just lost his cool for a moment, it might possibly have been, if not acceptable, at least redeemable, but that the turning off of the tape had potentially turned it into a premeditated assault.

Which Cooper was claiming via Albert Singer.

Though there was no witness to that, since there was no force on earth that could persuade Alejandro Martinez to back Cooper against Sam Becket, even if Cooper claimed that the earth was round.

Cooper was claiming that the rip in his jumpsuit and the bruising on his neck were down to Sam.

'I didn't rip his jumpsuit,' Sam said now, 'and I'd be surprised if I bruised him.'

'I'd rather hear you say that you know you did not bruise him,' Kennedy said.

Sam took less than two seconds.

'I know I did not bruise him, sir,' he said.

The captain nodded.

'You're suspended, Detective Becket,' he said, 'pending a disciplinary review.' He paused. 'Regrettably, none of this is new to you.'

'No, sir.'

Sam having been suspended a couple of years back for acting out of his jurisdiction, well aware at that time that he might have been demoted or even transferred out of the Detective Bureau.

'I'd like to apologize, Captain,' he said now.

'I'm sure you would,' Kennedy said.

'Too little, too late, I guess,' Sam said.

'Detective Martinez tells me you were provoked, and the tape backs that up.'

'It's no excuse,' Sam said.

'No, Sam, it is not,' Kennedy said.

At ten past eleven that same morning – the day before Richard Bianchi's funeral – Gina Bianchi, staying over at their parents' home in Fort Myers, sat on the bed in her brother's old room, opened the laptop computer which had been brought back from his Miami apartment, and switched it on.

First and foremost, she did so because she felt there might be practical matters to deal with that had not yet been considered, and if it were she who had died, her computer would tell those left behind most of what they needed to know in order to settle her affairs.

Besides, Gina had an urgent need to feel close to Richard.

She opened up Word, browsed his creative writing folder, hit on one of his short stories – titled 'Ground Control' – and began to read.

And, before long, to weep. Not just because he was gone, nor just because reading this piece proved to her again that her younger brother had possessed minimal talent, but mostly because she knew that Richard had known that too, which had made him less happy than he might otherwise have been.

He had wanted to write a novel, and Gina bet that if she looked a little harder, she'd find some attempts at that, and she would look in time, but not today, because finding something would only make her more sad. So she came to the end of the short story and then, feeling intrusive but pushing on anyway, browsed his mail.

The usual stuff was still coming in: shopping websites, junk, an email from someone called Rebecca, who sounded chatty and clearly had not heard the news, so Gina sent her a kindly worded note, telling her that Richard had passed away and that the funeral was tomorrow, and that, if Rebecca was anywhere near Fort Myers, she would be welcomed.

That done, she checked his calendar for appointments to be cancelled, but found that Richard had apparently not used that application, so she moved on to her brother's bookmarks: his bank, already dealt with; a doctor's office she'd never heard of – no reason she should have; a couple of book websites and a whole bunch of weird-sounding sites that she guessed Richard had probably used for research purposes, the kind that some novelists presumably frequented . . .

Gina returned to Word and looked for any letters or notes that her brother might have left for her or their parents, found none and was sadder still, yet not surprised, for why should a man of twenty-eight have had intimations of mortality?

Nothing to make her feel useful to him now.

One lousy email to this 'Rebecca', who might not even have been a real friend.

Gina shut down the computer and returned it to the closet, knowing that the sight of it would upset her mother.

As everything had, since it had happened.

Not least that bastard Becket's visit on Sunday.

FORTY

May 27

The day of the funeral passed slowly.

A posse of reporters tried to get close to Névé early Thursday morning, buzzed Mike's car when he drove out with Robbie, but for the most part the security system, combined with a little help from the Key Biscayne police, kept them at bay.

Daniel came and found Sam in the kitchen, where he was sitting after speaking to David about the results of his blood test, which had been clear. Like his throat and head, both fine now.

More than could be said for his conscience.

'We're not sure how you guys want to deal with today,' Daniel said.

'I wish I knew,' Sam told him.

'Claudia tried talking to Grace a while ago and had to back off.'

'It's a tough day for her.'

And many more to come.

'We both know that.'

'At least I'm not working,' Sam said wryly.

Cooper's arraignment today, too. Martinez attending instead of him.

'Every cloud, I guess.' Daniel paused. 'We're thinking we might leave you in peace for a few hours.'

'It should be us doing that for you,' Sam said.

'We figure you won't want to go out, with the paparazzi out there.'

'I'm not sure we qualify as celebrities,' Sam said. 'But you're not wrong.' He forced a smile. 'At least you and Claudia can escape for a while.'

'We could bring back some takeout for dinner,' Daniel said.

'Seems to me there's no way we're ever going to be able to thank you enough, Dan,' Sam said.

'It's just takeout.' Daniel smiled.

'If only,' Sam said.

'They've escaped,' Grace said after they'd gone.

'That's what I said.'

'You should go too,' she said.

'Stop that,' he told her, gently.

'OK,' she said.

'We'll take it quietly. Be with Joshua, be together.'

'While we can,' Grace said.

'Don't you know,' Sam asked, 'how much that hurts me?'

'I do know,' she said. 'I'm sorry.'

The guilt well still filling up and spilling over.

Then again, she told herself, if not today, when?

FORTY-ONE

May 30

On Sunday morning, a phone call from Chicago.

Frank Lucca, the sisters' father, who had suffered two strokes while his second wife, Roxanne, had still been alive and torturing him, and who had been in a nursing home since June two years ago, had suffered another stroke, this time described to Claudia as 'massive'.

He was not expected to pull through.

'Will they let me go?' Grace asked Sam.

Not a trace of love surviving between herself and the man who, during their childhood, had abused Claudia until the day Grace had fixed it for them to escape to Florida. Even if he had paid for his sins, courtesy of Jerome's mother.

'I need to be there for Claudia,' she said now.

Claudia had always been softer when it had come to their parents, had continued to visit Frank since the strokes – though if her visits brought him any pleasure, he had not shown it, what was left of his mind teetering between his own boyhood and the early years in his Italian grocery shop in Melrose Park.

'I'll call Jerry,' Sam said. 'Though I think we'll have to wait till tomorrow to get any kind of answer.'

Which made no difference, because less than an hour later there was a second phone call from Chicago, telling them that Frank had passed away.

The sisters sat up late, drinking Chianti and talking about the old days.

'It wasn't all bad,' Claudia said.

'Most of it was,' Grace said.

They talked, too, about more recent times, about their great good fortune, about their children and husbands. Claudia talked about getting over bad times, about how good she and Dan were now, how grateful she was to him for bringing her back here, to Grace, most of all.

'I think Dan's one of the kindest men I've ever met,' Grace said.

'He's the best,' Claudia said. 'Along with Sam.'

'I know it,' Grace said.

They fell silent for a little while.

'I wish I could help you more,' Claudia said.

'No one could have helped me more,' Grace said. 'Not just by sharing this beautiful, safe place with us.' She paused. 'You haven't judged. None of you have judged me.'

'Because we all believe in you,' Claudia said, and then she sighed, and shook her head.

'What?' Grace asked.

'Just thinking about Papa again.'

'If we're going to do much more thinking about Frank,' Grace said, 'I'm going to need more wine.'

Some time in the night, Sam and Daniel, both missing their wives, came downstairs and found the sisters asleep on the sofa in one of the nooks.

'Blankets?' Sam said softly.

Daniel nodded, disappeared, returning with a big patchwork quilt, and carefully they covered up the women and then headed for the kitchen.

'Drink?' Daniel said. 'I'm going to have a nip of something.'

'Sounds good,' Sam said.

'Malt whisky suit you?'

'Even better,' Sam said. 'And no work tomorrow.'

Daniel poured them a couple of fingers each, and they sat at the table.

'Mind if I say something?'

'Not a bit,' Sam said.

'Tell me to butt out any time.'

'Sure.'

'OK.' Daniel took a drink. 'Seems to me there are things we just can't control, no matter how badly we want to. Things we screw up ourselves or that just seem to get worse the more we throw at them. And sometimes, I guess you just have to let them happen and figure out what to do later.'

'I can't just *let* my wife go to jail,' Sam said softly.

'No,' Daniel said. 'That is just unthinkable.'

'The problem is, it's becoming all too thinkable.'

And this time, the other man had nothing to say.

FORTY-TWO

May 31–June 2

Permission granted, Grace and Claudia made the arrangements.

Frank would be buried beside their mother, Ellen.

Roxanne resting elsewhere.

A notice had been inserted in the *Melrose Park Journal*, giving details of the funeral for anyone left who might want to attend.

Cathy and Saul were coming, as were Mike and Robbie, though Joshua would stay with David and Mildred.

Leaving him the greatest wrench for Grace, though she was determined he not be exposed to anything connected with Frank Lucca.

On Tuesday – on what should have been Sam's first day back at work after a four-day suspension – they all checked into the Seneca Hotel on East Chestnut Street in Chicago.

'Nice room,' Sam said, looking around.

'Isn't it,' Grace said. 'We can almost pretend we're on vacation.'

He heard the note in her voice, irony mixed with panic.

'Do you want to get out of here?' he asked.

'No.' She sat on the end of the bed. 'Though, yes, I do feel a little claustrophobic, which is ridiculous, because it's a perfectly nice room.'

And because soon enough she would probably be occupying a cell.

Sam sat beside her, took her hand, and she leaned against him.

'One blow too many,' he said.

'My father?' Grace smiled, shook her head. 'I remember Claudia once telling me that she used to imagine Frank dying painfully and pleading for our forgiveness. Same with Ellen, who'd be begging Claudia to forgive her for not taking her side against Frank.'

Sam knew that neither parent had ever asked forgiveness.

'Claudia's the one who did the forgiving, of course,' Grace said. 'But it still hurts her, I think.'

'How about you?' Sam asked.

'Many things hurting at the moment,' she said. 'Not so much this.'

No one but family at the funeral, except for a representative from the nursing home, doing her duty.

'Your father was no trouble,' she told Grace and Claudia.

'You were all very kind to him,' Claudia told her.

'He seemed like a sweet man,' the woman said. 'He talked about you often.'

'Did he?' Grace asked.

'Especially about you,' the woman said, looking at Claudia.

Grace saw Daniel take his wife's hand, grip it tightly, was glad for her.

Glad for herself, too, feeling Sam close beside her.

Almost everyone who counted was here for her, except for Joshua, David and Mildred, and they'd be waiting for them when they got home tomorrow.

'OK?' Sam said, softly.

'OK,' she said.

Though it struck her abruptly as intensely sad that even now, after so many years, and even after all that Frank had endured, there was still only one word that came to her mind when she thought of her father.

Bastard.

* * *

There was little left for them to do.

The collecting of the very few remaining things that had belonged to Frank.

None of them keepsakes.

The house had gone while he was still in the hospital, before he'd been moved to the nursing home.

The house where the young Jerome Cooper had lived before he'd left Melrose Park to start on his first round of depravity. The house they knew from his *New Epistles* that he considered had been stolen from him.

They all went out to dinner at the Chicago Chophouse and Daniel protested when he found that Sam had paid the check, but Sam said it was the very least he could do, and the other man knew better than to argue.

'That's that,' Grace said as they got into bed later.

'All done,' Sam said.

If only.

FORTY-THREE

June 3

All sitting together on the American Airlines flight back to Miami.

Sharing a drink, a little good humor.

Grace and Sam looking forward to being with Joshua again.

Plenty of healing in that compact little body and in the sound of his laughter.

Tension rising steadily, though, the closer they got to MIA.

Only eight days now until the pretrial hearing.

Wagner had explained to Grace that the primary purpose of that hearing was generally to help make for a fair and expeditious trial. The attorneys getting a chance to raise issues ahead of time, preliminary stuff. Some testimony from witnesses, the judge asking questions, perhaps of her, should he wish to, with no jury present.

'How long does it usually last?' Grace had asked.

'Can be a day,' Wagner had said. 'There was a preliminary hearing in California a couple of years back that lasted six months.' He'd patted her hand. 'A big, complex case. I'd guess two days for ours, but it's just a guess.'

Ours.

Thinking about it even thousands of feet up in the air, Grace was so afraid of June 11 that she could hardly breathe, so she forced it to the back of her mind, returned Sam's concerned, loving look with a semblance of a smile, and took a sip of mineral water.

Eight days in which she knew she had to make the most of every minute – just as she would need to do between pretrial and the real thing. And she would do her very best, for Joshua and Cathy and Sam, all the while mentally marking off the days from one terrifying milestone to the next.

With only one ultimate destination that she could seem to picture.

A cell.

Sam saw past the smile to the pain behind it.

Her fear was the worst of it.

And not a damned thing he could do for her, except to stay close, let her know he still had faith, in her, if nothing else.

He'd thought, last year, when they had both thought they might not live to see any of their family again, that nothing could feel worse than that.

He knew differently now.

This was hell.

Watching the woman he loved most in all the world falling deeper and deeper into the pit of a nightmare, and not being able to do a damned thing to help her.

Hell.

FORTY-FOUR

June 7

The following Monday at around two p.m., a hot, humid afternoon, storms threatening, Sam and Martinez had just left the station, heading across Rocky Pomerantz Plaza on their way to Markie's for a bite, when Sam stopped in his tracks.

'What's up?' Martinez asked.

Sam didn't answer.

His eyes were on a small, bright-blue Honda parked on the opposite side of Washington Avenue.

'My, my,' he said, softly.

Martinez followed his line of sight. 'Who's that?'

'Bianchi's sister,' Sam said. 'Wait for me, Al.'

He began moving again, slowly, not wanting to spook her.

She was in the driver's seat, looking through her open window right at him, and she knew now that he had seen her, but that was all Sam could tell. He could not read the expression in her eyes, and the rest of her face was immobile, giving nothing away.

The lights were against him, but as he waited to cross, suppressing the urge to sprint and dodge traffic, he had the impression that she was steeling herself.

The lights changed.

He started walking again.

He could see those dark eyes more clearly now, locked on his but still unreadable.

And then, suddenly, she seemed to take a shuddering breath, and now it was all there in her face, a kind of violent pain, and Sam quickened his pace.

'Ms Bianchi,' he called out to her.

She gunned the gas pedal, and the Honda took off.

'Goddamn,' Sam said, staring after it.

Martinez crossed against the lights, joined him on the west side of the street.

'What the hell was that about?' he asked.

'Damned if I know,' Sam said.

'More anger to vent?' Martinez said.

'I don't think so,' Sam replied.

'You sure?' his partner said, thinking about revenge, a grieving woman maybe packing a gun this time, instead of a slap.

'I think,' Sam said, 'she wanted to talk to me.'

He turned it over and over during lunch, ate his sandwich without tasting it.

'Nothing you can do, man,' Martinez told him.

'I know it,' Sam said.

'So why do I get the feeling you don't really believe that?'

Sam downed half a bottle of Coke.

'Something's happened with her,' he said. 'Something's changed.'

'Tell Wagner,' Martinez said.
'Sure,' Sam said.
'Call him now.'
'I'll call him,' Sam said.
'What are you planning?' Martinez was uneasy.
'I don't know,' Sam said.

He waited till he had a moment alone, and then he called Angie Carlino in Tampa.
'What do you need, Sam?' No preamble.
'Couple of Naples addresses,' he told her. 'Gina Bianchi's, home and work. Her home's unlisted.'
'No problem,' she said.

FORTY-FIVE

June 8

Three days to go before the pretrial hearing.
If he was going to do this, it needed to be soon.
Today.
All through yesterday afternoon and evening, he'd waited for Gina Bianchi to surface again, had checked his cellphone constantly, had looked everywhere for bright-blue Hondas, parked or cruising.
Martinez said nothing, and if Grace or anyone else had noticed his preoccupation, he guessed they'd assumed it was connected with the hearing.
Grace, in any case, was in another zone altogether.
Loving with Joshua, then backing off – that cycle again, only more so.
He knew that going to see Bianchi's sister was risky.
But if – and it was a *big* if – Gina Bianchi had learned something significant about her brother, and if she'd considered sharing it with Sam, but had changed her mind, chances were she might never share it with anyone else either.
And that, it seemed to him, was an even greater risk.

* * *

He left Key Biscayne early, called Martinez en route.

'I'm taking a sick day,' he said. 'Need you to cover for me.'

'You're going to Naples,' his partner said. 'You don't want to do that.'

'I have no choice,' Sam said.

'Call Wagner,' Martinez said again.

'And tell him what?' Sam said. 'I need to know why she came.'

'Probably because she hates you, man.'

'Of course she hates me,' Sam said, 'but she wanted to talk.'

'Maybe she wanted to shoot your stubborn ass,' Martinez said.

Sam smiled. 'I don't think that's her style, though I could be wrong.'

'Jesus,' Martinez said.

His thoughts raced all the way back along Alligator Alley, part of the same journey he'd taken with his father a couple of weeks back, and he could only hope for a better outcome. He remembered what Grace had said after he'd screwed up the last interview with Cooper; that thing about them both having lost their direction and self-control. And he wasn't sure if his judgement was any less skewed today than it had been then, only that he felt – knew – that he had no viable alternative but to try.

He was standing on the sidewalk outside the offices of the Stephen L. Jacks Foundation on 6th Avenue North, when Gina Bianchi arrived at ten to nine. She did not see him until she was about fifteen feet away.

She stopped dead, and her face froze.

And then she shook her head with real violence, and came toward him.

'I'm sorry,' Sam said.

'You will be,' she said.

He registered the threat, knew he had to get past it somehow, knew he had to get through to her here and now, outside on this concrete sidewalk.

'You came to me first,' he said.

'I did not come to you,' Gina Bianchi said.

'I think you changed your mind,' Sam said. 'But I had the strongest feeling that you'd come to Miami Beach because you had something to tell me.'

'You were wrong,' she said, and started to turn.

'My wife is going to be in court this Friday.'

She turned back. 'Because she killed my brother.' Her voice was low, but the rage still burned.

'And she's ripping herself apart because of it, and she is— we are both so deeply sorry for you and your parents. I nearly lost my own brother a few years ago, and words don't cover how that felt, so I can only begin to imagine your loss.'

Two men in suits passed them on their way into the building, and one of them glanced, first at Gina, then at Sam.

'The truth is Grace believed that he was going to kill her,' Sam said. 'Even worse, from her standpoint, she believed he was going to harm a young frightened boy.' Barely hanging on here, and he knew it. 'And I think you came to Miami because you might have found out something important.'

'I'm going inside,' she said. 'I'm late.'

'Just one more minute.' Desperate man. 'After that, I'm gone.'

She shook her head. 'One minute and *I'm* gone.' She raised her wrist, checked her watch.

'Thank you,' he said.

'You're wasting time.'

On the clock.

'I'm not asking you to make a decision right now, Ms Bianchi, because if you have found out something disturbing, I imagine—'

The expression in her eyes halted him, was harder, angrier.

Though maybe that was good news, because if he'd been wrong about this, if she'd found out nothing, then she would surely have ended this immediately, either have slapped him again or just told him to get lost and walk away.

Clutching at straws.

'If you don't want to tell me – and maybe I'm the last person you would tell – but if there is anything you're not sure about, just the smallest doubt, then please, I beg you, tell *someone* before it's too late for my wife, for our little boy.'

She raised her watch again.

'I know you have every reason to hate us.' He sped up. 'But my wife's whole life is about trying to help people, and I'm watching guilt consume her, and I am scared as hell for her. Just as you must be scared for your parents, if the truth comes out.'

He took a step back, both hands up in surrender.

'You've listened,' he said. 'For that alone, I'm very grateful.'

Gina Bianchi stood in silence for a moment.

'What will happen to you,' she asked, finally, 'when I report this to your superiors?'

'Trouble,' Sam said. 'A heap of it, I imagine.'

'You've been a detective a long time.'

'Yes, I have.'

'You like your work.'

'I love my work.' Sam paused. 'Most of the time.'

'Then perhaps you should have thought twice,' she said.

And she turned, and walked into the building.

Sam waited another moment, and then he headed slowly back to the parking lot beside the building, got into the Saab.

He started the engine.

Grace's face came back to him, the way she'd looked in court at her arraignment. The whiteness of her face, the fear in her eyes.

The fear he'd seen too many times since then.

'Oh, God,' he said, softly.

And then he put his hands on the wheel, laid his face against them.

He'd achieved nothing, had only made it worse.

Nothing more to do now than wait.

FORTY-SIX

June 11

'All rise. Court is now in session. Judge Arthur Brazen presiding.'

Last night, for the first time, Grace had asked Sam what he knew about the judge, and Sam had said that he was reputed to be a fair man.

The same word Wagner had used when she'd asked him. 'Fair.'

A fair judge would have to find against a woman who had run down a man in cold blood.

Grace had thought she was trembling inside when she'd got out of bed this morning.

Forget trembling.

This felt more like 7.5 on the Richter scale.

* * *

It had begun.

Grace, sitting beside Wagner, looked around the courtroom, trying to still the buzzing in her ears, to slow the pounding of her heart.

The room seemed larger and more impressive than the one in which she'd been arraigned. The wood more highly polished, the judge more loftily elevated, presiding over the court.

Over her.

She took in the area where a jury would sit at her actual trial, suppressed a shudder, looked away; took in the two witness boxes, one on either side of the judge's bench, one presently occupied by the court clerk.

A court reporter sat at a table below the bench.

Grace looked up at the two flags behind Judge Brazen. The state flag, emblazoned with its large red 'X' and the state seal with its brilliant sun, palmetto tree, steamboat sailing, and Seminole woman scattering flowers. She thought about all that Florida had done for her and Claudia, the freedom that their escape into sunlight had brought them.

She looked away, past the judge, to the American flag, tried to recall the symbolism of red, white and blue, could remember only blue for justice and . . .

Panic seized her, and she tore her gaze away, and now she was searching for her family on the public benches, but there were so many more people here today than at the arraignment, more strangers . . .

She found them, the ones she needed, and Cathy looked scared, but Sam's eyes were on her, loving and supportive, and suddenly she wanted to weep, so instead she stared down at her hands in her lap, but they felt numb, as if they did not belong to her, and panic surged again . . .

'You're OK,' she heard Jerry Wagner say, very quietly.

Her eyes traveled, at last, to where she was most afraid to look.

At a blonde woman and a dark-haired man, both in black.

Josephine and Robert Bianchi.

No one with them who looked like their daughter, Gina.

Sam had told her on Tuesday evening about his visit, and Grace had seen his wretchedness and had consoled him, had told him she understood that he had felt he needed to try. And if Gina Bianchi had reported him to the department, the repercussions had not yet been forthcoming, though maybe Captain Kennedy was being kind, waiting till today was over.

Richard Bianchi's parents looked back at her now, their hatred searing.

No forgiveness in them.

Or in herself.

More shame from the bottomless well.

'Grace,' Wagner said, softly. 'Focus.'

She looked back at him, at his eyes, not piercing now, but calm and kindly, and she knew she had to grab on to that, knew there was no escaping from this process, and someone was speaking, though she could not quite hear because of the pounding in her ears.

She thought of Pete Mankowitz and his panic attacks.

'Breathe,' she'd always told him.

When she was still his psychologist.

Breathe.

Easier said.

She knew that now.

Poor Pete.

Judge Arthur Brazen was speaking.

'For those of you unfamiliar with what goes on at pretrial hearings, the way I sometimes like to look at it is as a last chance saloon for both sides to find a way to reach a resolution before we go forward for a long, torturous and costly trial.' He paused. 'There's no jury, so I get to make all the decisions, the most important of which is whether or not there's sufficient probable cause to go ahead.'

Breathe, Grace instructed herself again.

The judge looked at Elena Alonso, the prosecuting attorney, a stocky woman with short, wavy highlighted hair, dressed in a dark suit.

'Go,' he said.

Testimonies began.

A police officer was first, one of those who'd come to the scene on the evening of Richard Bianchi's death.

Then Sara Mankowitz, who did not once look at Grace.

Poor Sara, Grace thought, knowing that Pete's mother had no alternative but to tell it as she had seen it.

Then one of the people Sara had brought back with her from the highway: the husband of the woman who'd looked after Pete while Richard Bianchi had lain, dying . . .

All of them telling what they had witnessed, none of them meaning her any special harm, just speaking the truth. Enough truth, Grace supposed, to put her away for years, more years than she could bear to imagine.

Time passed. Her left foot prickled with pins and needles and she tried to wiggle her toes, but her shoe was too close-fitting, so she pushed its leather sole into the floor, trying to ease it that way.

Somewhere behind her a door opened and closed again and someone entered. A woman Grace did not recognize.

Another witness, she supposed.

The young woman sitting on Wagner's other side rose to acknowledge the newcomer, and Wagner turned too, nodded at her.

Someone for their side, apparently, maybe an expert witness, a psychologist, perhaps, hoping to lend credence to their case.

Elena Alonso stood.

'The prosecution rests,' she said.

Wagner rose.

'May I approach, Your Honor?' he asked the judge.

Alonso rose again, too, walked with Wagner to the bench.

They talked for a while, too quietly to be overheard.

Grace looked at her family – everyone here but David and Mildred, who were taking care of Joshua again – and at Magda, too, who'd insisted on coming, and she thought again how kind they all were, how loyal. And that, at least, was some comfort, knowing that Joshua would never go short of love and care . . .

She glanced back at the newcomer in the courtroom.

She was dark-haired, slim, wearing a dark-blue suit, and she seemed uneasy, nervous, even pale.

Not an expert witness, after all.

Wagner and Alonso were disagreeing over something.

If this were a movie, Grace thought, it would probably be an attempt to introduce new evidence, perhaps too late in the day, though this was not a trial . . .

Nor was it a movie.

Her stomach lurched and her heartbeat sped up again.

She looked at Sam, saw that his eyes were on the newcomer.

And suddenly she knew who she was.

Had to be.

She found herself praying that Arthur Brazen was an open-minded judge who might consider bending rules, who would allow whatever this woman had brought into the courtroom. *His* courtroom, his interpretation of law. Grace absolutely in his hands.

The lawyers returned to their tables and sat down.

Wagner shuffled papers around for a moment or two, scribbled a note, then put away his pen, nodded and rose again, with nothing in his hands.

'I call Gina Bianchi to the stand,' he said.

Sam and the others were sitting rigidly upright.

Grace felt as if life was happening around her, as if she were experiencing an out-of-body experience, observing the courtroom remotely.

Gina Bianchi had been sworn in.

The dead man's – Grace's victim's – sister. The woman who had slapped Sam when he had gone with David to visit her parents.

Those parents now sitting in court, new devastation in their eyes.

Gina Bianchi, who had totally rejected Sam's plea when he had gone to talk to her three days ago in Naples, still had every reason in the world to wish Grace in jail.

Or worse.

Jerry Wagner had begun his questioning.

'Can you tell us, Ms Bianchi, why you didn't come forward earlier?'

'I've been in mourning,' she said. 'And I didn't realize until quite recently that I had any information to give that might be relevant to this case.'

'And you didn't want to do anything to harm your brother's memory.'

'Objection.' Elena Alonso stood.

'Sustained,' the judge said. 'Though since this is not a trial, let's just get on with finding out why Ms Bianchi is here.' He smiled at her. 'In your own words.'

'Thank you,' she said. 'This is very hard for me.'

'Take your time,' the judge told her.

She nodded, composed herself. 'I saw some news items around the time that Jerome Cooper, the murderer, was arrested.'

'The alleged murderer,' Judge Brazen corrected her.

'Yes, Your Honor,' she said. 'I'm sorry.'

'Don't worry about it,' he said.

She shook her head. 'I'm trying to keep things in chronological order, but it's hard. I was trying to help my parents deal with my brother's death, and then suddenly questions were being asked about Richard that had nothing to do with him having been killed. People talking about his car, wanting to see his computer, search his apartment.'

'Go on,' Wagner prompted her, gently.

'Detective Samuel Becket, in particular, came to visit my parents just a few days before Richard's funeral, because I think he was hoping he might persuade them to let him see the computer. I'm afraid I became very angry. Too angry to listen properly to what he was saying.'

'What was Detective Becket saying?' Wagner asked.

'He was saying that he thought my brother might have been used by Jerome Cooper.'

'And you felt that was untrue?'

'Of course I did. I felt – I knew – that the real reason behind his visit was that he was trying to get his wife off the hook for killing my brother.'

Wagner waited a moment.

'And has anything altered since then, Ms Bianchi?'

'Yes.' Her voice was softer.

'I'm sorry, Ms Bianchi,' Judge Brazen said, 'but you will need to speak more distinctly.'

'Of course,' she said. 'I'm sorry.'

'We understand how difficult this is for you,' Wagner said.

'Just let the witness continue,' the judge said.

Wagner nodded, waited.

'The day before my brother's funeral,' Gina Bianchi went on, 'I turned on his laptop computer partly because I wanted to see if there were any people who still had to be contacted, and partly because I felt a need to read some of his work. Richard wrote short stories among other things, and I thought it might be a way of feeling close to him.'

Wagner waited a moment, but the young woman was looking at her parents. Her mother was pale, her father strained.

'Did you notice something else on Mr Bianchi's computer?' he asked finally.

'Yes.' She paused. 'Some unusual websites in the search history.'

'What kind of websites?'

'I didn't look at them,' she said, 'but their names indicated they had something to do with organ transplantation.'

'Did that strike you as strange?' Wagner asked.

'Not especially,' she said. 'I assumed they were research for his writing.'

'Was your brother writing about organ transplantation?'

'Not that I knew of,' she said. 'But that was what I assumed at the time.'

'And now?' Wagner asked. 'Do you still assume that?'

The young woman looked sick at heart.

'No,' she said, softly.

'Why is that?'

'I found other things, after that,' she said. 'Not that day. Some time after the funeral, when I turned on the laptop again.'

'What did you find then, Ms Bianchi?'

She took a moment. 'I found some material that Richard – or someone else using his computer – had downloaded from the Internet.'

'What kind of material?'

'It was about heart surgery,' she said. 'In particular, it was about heart excision for transplantation purposes.'

Now Wagner took a moment.

'You were kind enough, Ms Bianchi,' he said, 'to email me a copy of that material shortly before this hearing.'

'Yes,' she said.

'Were you aware that it is the exact same material that was found, in printout form, on the houseboat called the *Aggie*, on which Jerome Cooper was arrested?'

There was a stirring in the courtroom, murmurs and what sounded like the tapping of fingers on laptops, or might have been the court reporter, but Grace did not look around, just sat, frozen, waiting for Gina Bianchi's reply.

'No,' she said. 'I had no way of knowing that.'

'What else did you find, Ms Bianchi?'

There was a pause.

'Ms Bianchi?' Wagner prompted.

'I found an email confirmation of a purchase of surgical instruments.'

Grace, unaware that she had been holding her breath for several moments, took a sudden intake of air that sounded to her own ears like a gasp, which, in turn, made her cheeks flush. And she wanted to look at Sam, but she didn't dare to move, did not want to do anything that might risk halting the momentum of what was happening.

'Go on, Ms Bianchi,' Judge Brazen said.

'I remembered then that, among other things, Jerome Cooper had been arrested in connection with those "heart murders" – the horrible story of the heart that a child found in a pool at a hotel.'

'Was there a date on the email confirmation of the purchase you told us about?' Wagner asked.

'You know there was,' she said. 'I sent it to you this morning.'

'Please could you answer the question.'

'Yes,' she said. 'March eleventh.'

'March eleventh of this year?' Wagner checked.

'Yes.'

'And did you make any connection between your brother's purchase of surgical instruments and those terrible crimes?'

'I don't know that it was my brother's purchase,' she said. 'Someone else may have been using his computer.'

'Jerome Cooper, perhaps?'

'I don't know,' she said.

'Do you know of anyone else who might have used his computer?'

'No,' she said. 'But that doesn't mean they did not.'

'Did the email confirmation specify the method of payment?'

'I believe it was a credit card of some kind.'

'I have to tell you,' Wagner said, 'that while it has still to be confirmed, preliminary communications with the company who sent that email to your brother's address point to the purchase having been made using a credit card belonging to Richard Bianchi.'

Gina Bianchi grew paler and swayed a little, and over in the public benches, Josephine Bianchi stared into her husband's eyes.

'Would you like to stop for a while, Ms Bianchi?' Wagner asked.

'No,' she said. 'I'm OK.'

'Would you like a glass of water?' Judge Brazen asked.

'Yes, please.'

A glass of water was swiftly poured by Wagner's assistant, brought to the witness box, and as she took the glass and held it to her lips, her hands were trembling.

'Are you all right to go on?' the judge asked. 'We could take a break.'

'I'd rather go on,' she said.

'Ms Bianchi,' Wagner said, 'what else did you find of particular note in your search of Mr Bianchi's laptop computer?'

'I found some notes that were hard to understand.'

'Why was that?' Wagner asked.

'They were in a journal I hadn't noticed the first time I'd looked, and they were kind of cryptic. Mostly, they seemed to be blocking off dates, the way you do when you have something specific to do that could take time, but all that had been typed on those days was "The Boss".'

'Did your brother have a boss at the time? An employer?'

'Not to my knowledge. So far as I know, Richard was self-employed.'

'Anything else?'

'What seemed to be shopping lists,' she said.

'What was on the lists?' Wagner asked.

'All kinds of things. Food, pain medication, cleaning stuff, all kinds. I can't remember.'

'Why did you notice them at all?'

'Because they were in a file named "The Boss".'

'All of them?' Wagner said.

'No,' she said. 'One of the lists was headed with some initials.'

'What were the initials?'

'T.O.H.' She paused. 'It was a capital "T", then a capital "O", then an apostrophe, then a capital "H".'

'Did those initials mean anything to you, Ms Bianchi?' Wagner asked.

'Not until I went back and checked some of the newspaper articles about Jerome Cooper's arrest.' Her voice was growing huskier from strain. 'And I saw that the boat he was arrested on was registered to a man named O'Hagen.'

'Tom O'Hagen,' Wagner said.

'Yes.'

'And what, if anything, have you concluded from all these discoveries?'

Gina Bianchi's eyes seemed filled with pain.

'That when Detective Becket said he thought my brother might have been used by Jerome Cooper, he might have been right,' she said.

'Thank you, Ms Bianchi,' Wagner said.

'Is that all?' Judge Brazen asked the attorney.

'I do have one further question for the witness, Your Honor.'

'Ask it,' the judge said.

'Are you aware of any physical resemblance between your late brother and Jerome Cooper?'

'No,' Gina Bianchi said.

'What was your brother's natural hair color, Ms Bianchi?'

'Brown,' she answered.

'But at the time of his death,' Wagner said, 'his hair was a silvery blond, wasn't it?'

'Yes,' she said. 'It was.'

'Do you know how long it had been that color?'

'I don't,' she said. 'I hadn't seen Richard for some time.'

'What color was his hair the last time you saw him prior to his death?'

'It was brown, as it had always been.'

'So your brother was not, to the best of your knowledge, in the habit of tinting his hair different shades?'

'Not that I knew of,' she said.

'Were you surprised then when you saw his hair after his death?' Wagner paused. 'I am very sorry to ask you what must seem a very insensitive question.'

'It's damned insensitive,' the judge said.

'I don't mind answering,' Gina Bianchi said. 'I was surprised, yes.' For the first time since entering the witness box, there were tears in her eyes. 'Though I did have other things on my mind.'

'Of course you did,' Wagner said. 'I'm sorry.'

'Get to the point, Counselor,' Judge Brazen said.

'Are you aware, Ms Bianchi, that Grace Becket stated that she believed, when your brother came toward her car in a threatening—'

'Objection.' Elena Alonso was on her feet.

'Sustained.'

'Mrs Becket says that she believed your brother was Jerome Cooper, Ms Bianchi.' Wagner paused. 'And the last time he had been seen, his hair had been dyed silver.'

'Millions of men have silver hair.' Alonso was up again.

'But they were not all there that evening, coming at Mrs Becket's car in a taunting and threatening manner,' Wagner said.

'Objection,' Alonso said.

'In a manner perceived by Mrs Becket as greatly threatening,' Wagner amended.

'I don't know what you want me to say,' Gina Bianchi said.

'Of course you don't,' Judge Brazen said.

'I have no more questions for you, Ms Bianchi,' Wagner said. 'But I would like to thank you for coming forward. It must have taken great strength.'

In the witness box, Richard Bianchi's sister let go for the first time, leaned forward, buried her face in her hands and wept.

'Court is adjourned,' Judge Brazen said. 'One hour.' He paused. 'At which time, I think I'd like to hear a little summing up of exactly where both counselors feel they stand after all we've just heard.'

'What just happened in there?' Cathy asked Saul out in the hallway.

'I'm not exactly sure.' Saul looked at Daniel. 'What do you think?'

'I hardly dare say what I think,' Daniel said.

'Me neither,' Claudia said.

'Where's Sam?' Cathy asked.

'He went someplace with Grace and Mr Wagner,' Saul said.

'What do we do now?' Mike asked.

'I promised to call Dad and Mildred,' Saul said.

'And then I guess we all wait,' Claudia said.

'Anyone hungry?' Robbie asked.

No one answered.

'I could use a cup of coffee,' Magda said.

'There's Sam,' Saul said.

Walking slowly toward them. No clues in his expression.

'What's happening?' Cathy asked.

'I have nothing to tell you,' Sam said. 'Except Wagner and Ms Alonso are talking.'

'Jerry must have told you something,' Cathy said.

Sam put an arm around her. 'I'm the last person anyone's going to talk to right now.'

'Is Grace with them?' Claudia asked.

Now Sam's face showed a little of his strain. 'We had a moment together, but now I think they've given her a room to rest in.'

'Not a cell?' Cathy's anxiety was mounting again.

'No way,' Sam told her.

Not that he knew that for sure.

Cathy drew away from Sam, leaned against the wall.

'What just happened has to be good, surely?' Claudia said.

'You'd think,' Sam said.

Finding it hard to speak now.

'What do you mean?' Cathy asked.

'Hey,' Daniel said softly, checking out Sam's expression, seeing how close he was to the edge. 'It has to be good, but there's no way of knowing how good, so we'll all have to wait it out now, sweetheart.'

Sam caught Daniel's eye, nodded thanks.

It seemed to him that Grace's brother-in-law just got better with time.

He made a mental note to tell that to Grace.

When today was over.

For better or worse.

When Elena Alonso rose to address the court after the recess, it was to state that in view of the morning's developments, she wished to ask the judge's indulgence in allowing the defense attorney to speak first.

'I'll allow it,' Judge Brazen said.

Sam sat with Cathy on his left, Saul to his right. His legs were crossed, his hands folded over his right thigh. His eyes followed Jerry Wagner as he rose from his seat, then tracked back to Grace.

She was looking at him.

Her eyes seemed to him bluer and clearer than ever.

He felt a violent, futile urge to go grab her by the hand, get her out of here. Instead, he sat quiet and still, wired to the hilt.

His eyes left Grace, returned to Wagner.

He willed the lawyer to do the best job he'd ever done in his career.

And then some.

'On the evening of May sixth,' Wagner began, 'in a dark, narrow road off Crandon Boulevard in Key Biscayne, to which Grace Becket had been called to help one of her patients – a distressed, vulnerable boy – a man approached her car in what she perceived as a terrifying and threatening manner. At the time, Mrs Becket believed the man to be Jerome Cooper, a known murderer with an obsessive hatred for her family. Unable to escape him, and in desperate fear for her own life and that of her young patient, she defended herself in the only way she could, by striking out with her car.'

Wagner paused, looked around briefly, then returned his focus to the judge.

'Mrs Becket's remorse and horror when she discovered that the man was not, in fact, Jerome Cooper, but Mr Richard Bianchi, was and remains vast. Other than the very occasional parking ticket, Dr Grace Lucca Becket has never committed a crime or misdemeanor in her forty years, and her reputation as a child and adolescent psychologist is second to none. Mrs Becket is a loving wife and mother of two children: her adopted daughter, Cathy, and two-year-old Joshua. It is a matter of record that less than two years ago, Jerome Cooper abducted baby Joshua Becket from his family's home, and that Joshua was only narrowly saved from death when Cooper blew up the boat in which he had been keeping the baby prisoner. Cooper was believed dead, but he has since horrifically resurfaced and is currently in custody charged with two brutal murders, the attempted murder of Mrs Mildred Bleeker Becket, and the kidnapping of Joshua Becket. Numerous additional charges pending.' Wagner paused. 'A dangerous and frightening man, Your Honor.'

'Waiting again,' David Becket said to his wife, watching her as she sat on the rug on their sitting-room floor, playing with his grandson. 'Seems all we're good for these days is waiting.'

'We're minding Joshua,' Mildred said. 'Seems to me that's pretty important, old man.' She paused. 'It's going to be all right, you know.'

She looked up at her new husband, thinking how well he'd looked on their wedding day, just fifty days ago, compared with how *worn* he looked today, and how they'd all been through so much, and when did that finally turn into *too* much?

She prayed never to find that out.

She prayed, too, for Grace, and for her beloved Samuel, her dear friend before he'd become her son-in-law, and she never ceased wondering at the strangeness of such gifts of life, and she supposed it was simple greed to hope for more.

Or maybe it was just human.

'On April twelfth this year,' Jerry Wagner continued, 'a package containing a human heart was left outside the Becket family home. On May third, another human heart – which it is now known had been carved out of the strangled body of nineteen-year-old Ricardo Torres – was placed in the Becket family's bathtub. On May sixth – during the very evening that Richard Bianchi lost his life – Samuel Becket, Mrs Becket's husband, a detective with the Miami Beach

Police Department, discovered a threatening note left for him by Jerome Cooper.

'The prosecution would have you believe – and it's not unreasonable for them to have believed it themselves, until Ms Gina Bianchi gave evidence this morning – that Richard Bianchi was an innocent man. He was unarmed on the evening of his death. It appeared to Sara Mankowitz and the other witnesses arriving on the scene while Mr Bianchi lay dying, that he might have been approaching Mrs Becket in a conciliatory manner – indeed, that was what he told them. That he was "just trying to help".

'Mr Bianchi, it has been said, was a man with a loving family, a writer doing what many struggling writers do to make ends meet: copy editing to pay his bills while waiting for his big break.

'Had Gina Bianchi come forward sooner, I believe that the charges brought against Grace Becket would have been dropped, because what Detective Samuel Becket already suspected would have been borne out. But until Ms Bianchi found the evidence on her late brother's laptop computer and made her courageous phone call to my office, it seemed there might be no way to prove Detective Becket's suspicion: that Richard Bianchi was being used by – was perhaps in the pay of – Jerome Cooper.'

Wagner paused to clear his throat.

'Your Honor, I'd like to share with you some of the issues that had already aroused those suspicions. Richard Bianchi had, according to Sara Mankowitz, first introduced himself to her in a coffee shop near her son's school right after she had dropped him off one morning. He had – also according to Mrs Mankowitz – identified himself as Charles – Charlie – Duggan, a fictitious name he stuck with all through their friendship until his death. Nothing about Charlie Duggan was real, in fact. Neither the occupation he claimed, nor his address, nor the father he said was deceased, or the mother he said lived in North Miami.

'Sam Becket believes this was a friendship that Richard Bianchi probably engineered for sinister reasons. It was certainly a friendship which alarmed young Peter Mankowitz, because he said that Charlie Duggan took pleasure in frightening him and, as Peter ultimately confided in Mrs Becket, Mr Duggan – Richard Bianchi – also physically hurt him on more than one occasion.'

FORTY-SEVEN

In his cell at Miami-Dade County Prison, Jerome Cooper was writing another *Epistle*.

He was writing about death.

His own.

The death penalty being alive and well in the great state of Florida.

If it were not for the prospect of hell, which he knew – had always known – was waiting for him, he thought he might not mind dying one bit.

He remembered what he'd written about jail in one of his early *Epistles*.

Describing 'wickedness stealing around corners, oozing at him out of the night, flicking like snakes' tongues through cell doors.'

He remembered it because he'd been proud of his writing back then.

And because he'd been so damned scared that he could hardly breathe.

There was something to be said for being a known multiple killer.

Seemed that some of those low-life baby rapers and chicken hawks were scared of *him* now.

> Mind, some of the guys on Death Row have been there for twenty years or even more. Someone told me the food is better there too.
>
> Couldn't be worse.
>
> Twenty years in a place like this?
>
> Or hell right away?
>
> I guess I have to pick Death Row.
>
> And hell can damned well wait.

FORTY-EIGHT

'It was early evening on May sixth, after Pete had felt scared enough of "Charlie Duggan" to jump out of his open-topped car on Crandon Boulevard, when Sara Mankowitz called Grace Becket and implored her to come out to the scene.

'The Becket family were staying at a place of safety, but nevertheless, Mrs Becket still felt compelled to help her young patient, so she did as Sara Mankowitz had begged, and drove to meet her. "Charlie Duggan" was nowhere to be seen, had, according to Peter's mother, dropped out of sight for her son's sake. So Grace Becket left her car, walked to where the boy had taken shelter beneath the trees, and began the task of trying to calm him.'

Sitting listening to Wagner telling the tale, Grace almost felt she was back there again. Under those trees in the dark.

Pete's eyes full of fear and need.

She knew that if she could go back in time, she'd make the same decision. To go there and try to help.

Not the rest.

No matter what Richard Bianchi was.

'And then, suddenly, Duggan's car appeared, coming very slowly around a bend in the road. A red convertible Volkswagen Beetle. The same make, model and color car Grace Becket had noticed first during an unnerving situation on April nineteenth, and again on May fifth – the day before the event in question – when she had believed that the vehicle appeared to be following her.'

Wagner paused.

'Except when Mrs Becket saw the driver on the evening of May sixth, she saw that it was not Charles Duggan at all, but Jerome Cooper.

'She was terrified, but even then, her patient came first. She told Peter to go straight to his mother, called out to Sara Mankowitz to take her son and to run, to get back out to the highway and to people. Mrs Mankowitz has testified that this was what Mrs Becket told her to do.

'Mrs Becket reached her own Toyota car, but the man got out of the VW and began walking toward her car. And she panicked. Her car wouldn't start first time, and by the time it did start, the man was right in front of her vehicle, so she went into reverse to try to escape, but it was pitch dark, and she hit something – a tree stump, it was later confirmed – and after that it was a case of forward or nothing.

'She could have sat in her locked car, called 911 and waited. That is what the State says she should have done, and I have to tell you, Your Honor, that Grace Becket believes that too, with all her heart.

'But she was in a state of high panic. Because the man was still standing right in front of her car, leaning over it, taunting her and blocking her escape. A man she believed to be a multiple *killer*, the man who had stolen her own baby from his crib, who had brutally killed several people, who was still continuing to kill. And at that moment, in that dark, frightening place, Grace Becket found herself in a state of genuine fear for her life – and so she used the only defense she had: her car.

'And it was only when she was finally capable of getting out of the car and seeing the man lying on the ground, that she saw it was not Jerome Cooper at all, but another man. The man who had called himself Charles Duggan. The man who was, in reality, Richard Bianchi.'

A small, low moan pierced Wagner's pause.

A grieving mother, in unbearable pain.

He went on.

'A man who, as it turns out, was driving a car which had previously belonged to a friend of Jerome Cooper's, a former madam in Savannah, Georgia. A man who, it is strongly suspected, though not yet proven, was the individual referred to in Cooper's own writings as "Toy", a man who the killer admits brought him his "*shopping*".'

Wagner turned, walked back to the defense table, picked up a sheet of paper, and read: '"Toy came to see me today and brought me some meat from his very own Fresh Market. I wonder sometimes how I'd manage without him."'

Grace shuddered at that word.

'Meat'.

She saw again in her mind the *thing* left in their bathtub.

Realized, as never before, the sheer profanity of Jerome Cooper's acts against his victims and against her own family.

Realized, too, that Wagner had not alluded to the fact that Cooper was her stepbrother, although the judge must know that, *everyone* knew that by now, but it might be another mark against her.

And mad as she knew it probably was, that fact brought another small gusher of shame from the well.

Wagner was continuing, relentless now.

'Richard Bianchi, a man whose personal laptop computer and credit card were used for the purchase of the kind of surgical instruments later found on the killer's houseboat, and which were almost certainly used to carve out the hearts of at least two, and probably more, victims. A man who either allowed his computer to be used to download articles about open heart surgery. Or worse, who did so himself.

'A man who was the last person to be seen with murder victim, Ricardo Torres, at a party thrown on the night of April twenty-fourth.

'A man who, it is believed, cultivated a friendship with Sara Mankowitz precisely because Jerome Cooper knew her son was one of Grace Lucca Becket's patients. A man who used a false name, and who took pleasure in repeatedly frightening and physically hurting Peter Mankowitz.'

Wagner turned again to the defense table, laid down that sheet of paper and took a sip of water.

And then he turned back again to face the judge.

'Yes, Richard Bianchi was unarmed on the night when he taunted and terrified Grace Becket in that narrow road off the highway. But Mrs Becket did not know that, and from her perspective in those moments, he might just as well have been pointing a loaded pistol at her head. She'd already tried reversing and failed, and so, with no other means of escape, she reacted by putting her foot on the gas pedal of her car. And for reasons that we may never comprehend, Richard Bianchi did not move out of the way.

'Which was a tragedy for him, for his family, and for Grace Becket.

'Self-defense, she truly believed, against one of the most violent, evil multiple murderers ever seen in South Florida.

'Self-defense, for sure.

'Your Honor, I move that the charges against Grace Becket be dismissed. And that this multilayered tragedy be allowed to end here.'

Wagner took his seat.

Elena Alonso rose.

'Is this going to be a rebuttal, Counselor?' the judge asked.

Sam, Cathy, Saul, Claudia and the others there for Grace ceased breathing.

Grace's heart was pounding too hard again, her palms damp.

'No, Your Honor,' Alonso said.

Her pause hung in the air.

'In light of the new evidence,' she continued, 'the State is prepared to accept a plea of not guilty by reason of self-defense.' She paused again. 'If I may, I would like to add that this comes with the agreement, given during the last recess, of Mr Bianchi's family.'

Judge Arthur Brazen nodded.

Made a number of notes.

Before looking up again.

'I am going to take this under advisement,' he said.

If Grace could have, she would have screamed.

If Sam could have, he would have screamed louder.

'I will give my ruling one week from today.'

The judge rose.

'All rise,' said the court clerk.

FORTY-NINE

June 12–17

The longest week in the history of the Becket family.

The day after the hearing, Cathy and Saul had moved back into Névé.

'There's no point our staying away,' Cathy had said. 'Our heads are here.'

'If Claudia and Dan and the guys don't mind,' Saul added.

'The more the better,' Daniel said.

'We thought David and Mildred might like to squeeze in too,' Claudia said. 'But Sam thinks it would be too much of an upheaval for them.'

'They're coming to dinner one evening,' Daniel said.

Mildred had been cooking.

Having lived for so many years without walls, let alone a kitchen, it had taken time for her confidence to grow, but the third evening after the hearing, she brought chicken soup.

'Best I ever tasted,' Sam said.

'Told you,' David said to Mildred.

'You made her blush,' Cathy said.

'Nonsense,' Mildred said. 'I don't know how.'

'So how are you doing?' she asked Grace later, finding her outside on the terrace.

Alone again, which was getting to be a habit.

'Truth?' Grace said.

'Of course,' Mildred said.

'I have no idea how I'm doing,' Grace said.

'Floating someplace over all this?' Mildred asked.

'Drowning, mostly,' Grace said.

'Please don't,' Mildred told her. 'We all need you.'

'You may have to manage without me.'

'I doubt that, after what happened at the hearing.'

'Apparently, the judge doesn't have to agree,' Grace said. 'He could insist on a lesser charge, according to Jerry Wagner. I could still go to jail.'

'I don't know why they'd bother,' Mildred said. 'There's no one on earth who's going to be punishing herself more than you.'

Martinez came on the sixth evening.

'I've been wanting to be there for you so badly,' he told Grace and Sam.

'Not possible,' Sam said. 'We knew that.'

One man down in the unit, a heap of work and Captain Kennedy in a grim mood. Nothing Martinez could do.

'Cooper still says he won't talk to anyone but you,' he said now.

'He will,' Sam said.

Which he thought was probably true, because the need to brag was part of the nature of his kind of monster, and maybe he'd just go on writing it down in his damned *Epistles*, but they'd get there in the end.

The image of Grace standing in court came back to Sam again. It filled him with fury to think of her being put through the same legal processes as that beast.

She was reading his mind again.

'At least I'm not in jail,' she said, quietly.

And then she knocked on wood.
'Not yet, anyway,' she added.

FIFTY

June 18

'In light of Ms Bianchi's testimony,' Judge Arthur Brazen was saying, 'and the circumstances outlined by the defense, and in the absence of objections by the prosecution, the charges against the defendant are dismissed.'

Grace stared up at him.

'You're free to go, Mrs Becket.'

She wanted to speak, to thank him, but her voice was trapped in her throat.

Seeming to understand, he smiled down at her from his lofty bench.

It felt like a benediction of sorts.

That feeling did not last long.

Not once she saw the Bianchi family outside.

They were trying to leave swiftly, but Josephine Bianchi seemed to be having difficulty walking, and there were reporters in their faces.

Gina Bianchi was not with them.

'You can write to them,' Sam told her quietly.

'I guess,' Grace said.

And then the press were on them.

'Be careful,' Jerry Wagner said.

He had told her back in the courtroom that he would remain at their side until they were safely in their car.

'We'll issue a statement later,' he said. 'We don't want anything coming back to hurt you.'

'I guess not,' Grace said.

And allowed herself to be steered on, scarcely aware of cameras or questions or jostling.

Floating again, above the crowd.

But not in a good way.

She was not going to jail.

Which ought to have been making her happy.

She was certainly relieved beyond words, but she could not imagine ever being truly *happy* again.

It was still there. Would remain the elephant in every room she inhabited, and in her own mind, for a long, long time.

For ever.

She had killed a man.

The law might have found a way to forgive her, but she would never forgive herself for that. Not if she lived to be a hundred.

Though she guessed that at least by then, her memory might be gone.

She *guessed.*

The closest to clear thinking she was likely to achieve for some time.

Except for that one, repeating thought.

'I killed a man.'

FIFTY-ONE

July 5

The Independence Day holiday was almost at an end, and Grace found, to her shame, that she was glad.

They had gone to Golden Beach, to David and Mildred, and everyone had made an effort to be light-hearted, but she knew she'd made it hard for them.

She was finding it difficult to eat much, had been losing weight ever since May 6, and David had remarked on that today.

Mildred had tackled her in the kitchen, a little more directly.

'It's more than just weight you've lost,' Mildred had said. 'It's your spark.'

'What do you expect?' Grace had said, hearing her own defensiveness.

'I think,' Mildred said, 'you need to start helping yourself move on.'

'I'm not sure I'm ready for that,' Grace said.

'Joshua is more than ready,' Mildred said.

'A little more guilt,' Grace said. 'Just what I need.'

But she knew Mildred was right.

It was time.

'I'm going to call Magda in the morning,' she told Sam that night.

They were back home on the island, with a brand-new bathroom, complete with Jacuzzi tub and new tiles on the floor and walls, and Sam had arranged for the whole house to be decorated while they were still at Claudia's. Even the deck had been pressure scrubbed with oxygen bleach.

Every trace of Cooper's presence wiped away.

Not from her mind.

Nothing felt the same.

Magda had called her last week, had told her plainly that if she did not embark on a course of counseling sessions soon, she might never feel able to get back to work.

'I can't imagine ever being ready for work,' Grace had said.

'You can't imagine it now,' Magda had said. 'But you will.'

'There won't be any patients,' Grace said.

No parents prepared to send their troubled children to a killer.

'They'll forget,' Magda said, 'in time.'

'But I won't,' Grace said.

'No, you won't,' Magda had agreed. 'But you'll learn to live with it.'

Grace had not argued with that, had hoped her friend was right. Not for herself.

Her family needed her to feel better.

'The trouble is,' she said to Sam on Monday night, 'I already know the things Magda will be trying to help me believe. That I need to be kind to myself. That my pain is proof of my own humanity. That I'm a victim, too, in a sense. That I need to learn to forgive myself.'

Sam heard her irony, hated it.

One more thing for him to lay at Cooper's feet.

Martinez had said to him after the hearing that the killer must have been mightily pissed off at the dropping of the charges against Grace, had said too that he figured Cooper might have been surprised by Gina Bianchi's honesty.

Scum like that having no comprehension of the decency of others.

Another strike against Cooper, but not nearly enough for Sam.

'I guess it's easier for me,' he said to Grace now. 'I have my hate to keep me warm.'

'I hope you have something better than that to warm you,' she said.

'You'd better believe it,' Sam replied.

They got into bed, turned out the lights, held each other close.

'What if I can't ever learn to forgive myself, Sam?' she asked.

'One step at a time, Gracie,' he told her, softly.

'What if I can't ever believe in myself again?'

'I have more than enough belief in you for both of us,' he said.

FIFTY-TWO

August 5

A month had passed.

Grace had been seeing Magda twice a week. The sessions were helping to a degree, she felt, because her friend was a fine therapist and because Grace trusted her completely.

Sara Mankowitz, who'd written to Grace after the hearing to apologize for her part in the tragedy, had called several times since then to ask her to consider continuing as Pete's psychologist as soon as she felt ready.

'Pete really needs you,' Sara said.

It should have helped, Grace knew, but it did not.

Long way to go.

Sam was working, temporarily, with Joe Sheldon, hunting a violent serial mugger, while Martinez and Beth Riley, by order of the captain, continued to work at building up the Cooper case. Sam missed his partner, but knew it was the right thing. His own workload was under control, and he was home most evenings, had been with Grace and their son most weekends.

Nothing felt the same though, either at the station or at home, but in time, he hoped, they would settle, feel more *themselves* again.

In time.

* * *

One undeniably good thing.

They felt safe.

Cooper remained in secure custody, from which he would not emerge.

More good things, too.

Joshua had become confused for a while after their return, but as his routines had re-established and his parents' tensions had eased, he had relaxed back into his happy self, and Grace felt good about that, accepted it was the kind of thing she could allow herself to feel good about.

As time passed, she hoped there would be more.

Now and again, she would think back to some small thing she had done that day – laughing at something on TV, or walking into a local store without imagining that people had recognized her, were condemning her – and she would realize that she had done those things without shame.

Normality creeping back slowly.

And maybe the guilt well was starting to seal up.

FIFTY-THREE

September 5

Cooper's mother had been coming to him.

Jewel.

Roxy the white-witch-bitch.

He thought he'd killed her back on board the *Baby*.

Over two years ago now.

Not dead enough.

She came to him at night, told him to lie down so she could *do* it to him.

Punish him.

The way she used to.

With a whip, most often, in those days. She'd thrash him and then she'd kiss the weals on his body and clean them with chlorine bleach, which burned worse than fire.

Purification was part of it.

Only part.

'Take it like a man,' she'd told him sometimes.
He'd taken it, all right, until the night he'd stuck a knife into her heart.

'I made you what you are,' she said to him one night, coming to him in his cell.
Like she was proud of the fact.
Jewel had never been proud of him in her entire life.
But she was right about that much. She had made him.
Made Cal the Hater.
'You're finished now,' she told him another time.
'I thought you were finished,' he told her back.
'Not yet,' Jewel said.
'I guess that means they won't be able to finish me either,' he said.
'You've always been finished,' Jewel told him.

He'd said to Albert Singer that he'd decided it ought to be Cal taking the rap for the killings, not Jerome Cooper, but his bastard lawyer had told him that multiple personality pleas were hard to prove.
Albert Singer was a little prick.
'What about Tom O'Hagen?' the lawyer asked him after that.
Cooper wasn't sure if lawyers were supposed to be sarcastic with their clients.
Singer would get his one day, Cal would see to that.
Not finished yet, good old, bad old Cal.
Whatever Jewel said.

FIFTY-FOUR

September 14

Sam had pronounced Joshua's third birthday a family holiday.
No work or college.
Claudia and Daniel were throwing the party, to which Grace had agreed because she didn't feel she was quite up to doing her son justice yet, and because Claudia said that since they'd all gone home, it seemed to her that everyone was staying away from Névé

either because they thought they'd outstayed their welcome or, more probably, because of the awfulness of the associations.

'Time to turn that around,' Daniel had agreed.

A party to remember, a bunch of Joshua's little pals from preschool turning the adults into semi-wrecks. A good time had by all. No one sick, no children injured and nothing of consequence smashed.

By six thirty, the little ones gone, they were all exhausted, and Martinez had only just shown up after a long day's work, but Joshua had fallen asleep, David and Mildred had gone for a nap up in the guest room, Cathy had gone for a run with Mel and Saul – not Saul's thing at all, but Mel had talked him into it – and the rest of the family were relaxing in the big, oval nook that overlooked the terrace and pool.

'Anyone want a beer?' Claudia asked.

'Sounds good to me,' Martinez said.

'How about we throw a few steaks on the grill?' Daniel said.

'Haven't we eaten enough?' Grace said, curled up on a couch, shoes off.

'I could eat a steak,' Robbie said.

'When couldn't you?' Mike said.

Claudia stretched. 'I'm feeling so lazy.'

'You're entitled, sis,' Grace said. 'What a great party.'

'I almost forgot,' Martinez said to Sam. 'My car was sounding a little off on the way over.'

'Want me to go take a look with you?' Sam said.

'My husband, the mechanic,' Grace said.

'He's no worse than me,' Martinez said.

'Here.' Daniel tossed him a Bud.

'Thanks, man.'

Sam had just opened the front door when the siren sounded.

'Jesus,' Martinez said.

'Probably something I did,' Sam said. 'Damn door.'

'I'll take a look,' Robbie yelled over the noise.

He sprinted across the great hallway over to the door that shielded the first-floor security system, checked the bank of monitors, instantly saw the familiar gray-hooded figure.

'Just our old pal,' he called back to the others, muted the sounder, called the usual numbers with the code.

'Happens all the time,' Sam told Martinez.

'We still OK to look at the car?'

'Sure,' Sam said.

In the security room, Robbie was taking another look at one of the monitors.

The old guy was still loitering.

Something in his arms.

'Jesus,' he said, took one more look to be sure.

And then he yelled: 'Dad, I think the wino's got Woody.'

Over in the nook, Grace, alarmed, scrambled to her feet.

'Where's Ludo?' Claudia said, up too.

'I don't know.' Grace was looking around for her sneakers.

'Dan, what's going on?' Claudia called.

'Did you have to yell so loud?' Daniel said, looking at the monitor over his son's shoulder. 'You'll freak everyone out.'

'It freaked me out,' Robbie said. 'It is Woody, isn't it, Dad?'

'I'm going out to take a look,' his father said.

Already on his way.

'Anyone seen Ludo?' Robbie yelled, behind him.

'Ludo's outside,' Grace shouted back, dragging on her left sneaker. 'He's OK.'

The three-legged spaniel was out on the terrace, coming their way. She opened the big glass door, and the dog skulked past her as she headed out.

'Grace, what do you think you're doing?' Claudia said.

'I'm going to get Woody,' Grace said, over her shoulder.

'Grace, leave this to Dan.'

It had been a while since anything had seemed quite this clear to Grace.

She was getting their dog back.

Now.

'Dan, will you please get out here,' Claudia yelled.

Upstairs, David and Mildred came out of the guest room.

'What's going on?' Mildred asked.

'Something about the dogs, I think,' David said.

'Oh, my,' Mildred said.

David heard her tension.

'I'm sure it's nothing,' he said.

'You think?' Mildred said softly.

David looked at her, took her hand.

'She's already through the gate,' Claudia told Daniel. 'She wouldn't wait.'

'It's OK. I'll go get them.' He stepped through the open door. 'Make sure the others stay inside.'

'Should I call the police?' Claudia asked.

'We got two of them out in the driveway,' Daniel said.

Claudia turned, saw Mike on the phone.

'Go get Sam,' she told him.

The two men had their heads under the hood of the Chevy when Mike opened the front door.

'What's up?' Sam asked Mike.

'I think the wino's got Woody,' Mike said. 'Aunt Grace went to get him back.'

'And you let her?' Sam pushed past the young man.

'It's OK,' Mike said. 'My dad's gone after her.'

Sam stopped, turned to Martinez. 'Give me your gun.'

'Out of jurisdiction, man,' Martinez said.

'Just give it to me,' Sam said.

Outside Névé now, through the gate in the fence, on the stretch of sandy grassland between the property and the beach, Grace stopped dead, a little breathless.

She could see the man up ahead, holding Woody in his arms.

Gently. Not hurting him.

Careful.

'Excuse me,' she called.

'Ma'am,' the man called back.

Over the wind, and cries of gulls, she thought she heard Woody whine.

'That's my dog,' she said.

Staying polite. Not going too close. Not certain why.

'Grace.'

Daniel had come up behind her.

'Let me,' he told her.

'It's OK,' Grace said. 'Woody's fine.'

She took a step forward.

'Grace, no.'

She looked around at her brother-in-law.

He looked calm, but resolute.

'I'll go get him for you,' he said.

'OK,' she said.

Daniel began to walk toward the wino.

'I don't know what happened to him,' the other man said, still cradling the animal. 'I just found him out here, and he didn't look right.'

Drawing closer, Daniel saw that the wino's beard was grizzled, but his hood cast a shadow over his eyes.

Woody whined again.

'Hope you don't mind that I picked him up,' the man said.

'I'm very grateful.' Daniel put out his arms. 'It's OK, boy.'

'Easy,' the wino said, and passed the dog carefully over. 'He's a nice boy.'

'Thank you,' Daniel said, getting a whiff of beer and sweat.

He half-turned, looked back at Grace to show her.

'I think he's OK,' Grace said to Sam.

Standing beside her now, breathing hard.

'You shouldn't have come out here alone,' he said.

She glanced at his face, saw the grimness in it.

'He's our dog,' she said. 'And anyway, Dan was right behind me.'

She turned her head and saw Martinez and Mike waiting near the fence, like back-up, and then she looked down and saw the gun in Sam's hand.

'Better put that away,' she said.

'It's OK, Mom,' Robbie told Claudia. 'Dad's got him.'

Both in the security room now, watching the scene on the monitors.

'We're going to have to check that fence,' his mother said.

And then she bent forward, over her son's shoulder.

'No,' she said, suddenly, sharply. '*No*.'

'Anything we can do?' David asked from the door.

'No!' Claudia pushed past him, flew across the expanse of white floor, out through the open door on to the terrace, saw Martinez and her older son standing out just beyond the fence.

'Someone go help Dan!' she shouted.

* * *

'Just there's where I think he's hurt,' the old man said.

He stepped right up close, and Daniel smelled him more strongly.

'There,' the wino said. 'See?'

Daniel bent his head, trying to see.

'I don't—' he said.

And stopped speaking.

'He's got a *knife*!'

They all heard Claudia's yell.

'Oh, my God,' Grace said.

'Get down,' Sam ordered.

Pushed her hard, down on to the ground.

She heard a sharp click.

Then the gunshot.

'Sam!' she cried out, got up on her knees.

He was yards away, and she saw Woody first, his tail down between his short back legs, running to her, barging into her, whining, needy.

'Grace, you OK?'

Martinez, voice low, urgent, crouched beside her.

Grace looked up again.

Sam was hunkered down on the grass, one hand compressing the wound in Daniel's chest. He'd seen the knife in the hooded man's hand as he fled, and maybe if the bastard hadn't pulled the blade out, there might have been some hope, though he doubted it.

Too late now.

His fingers against Daniel's neck confirmed it.

Nothing in this world to be done for him.

He stood up.

The guy was moving away, limping, hit in the leg, but getting *away*.

Sam raised the Glock again, yelled a warning.

The killer kept on going.

Sam had him in his sight.

Pulled the trigger.

He saw the man fall, saw his body jolt, then lie still.

Sounds reverberated in Sam's ears, vibrated through his head. The gunshot's echo, waves, the mewing of gulls, screaming. Woody's whining. People shouting, running.

Then the unmistakable sounds of Claudia keening and Mike howling.

Martinez was beside him, easing the gun from his hands.

'Stay here, man.'

Sam watched his partner until he'd reached the killer.

Saw Martinez checking the man over, for weapons first, heartbeat next.

He looked up at Sam, raised his right arm, thumb up.

Bad guy down.

Safe.

Sam looked back at the scene on the grass.

Tragedy building before his eyes.

Claudia weeping over her husband. Mike, who'd stopped making any sound, trying in vain for a pulse, for something still alive in his father, then staring up at Sam in his bewilderment. Robbie standing a few feet back, his face a mask of horror. David and Mildred coming out through the open gate behind the others.

Something inside Sam was sagging.

Grace was beside him.

He turned to look at her, saw that she was crying.

'Tell me this isn't happening,' she begged.

'I wish I could,' Sam said.

Grace gave a moan, and then she went to her sister, got down on her knees beside her and her sons, and the fallen husband and father.

And Sam started walking toward Martinez.

FIFTY-FIVE

September 15

There had been a new message scrawled on Jerome Cooper's cell wall yesterday morning.

Mostly, it had been gouged with a metal screw.

Some of the letters, though, appeared to have been written in blood.

His own.

They knew at the prison about the killer's self-abuse patterns, but until recently the habit had appeared to be dormant.

He'd started again a while back.

He liked using his blood as ink.

Hated it when they washed it off the walls.

The guard who'd seen the message yesterday had figured he'd better show it to his boss, but something had come up, trouble in another cell, and it had been close to the end of the day before he'd finally reported it.

The killer had scratched the same thing seven times.

Cal the Hater isn't finished yet.

And then, at the bottom – and this was the part he'd written in blood:

Tell Becket.

FIFTY-SIX

September 16

Their turn now to help Grace's sister and her sons, who had come to the island, told by the investigators to leave the crime scene. Everyone reeling, piling in to this small house, sleeping on couches and inflatable beds on the floors. Claudia in Cathy's old room, refusing sedation, refusing comfort.

They had heard her grief through the walls the last two nights, had tried to go to her, had been sent away.

There was and would be no consoling her or her boys, who sat staring like lost souls, still disbelieving.

'She's insisting they go home tomorrow,' Grace told Sam. 'She says Mike and Robbie need their space and their stuff, and however hard it's going to be, Dan put too much into the house for her to turn her back on it now.'

'If that's how she feels,' Sam said. 'And maybe she's right.'

'But it's going to be worse than hard,' Grace said. 'And if she won't even let us stay with her . . .'

'It would be too much like before for you,' was what Claudia had said.

'But this isn't about me,' Grace had replied.

'I know that,' Claudia said. 'But I have the boys, and I know you'll be there for us whenever we need you. But this is how it's going to be, isn't it, so I may as well let it begin.'

'That kind, gifted, gentle man,' Grace said to Sam, in bed late Thursday night. 'It makes no sense.'

'It rarely does,' Sam said.

They lay still. Downstairs, the TV was still on, the grieving young men probably unable to sleep. From Cathy's old room, there was silence.

'I know it wouldn't make any real difference,' Grace said, 'but I wish we could at least understand why Jones did it. Was he just crazy?'

Matthew Harris Jones was the name of the hooded man who had knifed Daniel Brownley to death, his prints matching up with a Jacksonville-born, small-time larcenist.

'Maybe,' Sam said.

Grace heard the note in his voice. 'What?'

He hadn't told her yet about Cooper's blood message.

He told her now.

'You think this was *him*?' The horror was so great it seemed to pump through her like floodwater. 'The wino was *his*? All that time?' She sat up, fighting to comprehend it. 'But Dan said he'd been a local character before they built their house.'

'No one knows yet if that "character" was Jones,' Sam said. 'It's unlikely, I guess, but not impossible that Cooper, or maybe even Bianchi, got rid of the old wino and put Matthew Jones in his place.'

Grace, shaken beyond belief, lay back, was silent again for a while.

'But that means,' she said, finally, 'that it should have been one of us.'

'Not necessarily,' Sam said.

'Of course it does. He took Woody, *our* dog, which made it more likely that we would go after him. And I did, didn't I? And if Dan hadn't come after me, hadn't taken over – and I let him.' The horror was pumping more forcefully with every thought. 'Dear God, I let him.'

'Stop it.' Sam reached for her hand, held it tight. 'Don't do this to yourself, Gracie.'

'How can I not?'

'You have to try. There's no real logic in it, anyway. If this is down to Cooper – and it's another big if – he hates our whole family.'

'He hates the two of us more than Claudia.'

Sam's mouth twisted. 'Me most of all. He's said it often enough.' He paused. 'That doesn't make me responsible for what happened to Dan, any more than it does you.'

'Have they questioned Cooper about it?'

'Not yet,' Sam said. 'But they will.'

They wouldn't let him near the scumbag, though, were right not to.

'Will we tell Claudia?' Grace asked.

'I don't think so,' Sam said. 'Not till we know something for sure.'

'If we ever do,' Grace said.

FIFTY-SEVEN

September 22

'I feel rage all the time,' Sam told Martinez the following Wednesday.

Taking a walk in Lummus Park at lunchtime.

'So talk about it, man,' Martinez said. 'Let it out.'

Sam glanced toward the bench a few yards away that had once been home to Mildred, and he was glad of the anonymity out here among the vacationers and locals, strolling with their children and dogs, clutching their bottles of water and sun cream.

'Nothing much to let out,' he said, 'except there's too much darkness in *here* right now.' He touched two fingers to his head. 'I can't seem to see any way to stop the rot, you know?'

'You're just depressed, man,' Martinez said. 'It'll get easier.'

'I need to believe that,' Sam said. 'My wife and son need me to.'

'I read something one time,' Martinez went on. '"One good feeling begets another." Something like that.'

Sam grinned. 'Begets?'

'You can mock,' Martinez said. 'But it's true. Out of nowhere, you'll get a good feeling, and—'

'You're not going to sing, are you?' Sam said.

They walked on.

'So what are you thinking now about Jones?' Martinez asked after a few moments. 'Paid by Cooper or just a whacko?'

The post-mortem had confirmed that the man's liver had been pretty much pickled, his brain showing enough damage to have made him a solitary crazy.

Though that did not, of course, preclude the possibility of Cooper having been paying him to keep watch on Claudia's house, and maybe he'd found a way, even from jail, to go on putting enough in Jones's pockets for a hit on the family he loathed.

Or maybe not.

'I don't know,' Sam said. 'Seems to me there are no limits these days to what I don't know.'

They went on walking.

'Only one good thing,' he said.

'Yeah?' Martinez said.

'Either way, Cooper's still going to death row.'

The case against the killer was building well despite his continuing refusal to talk.

They still didn't know how he and Bianchi had met, or exactly what their relationship had been, but Richard Bianchi's apartment on NW North River Drive had at last yielded a missing link.

Minute fragments of Jerome Cooper's skin wedged beneath the baseboard in Bianchi's small, steam-cleaned bathroom.

Cooper's hidey-hole on shore, it now seemed likely.

The place, they were guessing, where the murderer might have gone to punish himself after he'd killed and mutilated his victims, raking at his own body till it bled, the way his late unlamented mom had taught him.

All the remaining evidence needed to take the 'writer's' memory down into infamy alongside Cal the Hater. And if Bianchi had lived, his defense would have challenged on the basis that with so much time having passed, and the apartment not having been sealed, the skin fragments might have been planted.

Still, proven in court or not, a little more satisfaction, from Sam's point of view, for Grace's sake.

Nothing much else feeling satisfying to him now, Lord knew.

His sorrow for Claudia and her sons knew no bounds.

And they still had no absolute proof that Cooper had had anything to do with Matthew Harris Jones before he'd stuck that knife into Dan's heart and destroyed a happy family of good people.

Just another crazy seemed the prevailing opinion, as the days passed.
Sam was not, would never be, sure of that.
Only one thing he did feel sure of.
He wanted Jerome Cooper out of this world.
He didn't give a damn which way.
Lynching, plague, electric chair or lethal injection.
The sooner the better.

FIFTY-EIGHT

October 1

Grace wanted him dead.

She wanted it so badly that it was making her sick.

Shaking her core beliefs.

A taste for death.

That was what Cooper had done to her.

She blamed him now for everything, for Bianchi's death too, even more than she blamed herself.

Which was, she supposed, a kind of progress.

She had not yet shared those feelings with Magda, had cut back on their sessions, too preoccupied for now with trying to find ways to help Claudia and her nephews, doing what little she could, what little she was allowed to do.

The funeral had passed, and Sam had agreed with her soon after that they needed to tell Claudia about the unproven suspicion of a link between Dan's killer and Cooper.

'Do you think I hadn't already considered that?' Claudia had said.

'Why didn't you say so?' Grace asked her.

'What difference would it have made?' Claudia said.

'You should start seeing patients again,' Magda had told Grace yesterday. 'Maybe at my place, if you're not sure about working from home.'

Location seemed the least of Grace's uncertainties.

Dan's death had reignited all her own fears of losing Sam.

She knew it was a natural enough reaction: turning such tragedies on to oneself, playing self-torturing 'what if?' games. But her mind, it seemed to her, was still too jammed with other things for her to be ready to help troubled children.

Her sister's and those young men's agony. Her own loss, too, of the brother-in-law who had become such a staunch friend.

Her still-abiding guilt over her own crime.

And, paradoxically darkest of all, it seemed to her, her longing for the moment of Cooper's death.

FIFTY-NINE

December 11

Jewel had come to him the night he'd started doing it again.

Really doing it.

'Lie down,' she'd told him, the way she used to.

'I don't have to,' he'd told her.

'Lie down, dolthead,' she said.

'I don't have to do what you tell me anymore,' he said.

Because you're dead.

'Lie down and take it like the shit-for-brains you are,' she said.

That was how he knew it was really Jewel.

Just a couple of the names she used to lavish on him.

Along with the pain.

He had known then that there was no escaping her. Ever.

So he had done it.

Over time in this place, they'd tried stopping him.

They took away the hard brush he'd stolen from the cleaning store, the peeler he'd smuggled out of the kitchen, the scourer from the shower block.

He used his fingernails, so they cut and filed them down.

But they grew again.

There was always a way.

So Jewel had kept on coming, and he had kept on doing it.

He had known he was getting sick a long while before they'd noticed.

'Do it *again*,' Jewel kept telling him.

All the way from hell.

Except in the old days, when he'd *disciplined* himself, he'd poured bleach on his wounds, the way she'd taught him, and Lord God, it had hurt, but it had kept him clean, the way he liked.

So now he was real sick.

His blood was poisoned.

They'd taken him to the ninth floor, which he knew was the psych ward, and they'd chained him to a bed, stuck tubes in him and given him medicine, and some of them were decent to him, considering who he was.

All of them better than his own mother had ever been.

None of them as kind as Blossom.

He was glad she was dead, glad she'd never really known him.

Maybe they'd cure him, given time.

Though if they did, he'd just do it all over again.

It was what Jewel wanted.

To be with him again.

Really with him.

Coming closer.

SIXTY

December 24

'Cooper says he wants to see you.'

Martinez brought him the news.

'He's dying, and he's talking last wishes, and he wants to see you. I didn't want to tell you, but Alvarez said we have to pass it on, though the Lieutenant agrees with me, thinks you should just tell him to go fuck himself.'

'I'll go,' Sam said.

'Why the hell would you do that?' Martinez said.

'Maybe it's like they say,' Sam said. 'Closure.'

He might scarcely have recognized him but for the rows of old scars and fresher wounds visible on his chest.

Sepsis, a doctor had told Sam. Organs failing.

His own insanity killing him.

He was afraid of death, Sam knew, remembering the *Epistles*.
Afraid of hell.

'You came,' he said. 'I knew you would.'
'What do you want, Cooper?' Sam asked.
'Won't you sit down?' the dying man asked.
'I'll stand,' Sam said.
'How's Grace doing?'
'Mention my wife again,' Sam said, 'and I'm out of here.'
He said it coldly, flatly, was surprised by the absence of rage in him.
Pain gripped the man in the bed, made him shudder.
Sam felt no pity.
'I'm a little scared,' Cooper said.
'Can't say I'm surprised,' Sam said. 'With so much on your conscience.'
'She made me do this, you know,' Cooper said. 'My mother.'
'Your mother is dead,' Sam said. 'You killed her.'
'I killed a lot of people,' Cooper said. 'I think she was the only one who deserved it, though.'
'What do you want?' Sam asked again.
Cooper's lips were cracked, his skin yellowing, little oxygen tubes in his nostrils, fluids flowing into and out of him via other tubes.
'I was sorry to hear about Claudia's husband,' he said.
The rage came back.
Sam clenched his fists and took a step closer to the bed.
'Something you want to tell me about that?' he said. 'To confess?'
'That had nothing to do with me,' Cooper said.
Sam looked right into the dying man's eyes.
The evil still there.
'It was all Jewel, like I said.'
Sam stepped back again, away from the stink of the man.
'Last time,' he said. 'What do you want?'
'To talk to you,' Cooper said. 'Like always.'
'No,' Sam said. 'No more talk.'
'Come on,' the dying man said. 'Don't you want to know what I put in the hypodermic I stuck you with?'
'Are you planning to tell me?' Sam said.
Cooper took a long, shaky breath.
'I'm not sure if I recall,' he said.
Sam shook his head, started to turn.

'Don't I get a last wish?' Cooper said.

'You get nothing,' Sam said. 'But I do have one wish for you.'

'And what's that, Samuel Lincoln Becket?'

'That you get yourself to hell,' Sam said. 'The sooner the better.'

And he turned and began to walk away.

'You haven't told me how the family's doing,' Cooper said.

Sam went on walking.

'You can't just walk out,' Cooper said. 'I might have things left to tell you.'

Sam went on, heading for the doors.

'Don't you *dare* walk out on me, you black sonofabitch.'

Sam stopped and turned around.

Just long enough to smile.

'So you just walked the fuck out,' Martinez said outside in the Chevy.

'Uh-huh,' Sam said.

'Good feeling?'

'Matter of fact,' Sam said, 'it was.'

'More to come, man,' Martinez said. 'Like I told you.'

SIXTY-ONE

December 25

The call came just after seven fifteen next morning.

They were still in bed.

In another year, they supposed Joshua would be getting them up before dawn on Christmas Day, but as it was, Grace – with hours of cooking ahead of her – was still burrowed against Sam's back.

He groaned, picked up the phone.

Praying it was nothing bad.

Nothing to take him away from home.

'Becket,' he said.

And listened.

'Thanks for calling,' he said.

Put the phone back down.

'What?' Grace murmured.

'Cooper died,' Sam said.
And there it was.
Another good feeling, just the way Martinez had predicted.
'Thank God,' Grace said.
'Amen,' Sam said.